THE WEDDING CAKE

ISABELLA MAY

Copyright © 2022 Isabella May

Artwork and Design: iStock.com by Getty, and sam_4321, Fiverr

Editor: Alice Cullerne-Bown

All rights reserved.

No part of this book may be used or reproduced in any manner whatsoever without written permission of the author except for brief quotations used for promotion or inreviews. This is a work of fiction. Names, characters, and incidents are used fictitiously.

'The most dangerous food to eat is a wedding cake'

Proverb

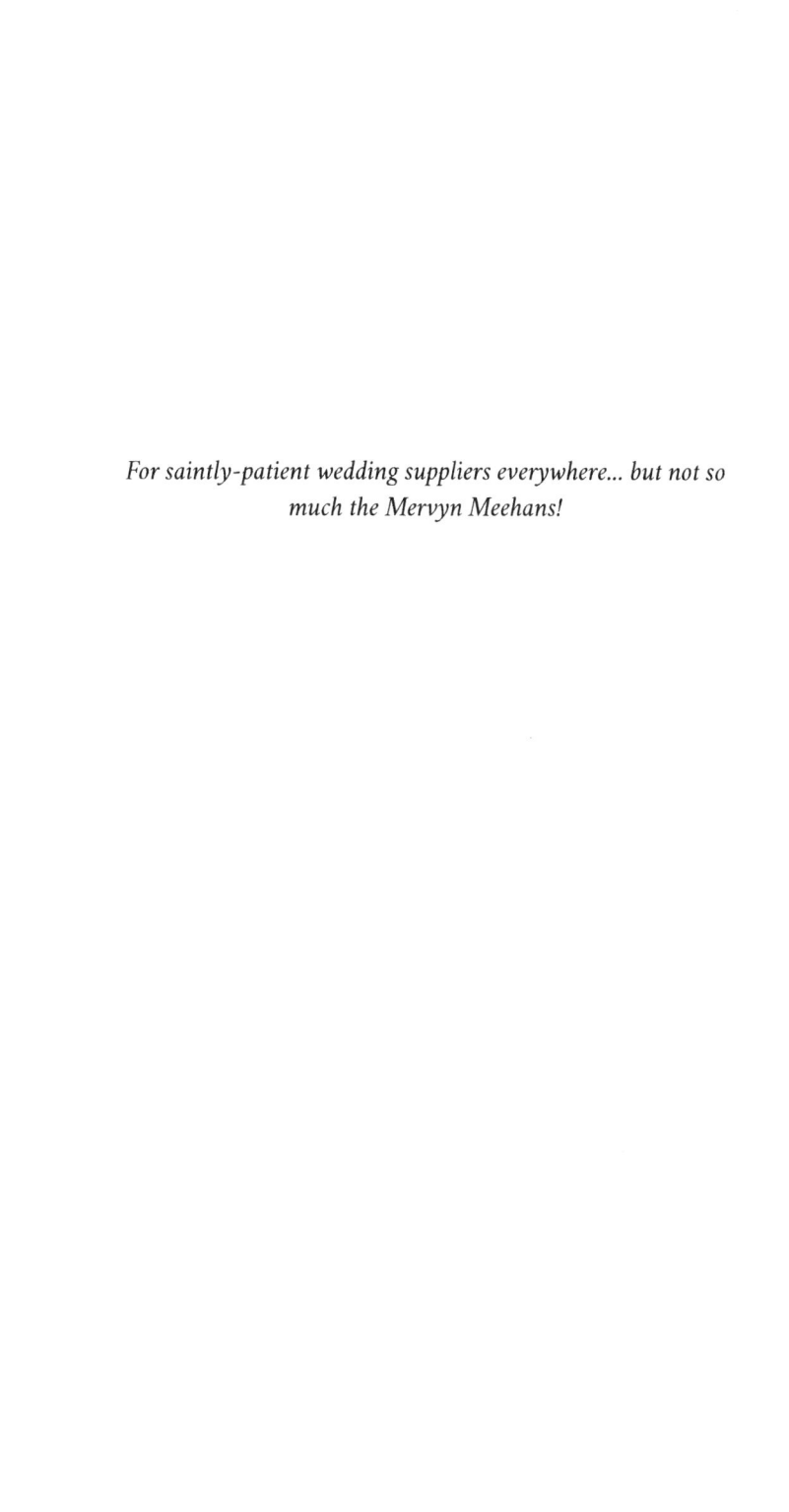

For saintly-patient wedding suppliers everywhere... but not so much the Mervyn Meehans!

ACKNOWLEDGEMENTS

I am always petrified that I will miss somebody out when I write this part of the book. And at the time of writing this, it is summer in Spain and I am absolutely melting! So I will say thank you to *everyone* who has made my author journey thus far so sweet.

But an extra special thank you must go out to Natali Drake - without her this story could never have been imagined! And I owe a huge GRACIAS to Cristina Hodgson for having the patience of a saint. She knows exactly why ;-)

FREYA

Freya Ashcroft let out a weary sigh. What she would give to have another hour in bed! The phone hadn't stopped ringing all morning, with orders and enquiries flying in from every dot on the globe. All she wanted to do was sink her bottom into a plush bucket chair at her favourite café in the orange tree square, soak up the weak winter sunshine, enjoy a *café sombra* and dive into a plate of churros dunked in a pool of velvety chocolate sauce, as was her usual Friday morning ritual. But that was December for you, when you ran an award-winning business in Marbella and everybody wanted a piece of your cake. You had to put your game face on and quit moaning, you had to accept you'd be lucky to get even a sip of coffee some days.

Now in its tenth year of trading, Freya's of Marbella not only rhymed (when you pronounced the town the Spanish way, *Mar-bay-ya*), it was also an institution for the local and international elite. The cakery – as Freya preferred to refer to it, since not a crumb of bread came out of its ovens – had won a glut of awards in the past decade and was the top tier foodie port of call for well-connected destination wedding planners and their equally well-heeled brides and grooms-to-be, priding itself on bespoke wedding cakes to die for. Figuratively speaking, of course.

Since opening the doors to her little shop in Marbella's gorgeous and iconic orange tree square, FOM, as Freya called her business when she was in a rush (which was most of the time) hadn't looked back, growing exponentially to take over two floors in two adjoining white-washed buildings that had been lovingly modernised with all the latest cakery gadgets. Nowadays, FOM consisted of a dozen hard-working part-timers and six members of full-time staff: Freya, who zipped from front of house to the mayhem of the kitchen to work her all-round magic; pastry chefs Jimena, Alejandro and Nicola; sugarcraft and cake decor expert Ricky (and his neon green spiral quiff and matching beard), and last but by no means least, Hannah, Freya's assistant. How she had coped without Hannah for nine full years, Freya would never know. Their latest recruit was worth her weight in edible gold. Cool, calm and collected, Hannah helped Freya keep the plates (or icing turntables) spinning.

Freya retreated to her office with the antiquated and battered order book under her wing. It had perennial pride of place in a hidey-hole behind the downstairs shop's till, where her biggest local wedding planner client, Mervyn Meehan, would still write in it to this day, adding his new requests the old school way with the pencil attached by string to the book's cover. Ridiculous, this far into the new millennium, you bet. But it was the way seventy-something Merv, the man who'd brought Freya her first clients, liked to do business, and he was a legend on the Costa del Sol. She couldn't afford to argue with him and the parade of couples he continued to bring her way. She tucked her springy, bob-length toffee-coloured curls behind her ear, shut the door to her office for a moment of solitude and perched on her desk to assess the entries Merv had added that very morning.

More often than not, brides and grooms, brides and brides, and grooms and grooms would arrange a taste test of Freya and her team's masterpieces via Merv's company, Weddings in Paradise. Nowadays, this rite of passage was par for the course in the upmarket wedding world – and Merv loved any excuse to stuff himself too, regularly joining his clients to get 'ambushed by cake' as they nibbled on moreish morsels. This would usually happen in the tiny courtyard at the back of Freya's premises. She would run around like a headless chicken to festoon the patio and its quaint water feature with fairy lights and tea lanterns, the old town's florist often lending her a gargantuan centrepiece to mark the occasion. But FOM's exceptional reputation preceded it. Since it was notoriously difficult to reserve a cake from Freya's emporium, such was the incessant demand from high-profile clients and the word of mouth in their inner circles, love birds would sometimes simply buy without trying.

Freya flicked through the pages until she reached August of the fast-approaching new year and nodded her head, satisfied that every wedding day in peak season was now full of sweet words.

Merv had added:

Wednesday August 3rd – *1 x three-tier milk chocolate ganache wedding cake with fresh fruit topping (nisperos, if you can source them) to be delivered to Cortijo Paloma on the road to Ronda.*

What was he like? Merv knew full well that nisperos, the tiny, sweet, orange fruit native to Spain, was only available April to June. And Merv was taking liberties with the journey, too. Freya had made it clear to him heaps of times that she preferred not to risk delivering to destinations on roads littered with potholes, hairpin bends, and vertical drops. A drive fit only for Alejandro (and not Ricky, *definitely not Ricky!*). Still, it was doable timewise since they only had one other simple creation going out the same day.

Saturday August 6th – *1 x eight-tier showstopper wedding cake with (starting from the bottom and working up) layers of salted caramel, Victoria sandwich, red velvet, and lemon curd with passionfruit – plus a waterfall (of Niagara Falls proportions) of pink and white sugar roses cascading down the side. Delivery to Finca Preciosa, near Mijas.*

Freya put her hands to her temples, willing the words to rearrange themselves. She closed her eyes hoping this wasn't happening. But when she peeped once again at the entry in the book, there it stubbornly remained.

Her *meh* reaction wasn't to the taste or the jaw–dropping finished look of the cake. Both would be sublime. It was the amount of work this number entailed. Freya would love to erase it from her repertoire altogether, having lost sleep over baking it numerous times. Yes, they'd be paid handsomely for constructing it. Seven thousand euros, plus TVA (VAT). But that little windfall came at a price to everyone's mental health, particularly in the height of a Spanish summer, when temperatures could hit forty degrees –– and so could tempers. Freya would need to have a word with Merv to try to convince him to steer his clientele away from her skyscraper creations in July and August in future. But Merv was also getting a cut of the proverbial cake for his efforts and naturally he wouldn't feel inclined. He had a high maintenance lifestyle to keep up, and an equally high maintenance wife, forty years his junior, to placate. Wife number six as far as Freya knew. Yes, Merv was quite the advertisement for his flourishing business, and quite the modern day Henry VIII, seemingly addicted to walking down the aisle himself. Nowadays, albeit with a diamante-topped cane.

And here was Freya, also almost forty years younger than Merv, but with barely a spare evening to go on a date, let alone build up to a marriage proposal. She had been on a grand total of two dates in two years. *Two dates!* When you were an above average-looking, young-ish female entrepreneur and you lived in Marbella, that was downright depressing.

At least they had been with two different guys. But now she stopped to think about it, Freya wasn't sure if that made things sound better or worse? And don't get her started on the subject of sex. Soon she'd wither and turn into a prune.

She'd spent ten years working her flip flops off. Money and accolades were all well and good, but she seemed to be creating everybody else's happy ever after, while her own ebbed further out of sight as she worked, quite literally, all the hours under the sun – and completed another of her own laps around its glowing orb. Soon she'd be in her mid-thirties, which was far from ancient, yet equally a whole world away from the carefree girl she'd been when she'd set up the business in her early twenties.

But now wasn't the moment to dissect her lack of a love or social life. She'd do that tonight. With Tiddles. As she frequently did. The poor tortoiseshell cat had heard it all before, and likely thought that if Freya spent less time complaining to her, and more time chowing down delicious (free) food of the fish and meat variety (*hello!*) with potential men instead of turning down their invitations – then she might have a better set of annual dating statistics in front of her. But Tiddles would purr along in agreement anyway, or pad at Freya's pyjamas with her soft paws, as if encouraging her to spill her woes. And then Freya would curl up with her book, Netflix humming along in the background, and the pair of them would fall asleep on the couch. Every morning Freya would vow it was the last time she'd allow herself to conk out on a work night as she massaged the painful kink from her neck.

This was the sad side of the wedding industry. Tiddles was the most gorgeous and patient feline to ingloriously infodump on, as she questioned why her own affairs of the heart had gone so tragically wrong. But there was no dodging it. Freya was living in a perpetual Groundhog Day…

ALICE

"Promise you won't be mad?" Alice Goldsmith fluttered her eyelashes at her fiancé, River, and swallowed down her nerves. "I've... kind of changed my mind."

River's face turned ashen and she quickly realised he thought she was about to strike a line through their wedding day. In a sense that was true. Just not in the way the love of her life was thinking.

"Not about us getting married!" Alice cried. "It's just that the nearer we get to the month of saying 'I do', the more I know with absolute certainty that *I don't* want the celebrations happening so close to my parents. Not only in the same county but in the same *country*. Something tells me we'd enjoy the day a whole lot more if we didn't have to keep looking over our shoulders, and if we sort of... escaped... abroad." Alice whispered the last bit then held her breath, petrified to take in River's reaction lest it should be a resolute 'no'.

"I know nine months before a wedding isn't the best time to turn everything on its head," she wittered on. "And I know we have a lot going on right now in prep for our future careers, but technically we *can* pull this off – and with minimal lost deposits for the things already booked. This must seem like a shock but I can't ignore my gut instinct: to be out of sight and out of my folks' minds. There's too much temptation for them to put in an unwanted appearance if we carry on with our current plans, and that would be a flipping disaster."

River's face slowly regained its customary hue – what could be seen beneath his beard, anyway. Before resuming her spiel, Alice drank in every inch of his rugged good looks: denim-blue eyes, wavy brown shoulder-length hair that looked great up or down, toothpaste advert teeth, and incredibly kissable lips, in spite of the facial hair. He was pretty damn phwoar. She was pretty damn lucky.

"I've already looked into it," she continued gingerly, hoping that the many hours she'd spent poring over possibilities wouldn't be for nothing. "There's this gorgeously rustic finca just inland from the Costa del Sol that would be perfect. Amazingly, it's free on Saturday the sixth of August!" Alice put her hands together as if praying. She needed all the support she could get and, if any angelic beings wanted to further her cause, she was not going to stop them. "It's got plenty of room for family and friends to stay. And the cute whitewashed village of Mijas is a stone's throw away for anybody else who decides to fly out. It's packed with B&Bs, sweet little hotels and apartments. It claims to have the world's smallest chocolate factory too. Hayley will be especially gutted if we don't do this."

Alice stopped and waited. She twisted her ethereal honey-blonde curls into a bun as rustic as the finca, and fixed it into place with a stray pencil from the kitchen worktop. If she added anything else to her campaign, it would sound way over-rehearsed. River didn't need to know that she'd actually gone ahead and paid the deposit on Finca Preciosa!

The tick of the kitchen clock marked several beats of painful silence. Alice couldn't take it any longer. She joined River at the dining table and reached for the salad tongs to break the interlude, claiming a heap of leaves from the bowl, tossing them onto her plate and drizzling them in dressing before cutting herself a wedge of her homemade chickpea and tomato quiche. River could help himself.

"I… *finca* it's a great idea," River finally replied with a megawatt grin. Alice let out a lengthy breath and circumnavigated the table for a celebratory hug (and a passionate snog). "To be honest, I'd much prefer to get away for our special day, too," said River once they'd come up for air. "I know we're not quite as famous as we used to be now we're back in Somerset for good." River and Alice had formerly been in the C-list rock band, Avalonia, before quitting music and the jet set scene for a quieter life. "But both of us could also do without the local press or die-hard fans sniffing around." Alice couldn't help but giggle at River's nostalgia. The pair of them were so rarely spotted nowadays, their fanbase largely to be found in South America. "And, if you're up for it, since we still haven't decided on the honeymoon part, we could have that in Spain too."

Now River's face lit up and Alice could tell he'd had one of his frequent brainwaves. Some of these were better than others. "Hey, we could drive over in 'Twinkle' and do a camper van road trip around Spain *and Portugal*. Obviously, we could book into a few boutique hotels along the way and make it a little more luxurious in between," he finished with a wink.

This was one of the many things Alice adored about River, and it was one of the reasons she couldn't wait to shuck off the Goldsmith part of her name and become a fully-fledged Jackson: they were almost always thinking the same thing, embellishing ideas from pipedreams to done deals within minutes.

"You're on!" said Alice, in the same carefree way in which she'd accepted River's flash mob dance proposal smack bang in the middle of Glastonbury high street. "A chilled out Andalucían wedding is so much more *us* than a formal 'do' in a posh Somerset castle."

She skipped to the drinks cabinet and pulled out a couple of wine glasses so they could celebrate.

"Hell, no. This calls for a cocktail, Al."

River did a swift assessment of their lunch ingredients, marched to the fridge and peered inside it, closed the door again (and his eyes), finger-jabbed skywards as if he'd just scored a goal (his new body language when about to make a decision – quite annoying, but not as tragic as leaving toilet seats up or dirty socks on the floor) and announced, "Cucumber watermelon mojito."

"Yes, please," Alice replied dreamily, already imagining how beautifully it would compliment the salad and quiche. River might have turned his back on the short cocktail career that had led him away from the music industry, but he definitely hadn't lost his impeccable taste buds. These could be relied upon to animate every meal at their kitchen table, from baked beans on toast to a Sunday roast. Oh, and now he would need to devise a whole new cocktail list to accompany their Spanish wedding breakfast. "Let the party planning begin!"

TIM

"And that's a wrap! Thanks everybody. Great bouncing session!" Tim Nutkins shouted down the hall through his microphone headset. His large, dark brown eyes peeped at his students through his floppy blonde side fringe. "As always, if you fancy staying behind to help pack away the equipment, I'd be much obliged. But if you have to cut and run, I quite understand. See you all next week."

Tim was thrilled with the evening's turnout for his trampoline class as things often tended to tail off in the run up to the festive period; thoughts turning to feasting, flavoured vodka, and work party frolics instead. But thirty fitness fanatics had shown up tonight, making use of all of his mini trampolines as they had rebounded – mostly in sync – to the greatest hits of Wham, Bananarama and Duran Duran. Admittedly, more than a dozen of them were late paying Tim this term, but if you couldn't make concessions during the season of goodwill, when could you? He was sure they'd reimburse him as soon as they could.

At six foot two, Tim's head (and airborne fringe) almost touched the ceiling when he put his class through their paces, but it didn't get better than this and he'd never been one to take himself too seriously. How could you when you'd gone through school being called 'Squirrel' on account of sharing your surname – well, minus the last letter – and your chocolate brown eyes with a certain Beatrix Potter character? And then there was Tim's rather outstanding ability at climbing trees…

At least *he* was happy with the way his career was progressing, as he mixed and matched his trampoline sessions with the new-fangled craze of bungee workouts. Piper would have other ideas. But that was why he adored her. They were a classic case of opposites attracting, and her enthusiasm for the stratospheric heights he could reach was infectious – if not a little overwhelming at times. Then again, Piper was eight years younger, and that kind of energy would help him keep a youthful approach to life as the years rolled by.

Piper had a late finish this evening. She was 'filming'. Tim put that bit in inverted commas because his bride-to-be wasn't an actor but an influencer. Whenever Piper was out of earshot and Tim was in a conversation, for some reason he would whisper the 'I' word. Not because he was embarrassed about his stunning fiancée's choice of career, promoting brands by gracing them with her presence (Piper's speciality tended to be luxury hotels and resorts, a little unfathomable given she'd started out endorsing cosmetics). It was just that it didn't particularly pique the interest of the grafters in his family and circle of friends. His circle prior to meeting Piper. Obviously, he was now on the periphery of his girlfriend's much wider and wealthier set too, when she let him tag along to events.

Tim saluted his thanks to the trio of exercise buddies who always stayed behind to help him, rolled up the mat at his feet and propped it against the wall, ready to be locked in the giant store cupboard along with the rest of the gym equipment. He ploughed a hand through his thick floppy hair and let himself drift back to that very first meeting with the woman who was soon to become his wife.

He'd been mesmerised the moment Piper had sashayed into his spin class in the gym of one of Manchester's top hotels. He'd picked up a few months of work there straight out of his sports management degree, prepping those who could afford the fifty-pound sessions for the benefit of their summer bikinis and trunks. Piper had looked exquisite in her skimpy workout gear – and still did, of course – with her blow-waved, glossy mahogany locks falling over her shoulders and trailing down to the middle of her back. Those smouldering jade-green eyes hit you for six; not to mention her Bambi-esque lashes, and her killer physique with every curve in just the right place. Curves that Tim had very much wanted to explore after the fade-out of the last tune on his stereo (modern day pop might favour the cold ending, but Tim played classic eighties hits during his classes). It was an animal attraction. Primeval and wild. Tim's previous romances had been slow burn tropes straight out of a movie, and they hadn't lasted once things had got started, so he could only take this mutual captivation as a good sign.

Before he knew it, Piper was sitting snugly at his side in the cocktail bar on the top floor of the hotel where they had both knocked back Cloud Nines. Then they were ripping each other's clothes off in Piper's executive suite, experiencing Cloud Nine in a much more intimate way. It still aroused him now just thinking about it. The sex had been frenetic, and he wasn't sure where either of them had found the energy after an hour of hardcore cycling to disco anthems on the exercise bikes.

Bedroom antics were still almost as fast-paced nowadays. There was just the *small* matter of Piper bringing up wedding plans increasingly frequently amidst their love making. Always at the most inopportune moments, too… like when things were building to a crescendo and he'd found her G spot. Why couldn't she just stay in the moment? He didn't care about balloon arches and doves flying out of cages, caricaturists capturing the hammed-up quirks of their guests on canvas, or magicians with such impressive sleight of hand that they'd performed for royalty and footballers – much less Piper's latest obsession: 'a showstopper of a wedding cake to rival all wedding cakes'. It was something of an enigma when she rarely touched sugar. He just wanted to marry her. That was the main event, surely? The love aspect, coupledom, and whatever came next. He supposed he wanted kids but, truth be told, he wasn't sure if Piper would have the time for them. Something would definitely have to give on the career front for one of them. Not that he was averse to being a stay-at-home husband.

Tim double-checked that everything was to his satisfaction in the now empty town hall. He was super grateful for the opportunity to run his classes here in down to earth (but hilly) Glossop. Yes, it was a trek from the luxury penthouse apartment he shared with Piper in the sought-after canalside area of Manchester, but it was refreshing. And it was a prime location to host a bootcamp. Next summer Tim planned to cash in on the fact that Glossop was the gateway to the Peak District and the Pennines by leading some group excursions there for outdoor activities. Climbing, foraging, wild camping and swimming all sprang to mind. Not that he charged anywhere near as much as Piper suggested he should for his sessions. 'Exercise Available to ALL' was Tim's motto.

He slung his sports bag over his shoulder, locked up the hall, and paced over to the carpark in the bitterly cold night, teeth chattering as he fumbled for the keys to his ten-year-old Volkswagen Polo. Another thing that Piper would upgrade in a heartbeat for him, probably to something like her six-month-old, frisky royal blue Mini Cooper. She was such a honey. Tim Nutkins was the world's jammiest man and there was no denying it. Piper and her big heart doted on him. That's why he hadn't hesitated to move in with his girlfriend after just six weeks, and that's why he'd popped the question after a whirlwind nine months together. He couldn't wait for them to live out their HEA in wedded bliss.

FREYA

Freya sighed and checked her reflection in the cloakroom mirror before grabbing her coat. She looked as good as it got, after a jam-packed day at work. Though being a little frazzled did make the freckles on her cheeks and the hazel of her eyes pop all the more. How had she been so naive as to let Jimena, Alejandro, Nicola and Ricky talk her into this, though? Why hadn't Tiddles given her a sign that it was a very bad idea? Last time she'd got ready for a date, her cat had deposited a live cricket on the bathroom floor, making her emit a blood-curdling scream, followed by a bout of shivers that she'd been unable to shake off all night. And the time before that, Tiddles had got stuck up the large lemon tree in her garden and she'd been out there until the twilight hours trying to coax her back down, cancelling on the furious guy in question; a sure sign that said date most definitely would not have been the One. Only Hannah seemed to get Freya, and was always so sweetly protective of her boss, reminding her she didn't have to go through with the crap she was about to embark on. Which was such a negative thought to leave the cakery with, that she

THE WEDDING CAKE

might just as well go home to Tiddles, tea on tap and Netflix. None of the men she'd met in the Costa del Sol's bars or eateries in recent years had whetted her appetite for more. Why would this evening's attempt be any different?

"It'll do you the world of good," said Nicola as Freya stepped back into the cake decorating room, feeling jittery for what would probably be nothing. "The dates you have the least expectation about always end up being the best."

"Yep," agreed her double act, Jimena. "Third time lucky."

"You look great, don't chicken out and waste all that effort staying here with us," Alejandro added, without taking his eye off the intricate process of 'glueing' his reindeer biscuits to the middle tier of a breathtaking Christmas wedding cake he was helping Ricky to assemble ready for its spot in the limelight. It was unusual for Alejandro, Jimena and Nicola to congregate in the cake decorating room – the baking room being their regular territory – but there was so much assemblage to tend to today; a number of the part-timers had come down with the seasonal lurgy, and Glaswegian Ricky was up to his eyeballs in fiddly piping.

"Awayyego! We are more than ready to cover for you if you end up getting so moolured you shag him and wake up with a head full of regret," hooted Ricky, who could always be relied upon to lower the tone.

Thankfully, he was far more respectful towards his precious cake styling; the precision on his beloved icing mirrored the attention to detail he gave his hair, and the decadent chocolate almond pine cones Ricky was planting on the top tier of the festive cake could have been real-life specimens from the Andalucían forest.

"The only thing I'm looking forward to is the outdoor heaters and furry rug seats," Freya replied candidly.

Every time she went on a date in Marbella it ended in either disaster or a dead end. If the guy she was out with wasn't interrupted by a VIP phone call just as she was about to deliver her punchline in a story, he had a back catalogue of relationships that screamed 'run for the Sierra Nevada mountains and never look back!' This whole escapade felt as pointless as every other.

"I can barely contain my excitement," Ricky quipped. "Maybe they'll have old granny throws and a couple of corgi dogs that can sit on your lap as you sip your way through a pot of Earl Grey like the queen."

Everybody laughed at this, Freya included, even if it did sound like a much better proposition. Although she had lived in Marbella ever since her parents had made the whole family up sticks from Brighton for a new life in the sun, Freya was notoriously grumpy in Spain's winter months, drinking endless tea just to survive. How she had coped with southern England's freezing temperatures from November to March until her early teens, she would never know.

"All right, I'll try to make the best of it," she pacified the gang, wondering for the hundredth time why she had fallen for the 'charms' of Tinder again. In Spain, like other countries, the App was renowned for being more 'hook-up', less bona fide date. "And no strolling past and rubbernecking through the window to keep tabs on my progress like last time."

A chorus of snickers ensued. Hannah, in the corner of the room packaging a Christmas cake for the town hall's annual party, shook her head in disbelief at her colleagues' antics.

"We only wanted to make sure you weren't out with a nutter," chirruped Jimena.

"See!" Freya flung her palms wide. "This is exactly why I cannot be arsed. I don't know if I want to go through the same old restaurant/café/bar routine, only to get the same old results."

Now she felt like a hypocrite, because at least her

colleagues were being proactive on her behalf. When had Freya ever done anything about trying to meet a man in less obvious circumstances?

"Somehow I can't quite see you getting it on with a guy halfway across the flimsy bridge over the Caminito del Rey's gorge, like the adrenaline junkies do," said Nicola.

"Is that so?" Freya arched her brow. "You'd be very surprised at my sense of adventure in that case. Well... my past sense of adventure."

It was true. Freya had relished getting a regular dose of fresh air and engaging in all manner of outdoor pursuits, prior to setting up shop. Those had been the good old days when she'd had a work-life balance – not that she could protest at what she'd achieved on paper, or in her bank account. This lot, though, appeared to have pigeonholed her as a homely little old lady who needed to get out more. Well, it was time they got to know the dark horse she had once been. The wicked cogs in Freya's brain started whirring and now she could feel a revenge team building event on paragliders coming on. That would soon shut their pie holes. Which was a pretty uncivilized thought, so best to leave it in her head. She loved her co-workers to bits really, except when it came to their incessant matchmaking banter. It was easy to toss this about like cheap confetti when you were either married, in a committed and loving relationship, or a player yourself (aka. Ricky).

"You wouldnae catch me putting as much as a wee toe on that scunnered walkway," Ricky shrieked.

"Don't be daft," said Hannah in her Yorkshire accent, ever the voice of wisdom. She didn't often contribute to group discussions but when she did she made her point known. "It requires more bravery to add the finer details to thousands of pounds worth of wedding cake. The Caminito is a literal rite of passage. You can't live in this part of the world without having conquered it. It's just a walkway in a gorge and the views are incredible."

See, Hannah was so in tune with Freya. She could even read her mind.

"And I'm just a twenty-seven-year-old standing in front of a gorge four hundred metres above frigging sea level, screaming 'no way, José!'" Ricky cried, putting his unique spin on the infamous Notting Hill movie line.

"I think you've planted a seed, Nicola. We'll definitely get something extreme booked up for the spring," Freya confirmed with a laugh, loving that she could sneakily pin the adventurous proposal back on her pastry chef.

"Count me right out." Ricky shuddered. "You're bananas."

"Me too," said Nicola, despite having suggested it in the first place.

"Me three," chorused Jimena, predictable as ever.

"Sounds fab! I'm up for it." At least Alejandro was enthused.

Okay then, maybe the idea was a little rad. But Freya was already determined that she would get the team away from these four walls and out into the great outdoors. Fine. They'd start with a spot of car racing on the world famous Jerez race track instead. She just wouldn't tell them yet.

"Off you go," said Hannah, ushering Freya out the door and down the stairs. "We'll be fine. And if the date doesn't pan out, for the love of God don't suffer a second longer than necessary; come straight back here and I'll make you a cuppa and order an Uber. Oh, and don't forget to text me the moment you arrive so I've a pin of your location to pick you up if need be, although the bar staff should really be drilled to help if the guy's profile doesn't sync with reality and you want to extricate yourself from the venue."

Again, Hannah was the model employee. She simply said

and did all the right things. Always and without fail. Freya couldn't have asked for more.

Freya did as she was told and left the building, not before picking up the weekly charity box of donations that she and her staff contributed to the town hall's food bank scheme. The bags of lentils, chickpeas and rice weighed her down but it was important they did their bit. Times had been tough for those who worked in the tourist industry in the last couple of years, with many still out of work or struggling to support families on part-time wages while they waited for visitor numbers to go back to their previous levels, and more permanent roles to arrive. Freya wasn't one to blow her own trumpet but this box from FOM's employees was just a supplement to the huge weekly charity supermarket shop she did privately online.

She inhaled the heady fragrance of the old town's square, marvelling at how superbly its clusters of trees loaded with dazzling ripe oranges blended with the vibrant red of Marbella's poinsettias. Luckily, the town hall was directly opposite the cakery, across the square, so she didn't need to test her muscle power for long, and she gratefully made the drop at its reception. Weaving her way through the narrow, flower pot-strewn lanes, Freya reached the main road and crossed it, heading toward the sea. It felt strange to be leaving work at such an early hour. 6.30 p.m. was practically after lunch in this part of the world, and she felt more than a little guilty for abandoning her employees, despite knowing everything was ship-shape back in the cakery. But this was a date with a Norwegian. He preferred eating early, he'd said. Freya knew this already set the tone for the date. He (thought) he wore the decision-making trousers, and therefore he couldn't hope to win a piece of her heart (or her esteemed cake). Still, nothing could have prepared her for his opening dialogue when she reached the upmarket tapas bar.

He was – disappointingly – sitting indoors so she couldn't even wrap herself up in a fluffy *hygge* throw to navigate the experience.

"You are five and a half minutes late." Lars, who turned out to be skinny, lanky and ash-blond, tapped his chunky Rolex. *What the actual eff?* He'd need to do better than that.

Then he stood and extended his hand robotically for a shake as if this was a business meeting. Not that Freya much wished to brush her cheek against the lazy stubble on his face. "It's great to meet you at last. I've heard so much about you," he said next. What in the frick was that meant to mean? She hoped he was only referring to her professional reputation, and he hadn't been fed reports from the sparse suitors of her past. Perhaps this was some kind of challenge to see if he could be the one to defrost her heart?

"So anyway, I made the executive decision to order," he continued before Freya could as much as open her mouth with her own greeting. "We are having fried eggplant with honey, alioli potatoes, fried squid and black pudding. The wine I have selected for us this evening is a vintage and oaky dry Rioja. The most expensive bottle on the menu." Lars added the kind of wink and skew-whiff grin he clearly thought would make Freya roll over into submission, begging him to take her right now.

Again, what the actual fuck? Freya was not going to censor the cuss words in her head. This wasn't some regency period drama where women were second class citizens, unable to formulate an opinion for themselves. She could have been a veggie for all he knew.

On the subject of drink, Freya wanted a gin and tonic. She was one of those 'curious' women who couldn't appreciate the dehydrating and vinegary attraction of wine, red, white or rosé. Not that she needed to justify herself. And how had Lars intuitively ordered every single tapa that she loathed? There were plenty of options on the menu that Freya loved. If only she'd been given the chance to choose for herself – but apparently she was a child.

Lars rolled up the sleeves of his blazer so that he looked like an eighties yuppie, finally lifted the aviator sunglasses from his eyes, tipping them backwards to rest on his tufty hair, and pinned Freya with his steely blue gaze. Oh, he looked exactly like his profile picture on her dating app. On steroids. This was like being in one of those live-action animation movies, where the cartoon character and human being generally tend to wind one another up to the point of volcanic eruption.

"I cannot tell you what an amazing day today has been for business," Lars crooned, oblivious to Freya's musing as they took their seats. He helped himself to a handful of breadsticks from a pot that he moved to his side of the table. Freya knew it was uncouth, but she would have loved to shove them up his backside. She chewed back her snort laugh.

"Well, that's great. I've had a pretty successful day myself, I¾"

"My Nordic kitchen design company has a contract for two million euros in the bag," Lars squealed like a pig, rubbing his hands together ferociously. "The biggest real estate company on the coast wants *my ideas* to run seamlessly through their showhomes and into every specification of apartments surrounding one of Spain's top golf courses. It doesn't get better than that." He grinned, seemingly into the distance, until Freya followed his gaze. He was scanning the figure of a Barbie-doll woman who would make the perfect accompaniment to Lars' Ken-like self.

Freya put her rapidly mounting disdain on ice and played along, indulging the braggart by listening intently to his one-sided conversation about his plans for retail expansion into the Canary islands. Something incredibly strange was happening today. Just like the spontaneous idea Nicola had planted in her head earlier, now along came another. She would bide her time though, sitting through this horrific monologue of boasts until the right moment.

"Simon Cowell has just requested a quote for a bespoke spin-off of our largest mega island to go in the middle of his new villa's kitchen."

Whoop-de-doo.

"I had breakfast this morning at the same café as George and Amal Clooney."

And probably gave them indigestion.

"Next week I'm going to a Gala dinner hosted by Penelope Cruz."

The poor woman doesn't know what she's let herself in for...

Freya had never been starstruck. Fame and fortune didn't impress her. People were people, no matter where they came in the recognition stakes. She'd designed and baked wedding cakes for a handful of A listers – and a profusion of B and C listers – ironing out the finer details with them over the phone when they were too busy to call into the cakery to see her in person. Though she appreciated the custom, the celebrity game was meaningless and those who got off on name-dropping to the extent of the man sitting opposite her really needed to get a life.

Then came Lars' most fabulous line to date, delivered just as the waiter lovingly placed the tray of assorted tapas before them.

"So, I was thinking… my kitchens and your cakes could make some *beauuuuutiful* music, Freya." Lars inserted a majorly cheesy wink into his pitch. "My stunning fjord- and forest-inspired kitchen table range would boost your profile enormously and elevate your finished products to the next level."

Lars' eyes bored into Freya's skull while her stomach

THE WEDDING CAKE

churned in protest. *Hardly* – the last time she checked, bridal couples tended to get married *outside* of the kitchen.

"I've been doing the maths: I like the HEA dream you've created for Marbella's destination wedding venue clients." Now his glance raked over her bust. "The towering *naked* layer cake you made for last weekend's wedding at the golf course sent shivers down my spine. Let's get something in the diary for next week."

Oh, if Ricky could be a fly on the wall right now. He was FOM's sole naked layer cake decorator. Freya could already hear the puns of retaliation flying out of his mouth.

Without waiting for her say-so, her date pulled his smartphone out of the inside pocket of his jacket with one hand, wolfing down a particularly slimy disc of aubergine with the other. The idiot was something else. Freya had seen and heard quite enough of his targeted lingo and shameless snooping. How long had she been the jackass's case study?

"*Perdona*," she caught the attention of a passing waiter. "*Una botella de Bollinger, por favor.*"

The waiter nodded and sped to the bar.

"Awesome, babe. I knew you'd agree," said Lars, assuming Freya had ordered a bottle of champagne to celebrate. "Now then." He started tapping through the days of the week on his gadget with a stylus. "Monday and Tuesday I'm in hot demand but Wednesday evening suits me fine. The question is," he paused to let the words linger on the air. "Your place or mine?"

Before Freya had the chance to reply, the waiter returned with an ice bucket and two glasses, his timing spot on for her to instruct him that only one glass was required, as she handed him a crisp fifty euro note. Lars' pencil thin lips struggled to hold a smirk on the edge of combustion but Freya didn't care. She took a sip of her Bolly, got her own more modest phone out, banged out a quick and belated 'I'm here and all is well' message to Hannah, held her glass aloft in a toast to thin air and then captured the image on her mobile's camera for posterity.

"Cheers to me and cheers to never again agreeing to a date in a restaurant, café or bar…" What had she just said to her staff about the predictability of foodie fraternizing? "In other words, *never again* will I fall for the empty promise of meeting a man in a *goddamn eatery* or anywhere else of a stereotypical pick-up nature. Lars, you have an incredible talent for making a woman wake up and smell the coffee… and the – *bleugh* – pongy garlic-laden potatoes."

Freya wrinkled her nose, ignoring the puzzled embarrassment on Lars' face. Out of the corner of her eye she could see she'd amassed quite an audience, everybody else's chatter having stopped to the extent you could hear a pin (or a grain of paella rice) drop. Next she positioned the bowls of tapas just so, as if she was directing a wedding cake photo shoot, hooking a squid ring over Lars' ring finger on his left hand – later realising it should have been his right hand since he was Norwegian: *minor detail* – and making certain her gawking subject was the centrepiece for a second shot.

"Stay right where you are, *babe*," she instructed him as she quickly set up the zoom lens on her phone's camera. "I've got a bigger social media following than your bank balance and we'll soon have this little *catch of the day* advertorial all over Marbs. The ladies will be queuing round the block now you're offering your hand." Freya snapped a perfectly gormless picture of Lars, and indulged in some speedy and expert hashtag priming, so that soon the desperate tableau was all over Instagram, Twitter and Facebook. Her date, meanwhile, remained speechless. Smirk gone, mouth wide open. "I would leave you with the rest of this bottle." Freya picked up the champagne and hugged it possessively to her chest, "But you deserve something as old as your chat-up lines, so you can keep the red. *Adios* and definitely not *hasta la vista!*"

Freya walked out of the tapas bar, stunned at her own over the top performance. But something had to give and she was not prepared to take a moment more of the smart-arse's bullshit. The champagne bottle she clutched tightly in her hand garnered her numerous looks of approval and disapproval as she paced through the streets, only stopping when she reached the wide boulevard flanking Marbella's beach. It was virtually empty of tourists of course, this being low season. The mildness of the day was fast dissipating in hues of amber and plum as the clouds scudded across the sky. She stood at the wall, took a swig of her drink to buoy her up, looked out to the horizon, took a deep breath, and, for the first time in a decade, she gingerly – then more decidedly – tiptoed onto the sand, ecstatic with herself for overcoming such a large hurdle, and not just of the walking-away-from-the-wacky-wooing-game variety.

Freya wouldn't even deliver a cake to a beach venue. The task was always passed to one of her colleagues, not that any of them seemed to twig that she had a phobia of the seaside. The very last time Freya had set foot on any stretch of coastline was the day of her own wedding. The day Sid had left her at the floral hoop altar.

Sid's eyes had been the giveaway. It's true, they are the windows to the soul. Freya's father had walked her towards the stunning circle of pastel peach and blush pink flowers that she and Sid had chosen to symbolise their unbreakable unity, but instead of looking starry-eyed at his fast-approaching bride, Sid couldn't meet Freya's gaze at all. Even from afar Freya, who was long-sighted, could see that Sid was looking just above her forehead. As if that wasn't unnerving enough, a nun had already crossed Freya's path just as she'd stepped out of the golf buggy that had dropped her and her father off at the beach's wooden boardwalk. Freya had immediately cursed herself for reading too much into old wives' tales. But with every step she took in her crystal-embellished flip flops, the sudden terror of what was to come engulfed her. This was worse than walking the plank. The sea would swallow her mortification, submerging her from the pity of her family and friends, if only she could have traded places with a pirate right now. To add insult to injury, the next thing she knew, a teenage member of Sid's side of the congregation had dropped their ring in the aisle. One of those gold-plated sovereign medallion rings that were the specialty of the high street. It wheeled along diagonally from Freya's left side, coming to a brisk halt on a petal in front of her. She stepped over it, knowing she had now received her three omens that this wedding was doomed: nun, Sid's shiftiness, ring drop. The minister could sense it too, his greeting dithery and wooden all at once. But it was Sid's calm and softly-spoken words that were the most tragic:

"Freya, I'm sorry, sweetheart. I can't be the man that you deserve. The thing is… I'm having a number of affairs. Three to be precise." The minister swayed at this point, emitting a very definite *mierda* under his breath, and Freya feared he might pass out on her. Still, she hung on Sid's words with misty eyes, as if he were saying his wedding vows. "I know this is lame and unbelievably weak. I know I should have come clean by now. You just got under my skin a little more than the rest. You're such a wonderful person, such a strangely beautiful and intriguing woman. I guess I thought I could have my cake and eat it until marriage put an end to my wild ways. But, despite how amazing you look today…" Sid paused and let his eyes rove over her. Freya blinked rapidly as if that might wake her from the strange out of body experience. "And despite the fact I know you would be an incredible wife, the truth is that standing here on the day I should be committing to you, I can't get Cecile, Ana or Simona out of my head."

Freya watched on, dread plummeting from her stomach to her toes as her fiancé spun on his heel, then ran as fast as he could across the rippling sand, past their small collection of nearest and dearest.

Strangely beautiful? Was that even a compliment?

The modern day Freya would have thrown a bucket of sand in Sid's face and put a spadeful of giant Spanish ants down his boxers. For starters. And how dare he bring her beloved cake into the mix? Merv might throw in his 'ambushed by cake' jokes in reference to one Boris Johnson and his unsavoury birthday party celebrations during lockdown in a pandemic, but Sid truly was using cake as his excuse: the very food that kept a roof over Freya and her employees' heads. She'd never felt so insulted. In Freya's world that made him just as immoral as the clown at Ten Downing Street. Thank God (not that Freya was sure God existed after that fateful day) none of the congregation overheard that bit – or any of Sid's fucked-up spiel. No, all Freya and Sid's friends and family got were the mumbles of an inept groom, the tears of a jilted bride, and an all-you-can-eat seafood buffet with sangria on tap. That was the real reason Freya hadn't gone near a squid ring or a glass of *tinto de verano*, the local name for sangria, since her twenty-fifth summer on planet Earth. Oh, and consequently, that was the reason Freya had banned cake pop wedding cakes from her kitchen. She couldn't bear to be within a thousand kilometres of the things.

She couldn't have looked more stunning on that wedding day. Her unruly curls had been tamed and half tied back in dried flower hair combs, and her flawless, natural makeup had been applied by one of Marbella's top artists. Admittedly, her casual white chiffon dress was understated to the max but it was also the epitome of less is more; everything Sid claimed to love about her. They were tying the knot on a laid-back beach, after all, not in some fancy colonial mansion or a luxury villa.

And what about those other women? Had they realised they were part of a harem?

Freya had pelted to the north of the beach seconds after Sid, her dad struggling along behind her with his arthritic hip, while the congregation froze in their seats. Which made it look as if she'd been desperately chasing after her ex-fiancé, but she could hardly sit it out on a deckchair and wait for a rescue ship, much less swim south to the haven of Morocco, even if the African coastline was just a few kilometres away. And Freya refused to veer east or west across the sand in her wedding dress to enliven the afternoons of July's sun worshippers either. That was the hot lifeguard's job.

Present-day Freya continued to walk closer to the shore. She'd done this a million times in her head but every single visualisation had resulted in grappling with a panic attack that she wasn't strong enough to overcome. Not today. How could she have let Sid take this freedom away from her for so long? This stretch of coastline was a human right. It connected Europe to Africa. It teemed with magic and the possibility of new horizons. Its waves twinkled serenely or ferociously, forever treating its onlookers to a panoply of blues, greens and greys through sunshine and storms. If only Freya had been brave enough to test the waters (or sand) in real-life before. Now the moment had arrived, everything about returning to the space where she'd been rejected was easier than she'd imagined. She felt completely free, in control, and stronger than ever. And far from being shunned, she felt embraced.

In hindsight she should have known Sid would screw up.

The clues had been flying in thick and fast for the longest time. Not so much the classic lipstick on collar or perfume lingering in the air. Not even his weekly business trips, which had been part of the routine since she'd met him; his lofty position with his UK company meant that he could be home *and* office-based, so he would fly in and out of Malaga airport like the breeze. No, it was the sudden fascination with Monet's art and Bordeaux wine (no matter how much more expensive it was than the Spanish supermarket's Rioja); the increasing appearance of Real Madrid football shirts (despite Sid pledging his allegiance to Malaga FC), and the crinkled tickets for Rome's opera house in his trouser pockets that piqued her curiosity. None of which added up, when Freya knew full well that Sid's clients were based in the UK and Ireland, the US and Australia.

Freya suspected that these *lucky ladies* had all met Sid in similar circumstances to her: a tried, tested and polished mid-aisle collision at a trade fair, followed by a trip to a conveniently close swanky bar. Sid worked in publishing, and when she first had the misfortune of clapping eyes on him, Freya had been in the early stages of promoting and developing her own business: high-end cakes. Bristol-based Sid had had a few business meetings to stay behind for at the end of his industry's trade show at London's Olympia (before the venue transformed itself for the food show) and had found himself lumbered with the task of packing up his company's stand – something that was not the norm for one of his rank. He'd made that abundantly clear during his and Freya's 'accidental' intro when he'd bumped into her, and dropped a mysteriously open briefcase of paperwork all over the floor. But the Martinis he'd later plied her with softened her perception so much that the slick performance was forgotten in a heartbeat. The rest, as they say, is history.

Freya no longer believed in marriage after Sid had humiliated her so badly. Not for herself, anyway. But she did believe in turning negatives into positives. That's why she'd gone full throttle with the business despite her own personal disaster, more focused than ever on ensuring that everybody else got their special day without a hitch.

Now she'd reached the shoreline. It wasn't the same section of sand. Her feet, out of her kitten heels, were digging into the cool, damp stretch of Playa de la Fontanilla, while her wedding had taken place on Ventura del Mar beach. Sid had chosen it specifically as it had been the playground of the sixties jet set. Extremely fitting. All of that hedonism, bed-hopping and free love.

Freya didn't care if she got a soggy bottom. She settled herself on the coarse, biscuity sand (despite all the paradise images of Marbella's coastline, it was actually nowhere near as enticing as neighbouring Costa de la Luz), swigging champagne from the bottle. Perhaps she should have taken the glass, but she didn't fancy the waiter chasing her. Although maybe that wouldn't have been so bad. He was kind of cute! Then she giggled and giggled *and giggled*. The scant few joggers and dog walkers could knit their brows and frown at her oddball antics all they liked. There really was something rather momentous and magical about today. As if the universe had marked the entry on a calendar long ago as the point in time when the curse would end, when Freya would snap out of her brain fog and open her eyes. It was only a Thursday, and there was never anything very outstanding about a weekday in winter on paper. Yet as the sun dipped beneath the crest of the mountains over her shoulder, Freya knew that when she woke up tomorrow morning, she would be a new woman.

She already was one.

ALICE

It was beyond flash but once that Mervyn Meehan guy had shown Alice the eight-tier showstopper cake, there was no going back. It was River's doing, really. All that exciting talk of a tour around Spain and Portugal for a honeymoon. Bear with her, and Alice would explain…

Yes, eight layers of cake was far too much for a newlywed couple and their guests to munch their way through – well, in small to average wedding terms, anyway. Even Hayley, their all-things-saccharine-in-vast-quantities friend, would probably struggle to find a home for it. But Alice missed last Christmas's foodie adventure with River in their retro, racing-green camper van more than words could say. As soon as it had become clear that their new life in Cornwall wasn't working out for them, the couple had returned to their childhood home of Glastonbury in Somerset, intent on getting to know it and the cute surrounding villages better. It had been an amazing sabbatical in the camper van (if a little chilly) and they'd enlisted the help of friends to supply them with gourmet gingerbread and hot chocolate, which they'd sold to villagers as they'd pootled about the countryside uniting communities and reigniting the previously flagging Christmas spirit. They'd even unwittingly played Cupid to two of their friends in the process. And on the subject of weddings, Alice hoped it wouldn't be long before Zara and Bruno would tie the knot...

Alice knew River missed every aspect of their wintery escapade too, hence suggesting they spend most of their honeymoon in 'Twinkle'. All of which meant they could do something similar to their Christmas jaunt, sharing a huge part of their wedding cake and bringing a little community spirit to Spain, handing it out to locals in quaint *pueblos* on the first leg of their holiday, giving something back to beautiful Andalucía, the vast southern chunk of the country where the finca was located. What better way to start married life together? After a suitably heavy night of passion, of course.

Alice had flinched when Mervyn sent her the quotation for the cake. It was one third of the finca's rental cost! But this was a one-off day. She did not intend to repeat it and River didn't need to know the way it had been funded. The other cakes Mervyn had presented via mouthwatering screenshots during their hour-long Zoom chat were delightful too, but something about the showstopper tugged at Alice's heart and purse strings and wouldn't let go. She'd just have to cut corners on her dress.

It would be incredibly vain to shout it out loud, but Alice knew she was a natural beauty, such had been her fate since birth. She didn't need anything pavlova-esque to jazz herself up. Simple would work best in the fashion stakes on her wedding day. In fact, she intended to head to a small business on Etsy and pair up a plain ivory gown with some baseball boots. Similarly, she wasn't overly fussy about her hair or her bouquet. The areas that deserved to have money thrown at them were those that included everybody's enjoyment: a finca with as many mattresses as possible for weary heads, perhaps a couple of glamping tents in the garden so nobody had to take out an overdraft just to be there. Then the meal, the wine, the styling of the venue, a Spanish guitarist, churros and ice cream carts, fun things to keep their friends' kids occupied; a couple of all-expenses paid day trips on a minibus… and, yeah, the cake.

Back home in their small town of Glastonbury, Alice and River were in the middle of converting a caravan park into stables and a café, having been left it in River's aunt Sheba's will, along with the old camper van. It had been quite a shock, especially as the bequest had coincided with the moment when River and Alice were wondering what to do with their lives next – aside from spending them together. The campsite had come with the proviso that River could make any changes to the land and its functionality that he saw fit (Sheba would have been the first to admit that the advent of Airbnb had sucked the profit out of her business), as long as her current staff still had jobs, should they wish to stay. Fortunately, every member of Sheba's workforce had been champing at the bit – pun not intended but appropriate – to help with the equine venture. This was to be a stables with a difference: fair-priced horse riding lessons available to the whole community, not just those born with a silver spoon in their mouth like Alice, hence her own level of proficiency in the saddle. Meanwhile, River's contribution to the enterprise would be a fair-trade eatery with a cracking view of the paddock and the iconic Glastonbury Tor. The kind of get-up that served local, organically grown produce; showcasing producers in a little farm shop tacked on to the cafe, encouraging folk to switch up their buying habits – at least occasionally. There was still a lot of work to be done but everything was shaping up beautifully and Alice couldn't feel more excited about married life now they'd put down some firm roots and created a joint vision for the future.

After talking at length online, Mervyn had booked her and River in for a taste test of the gargantuan wedding cake at FOM, baker extraordinaire Freya Ashcroft's mini emporium. How serendipitous was that! Alice knew from her wedding research, as well as past gloating by Tamara, her older sister, after attending many a society bash in and around Marbella, that securing a cake from Ms. Ashcroft was no mean feat. True, there were any number of cake makers Mervyn could have turned to, but Freya's company was his number one go-to and he 'knew her diary inside out and like the back of his hand'. As luck would have it, both the finca and the cake would be available on August the sixth. It was definitely meant to be.

On a dull, grey weekend in February, Alice and River hopped on a plane at Bristol airport, switching humdrum skies for cobalt blue ones.

"I don't think we've been here since our whistle stop tour around the Med," said River with a happy sigh. He squinted at the sun's golden rays across the tarmac as they walked to the Arrivals hall at the busy airport which serviced the Costa del Sol. "I'm so excited to see this part of Spain properly. Last time we were here it was with the band to support the Jackson Five at that posh tennis club, do you remember?" Alice winced, recalling how Jermaine had politely declined River's offer to step in as the fifth Jackson in the late Michael's place, since he had the same surname.

She went quiet at this point. Glenn, the wooden bit part American actor she'd unfathomably been enamoured with, prior to finally getting it on with the man who had always truly had her heart, had brought her to Spain on numerous occasions since the band's tour. But hedonistic Ibiza and bustling Barcelona were thankfully a world away from

THE WEDDING CAKE

Andalucía, so Alice wouldn't need to relive any of the memories associated with those tempestuous couple of years. She was here to make new Spanish memories with River.

After a leisurely brunch – and sex – at the gorgeously old-school Parador hotel that River had booked them into in Malaga city, Alice and River caught a taxi to nearby Marbella. They were to meet Mervyn at the orange tree square in the old town for refreshments prior to the all-important cake tasting. It seemed crazy to be focusing on the finer points of the day when they hadn't even seen the finca in the flesh yet, but Freya could only fit them in this afternoon, and back in England, building work was starting on the second stable block on Monday, so the pair couldn't extend their visit. Tomorrow Mervyn would take them to the finca, adding on a vineyard stop and two prospective caterers too. Then on Friday they'd go out for a late lunch with Mervyn (crunching numbers and firming up preliminary details) after visiting a potential hairdresser and makeup artist, florist, photographer and churros vendor. It was just as well that the wedding was in the summer because waistlines would balloon over the next few days – even slender ones.

"Dahlings! Over here," came a mild Irish accent. Alice and River looked all around, but there were so many people milling about they weren't even sure the call was aimed at them. "Yes, yoo-hoo! I'm talking to you, Al and Riv!"

Alice spun and almost knocked over the older man who had crept up from nowhere behind her. "I'd have recognised your stunning complexion a mile off, my dear," said Mervyn, tagging on a light chuckle, and Alice tried not to cringe. She could sense River's hackles rising, especially at such premature name shortening. This was not an ideal start.

"How lovely to meet you after all our correspondence," Alice greeted Mervyn a little more formally and offered her hand for a shake. "We're a bit early but we were keen to soak up the atmosphere of the old town before things get hectic with the visits."

"Oh, I insist that you do," Mervyn replied, kissing Alice's cheeks an excessive number of times and then diving in for a handshake with River. "I've secured us a table over yonder. Follow me." Off he tottered with his bling-encrusted hand capping his bling-encrusted cane. Now Alice could sense River recoiling, not wishing to be too closely associated with the curious man, although he certainly didn't look out of place in the swish environment. Alice and River were in casual shirts and jeans but many of the locals wore seriously expensive-looking suits and dresses, flaunting accessories to match, as if they'd stepped fresh off the catwalk via Tiffany & Co.

Once everyone was seated, their wedding planner ordered them a round of non-negotiable Pedro Ximénez sherry. Alice guessed this little routine was part and parcel of the theatrics: get your clients merry, all the better to sign on the dotted line for all manner of wedding extras. She'd have to be on her guard, although it would be impossible for Mervyn to talk them into upgrading their cake this afternoon. It was FOM's most expensive and nothing surpassed it.

"We wouldn't normally touch alcohol in the daytime," River muttered as the waiter returned at lightning speed with their order. "But thanks, Mr Meehan, I salute your choice. I'm a bit of a connoisseur myself, having set up Glastonbury's flagship cocktail bar back home." Hmm, and one utter nosedive of a cocktail bar in Cornwall, thought Alice, although they didn't tend to talk about that nowadays if they could avoid it. River took an appreciative sip of the light mahogany liquid and further perked up. "The Pedro

Manhattan is one of my specialties, as it happens." He arched a brow.

"The name's Mervyn... and is it now? How very fascinating. I'm quite partial to a Rob Roy myself," he said, adjusting his lilac cravat. "I know one of the grape producers up in Jerez rather well. Remind me to give you their card later. Alice mentioned that you're keen to do a touring honeymoon of southern Spain after the wedding. Such a charming idea. A visit to my pal and his vineyard is a must!"

And relax... Alice could finally shake off the dread she'd been carrying for weeks building up to this trip. These two were going to get on like a house on fire. There was no way River would quibble over the price of the cake today, or the cost of the finca tomorrow, or start calculating all the jobs that could happen at the stables and café with the money instead – the jobs that Alice's secret windfall was supposed to be contributing to. Another round of sherry, and all of her boyfriend's financial concerns would dissolve in a puff of Dragon's Breath (the cocktail, not the mythical creature; wedding planning didn't need any more unnecessary challenges).

"Excuse me," said Mervyn, whose mobile phone had buzzed into action. He twisted himself sideways in an apparent bid to be discreet but Alice could still hear his conversation. "Yes, yes of course. Don't you fret, my dear. We're all raring to go and as famished as those hippos in that dreadful plastic ball-eating game the grandchildren rope me into whenever I visit. We'll see you in approximately two minutes."

Oh, there went the no-cake-price-quibbling guarantee then. What a shame Mervyn hadn't ordered everyone a double. Alice should have sipped at her own goblet instead of downing it, then she could have topped River's glass up when he wasn't looking. It sounded suspiciously like Freya Ashcroft was ready for them now.

"So that was the lady herself," said Mervyn on cue. "She's all set up in the courtyard and wants us to head to her for the tasting asap."

River really must have warmed to Mervyn – he'd pulled out his wallet and extracted a note.

"It would be on me even if cash was required, River," Mervyn held his hands up in protest. "Fortunately, I have an account here that doesn't need settling yet. Chippety-chop, off we pop."

Hello? *Did he really just say that?*

Apparently yes because River's eyes were on stalks at this man and his eccentricities.

Crossing the square and navigating the throngs of people moving at turtle speed, the three of them made their way to the Freya's of Marbella shop. The stylised font finally came into view through a knot of gnarly orange trees.

Mervyn pushed open the door to the cakery and they were immediately hit by a heady and magical aroma of vanilla, sugar and chocolate. A stout young woman with a heavy copper, ruler-straight fringe stepped forward to shake everybody's hands, introducing herself as Hannah in a delightful Yorkshire accent. It was kind of a homely touch, but Alice hoped Freya employed Spanish people too.

"Freya's upstairs. She won't be a moment. Let me take you all out to the courtyard and get you seated, then I'll fix you up with some tea and coffee, and we'll bring the cake out."

"Fabulous!" Mervyn patted his stomach, nudging past Hannah to lead them through the shop. "This way, please." He twirled his cane in the air and Alice couldn't miss Hannah's grimace at its proximity to the rotating cake display on the counter. The man put her in mind of an older version of the original Willy Wonka actor, Gene Wilder.

Mannerisms and looks-wise. It was evident he'd been facially nipped and tucked. She hoped there wasn't a chocolate river awaiting them out the back.

Thankfully the small courtyard was as serene as it was pretty, with no evidence of edible props. Straight out of a bridal magazine. Freya and her team had decorated it alluringly. A spider's web of tiny, sparkly fairy lights created a mini sky-at-night above them, whilst petal confetti created a fetching carpet on the patio's tiles. A water feature soothed Alice's last minute nerves regarding all things financial. Elegant harp music serenaded everybody gently from a hidden device, and a vase of the most incredible white flowers Alice had ever seen sat beguilingly in the middle of the table.

"Wow, wow, WOW," she said. "What a feast for the eyes, and we haven't even started on the cake."

On taking in a three-sixty panorama of the spectacle himself, River seemed to have disappointingly sobered up. *Completely.* Fortunately, Freya appeared before he could suggest they'd come to the wrong place and that their budget didn't quite extend to this.

"Good afternoon, everybody. It's a pleasure to meet you. I don't usually get starstruck but I must admit to being a fan of your music, guys! When Mervyn added your details to my order book," Freya raised a wing like a chicken, referring to the tatty green thing tucked under her arm, "I didn't for one minute twig that a Jackson-Goldsmith wedding would mean we'd have the honour of baking a wedding cake fit for rock stars. I'm beyond thrilled!"

Freya stuck out her free hand for a shake. She seemed so genuinely warm and friendly, and she and Alice shared exactly the same corkscrew curls, albeit Freya's were super bouncy, given her bob cut, and as caramel in colour as the kind of stuff she no doubt simmered on her stove.

"Before we get down to business... can I just inquire as to the cost?" asked River, throwing Alice into a mammoth tailspin, setting her teeth on edge just like the grimacing Emoji she often used in WhatsApp messages. Flipping heck, they hadn't even taken their seats yet.

Alice was determined not to catch Mervyn's eye. She knew that he knew full well they had covered this aspect in great detail during their on-screen chat.

"The show stopper is seven thousand euros plus VAT," Freya stated calmly.

Damn. Alice had imagined River okay-ing the expense in a sugar haze after he'd sampled each of the four scrumptious layers of salted caramel, Victoria sandwich, red velvet and lemon curd with passionfruit. Her timing was so out. If only they'd got to that last layer. She knew it would be the most delicious, instantly rendering all thoughts of price tags obsolete. She would have flinched, but they were here now and she'd just have to find a way to persuade her other half.

"Seven thousand euros! *Sheesh.*" Argh, River didn't half remind Alice of Kermit the Frog when he came out with that word – which wasn't too often, thank goodness. Why did he have to make her feel so unnecessarily Miss Piggy about everything, and in front of strangers, too? "Al, are you quite sure about this?"

"Merv?" Quick as a whip, Freya read the situation and commandeered the beaming wedding planner, pulling him back inside the cakery, with Hannah following closely behind. "We'll just leave you both to it and plate up the samples."

Alice was mortified. This was the first time River had questioned her over any kind of spending and dammit, it would be the last, even if there was technically a revelation she should be sharing with him.

"Look, I know I've done the stereotypically blokish thing

and left all of the organisation to you, for which I can only apologise again." River outstretched his palms. "But it's been so hands-on with project managing the building of the stables, café and shop while you've been sorting out the horses, the riding instructors, and the marketing… Which isn't to say that your work to get everything up and running back home has been lighter than mine." River stopped for a breath and Alice steeled herself for the giant BUT that was sure to hit her any moment now. "I know you're way more clued up about prices and all of the finer detail that's needed to make it an amazing day… b-but *seven thou*… is rather a lot to spend on a cake, which will soon become crumbs! Surely, the old dude mentioned the cost before? Couldn't we go for something a bit… you know… smaller?"

Now Alice sighed deeply. It was unfair not to be straight with her fiancé but she really wanted the reason for the cake to be a surprise and, until the stables, café and shop were finished and everything had been given that final lick of paint, she did not intend to reveal the identity of the benefactor funding their riding business. River would go nuts. He'd made it clear that the person in question had crossed a line and was undeserving of a second of Alice's time. Her groom-to-be thought the frequent contributions to the works were coming from her own modest income pot from their music days, and she didn't plan to disabuse him just yet.

"You're going to have to trust me on this, Riv. We can afford it. I've done the maths. I know it might seem out of character for me to splash out but," she thought on her feet, remembering something she'd read in a wedding magazine, "the wedding cake symbolises prosperity, good luck and *fertility*."

The abundance of spotlights in the courtyard revealed River's flush within seconds.

"Oh, right. I see," he whispered, blue eyes growing ever wider, jet-black pupils dilating.

Typical man. Alice eye-rolled inwardly, detecting the cogs set in motion in River's brain. Yes, she wanted kids but not a platoon of them. However, since things were going so well, she added, "And it's really important that it's made from the highest quality ingredients in order for those things to come to pass."

"Okay. You've converted me." River winked, hands aloft to cease Alice's explanation. "But never mind eating it, now I'll be whisking you off to the finca's master bedroom the moment we've cut the cake, sweetheart."

"Shh. Keep your voice down! They're coming back."

River filled a water glass from the crystal jug on the table and gulped it in one. Thank goodness. It was like a power shower to the crimson hue of his cheeks. Meanwhile, Hannah and a tray of aromatic coffee and tea led the procession back to the courtyard. A tentative Mervyn appeared next at the doorway with a demi-smile as he eyed the magnificent cake stand of morsels in his hands; he seemed to be sauntering about rather nicely without the aid of his posh walking stick all of a sudden. And Freya brought up the rear with a tower of plates, a further cake stand bearing yet more precision-cut squares of layer cake, and a collection of forks. Alice was drooling.

Once everything was arranged on the table, Freya invited everybody to take their seats and Hannah served up their drinks, adding:

"As I always say, if anybody would prefer a special herbal infusion, just shout!"

"I can't speak for myself," said Mervyn, knitting his brow. "But you really are quite a puzzle, Hannah, throwing that line in every time I bring my clients here. Pure caffeine is just fine. Nobody wants any of that murky witch's brew," he scoffed.

Sheesh, to borrow that annoying word of River's from moments ago. Alice couldn't see any harm in Hannah's innocent and thoughtful query.

"Merv!" Freya admonished. "It was good of Hannah to offer up an alternative. Some people prefer non-caffeinated drinks. Alice and River, are you happy with your bog-standard tea and coffee?"

"Perfect as we are, but thanks for asking," Alice answered for both of them. Whilst they hailed from Glastonbury, the town of all things alternative, Alice and River couldn't bear herbal tea.

Hannah skulked back towards the cakery and Alice's heart went with her. What a sod Mervyn was to talk to her like that. Maybe he'd been sinking the sherries before they'd met him. Hannah peered over her shoulder then, and if Alice wasn't imagining things, the assistant's eyes appeared to glimmer. Alice looked again to be sure, but Hannah had turned away. Ah, well. Perhaps it was just the effect of the copious illuminations, the sherry from earlier, and all the cake excitement.

Freya tentatively recapped on the pricing and Alice could hardly believe the updated and carefree version of River sitting next to her. He happily signed the paperwork along with Alice and Mervyn, and the deposit was paid. Not before some orgasmic sounds were made around the table. Alice supposed Freya was used to them by now but it was a bit embarrassing given they were coming from Mervyn as well.

The base cake layer – and the biggest in terms of circumference – would be salted caramel. Freya had placed the crystal plate loaded with that flavour in the centre of the table.

"Only the very best dulce de leche caramel – a secret

recipe from South America – goes in this," Freya told them as she nudged the plate closer to Alice and River and gestured for them to help themselves.

Alice couldn't wait to dive in and was more amused than irritated to see Mervyn had beaten her and River to it. But then who could blame him, if this was the fusion of flavours he got every time he chaperoned his clients? Within seconds Alice felt as blissed out as the sultry rabbit cartoon character who used to appear in the Cadbury's Caramel commercials. She flicked her gaze to River and stifled a laugh at the look of ecstasy on his face. Their guests would be rendered speechless over this all-important foundation of the construction. As would the Spanish villagers.

Next Freya wowed them with the Victoria sandwich tier. Alice honestly thought she'd died and gone to heaven. Growing up in a quintessentially English village, she had tasted many a Vicky sponge in the village hall and at the country house tables of her horsey friends, but nothing would ever again compare to FOM's version.

"I always use Asturias butter from the north of Spain," Freya explained. "If you've ever been to that area and you've seen the lush, green grass the cows eat, you'll understand why the sponge and the buttercream taste so sublime."

"We'll have to take a detour that way with Twinkle on the way back to the port after the honeymoon." River smiled.

A quick swig of tea cleansed everybody's palates and Mervyn wasted no time in pilfering a cube of the red velvet sponge next.

Freya assured them she only ever worked with the traditional recipe for red velvet cake, sourcing her anthocyanin cocoa – which gave the cake its colour – from the best supplier. The shade of the crumb was the proof of the pudding. The sponge was a deep, delectable scarlet; its thick smothering of cream cheese frosting was a bold contrast.

THE WEDDING CAKE

Finally, Freya offered the lemon curd and passionfruit sponge to Alice and River, before Mervyn could get his mitts on it. The wonderful smell and taste of lemon was enough to overpower the orange trees in the square outside.

"Okay, you can certainly bake, Freya," said River and everybody laughed.

Couldn't she just? Alice wasn't cake obsessed. She had a steely dietary willpower most human beings would crave almost as much as sugar cubes. But equally, when circumstance dictated, she was rather partial to a sweet treat, and, having been in a relatively successful band, naturally she'd had the opportunity to sample cake in many luxury destinations. Yet despite all those impressive morsels savoured around the world, she didn't think anything could beat the delicious samples she'd devoured today. This cake would be the focal point of the wedding and the perfect gift to everyone they encountered on the road. How much tastier things had become since her dreary days as a bridesmaid, when it had been all glacé cherries, super sweet marzipan and stodgy icing.

"Thanks!" Freya replied. "But I really can't take the credit. I have a brilliant team."

A loud snore made them all jump and Freya's face contorted as she gently nudged Mervyn out of his post-party slumber.

"Oh. I-I was just resting my eyes, that's all. Right." He sat bolt upright as if pulled up by invisible strings. "If we're all done here then chippety-chop, off we pop."

No, Alice and River hadn't mistaken the cringeworthy catchphrase the first time around. Freya cleared her throat as if to avert their attention. Alice guessed this was another of Mervyn's oddities she was accustomed to. Freya stood to shake their hands, took Mervyn under one wing and the ancient-looking order book full of their details under the other, leaving Alice and River to follow them through to the shop floor and back out into the orange tree square.

"You were right, and I will never doubt you again," said River with a gigantic smile. "This is going to be the best wedding ever – and we deserve to have our cake and eat it."

TIM

Tim couldn't believe it. Piper had booked the visit to the destination wedding planner in Spain without consulting him! It wasn't that he didn't fancy the idea of them exchanging their vows in the sun. It sounded perfect on the surface. But it wasn't so ideal that he'd had to rearrange all his fitness classes for the coming week, so he and Piper could flit about to supplier appointments. He hated messing with his clients. It wasn't in his nature, especially when it had taken him so long to build up a loyal tribe. Why did they have to travel overseas for their big day at all? It would be far from ideal for his mam who was in a wheelchair, or for his dad who suffered from travel sickness. There were plenty of impressive locations closer to home which would have made the logistics easier for both his and Piper's families – not to mention his friends. Nath, Josh and Kyle had been Tim's best mates since primary school and none of them were what you would call flush. Piper could more than afford to foot the bill for anybody struggling to finance their hotel and travel, of course. She could probably even put out some feelers with her contacts in hospitality to bag them a free hotel room. But nobody wanted to find themselves in such a humiliating predicament, did they?

Still, as the limo pulled up outside their hip and trendy hotel in Puerto Banus, the affluent harbour-side resort that merged into Marbella, he had to put all of those worries to one side for the moment and acknowledge his better half's stroke of genius. Not on account of the fancy building awaiting them, but because of the weather. February in Spain was a whole world away from February in Northern England. Hello blue skies and almost T-shirt temperatures. Hello morning runs that didn't chill you to the extremities. Tim might even hire a paddle board and hit the Mediterranean's sparkling turquoise waves while he was here. It would be good to infuse a little variety into his daily workout, in the absence of any visible trampolines or bungees. He was sure he could pick up a wetsuit somewhere near the port.

He'd jetted off with Piper on a string of all expenses paid trips since they'd become an item, which meant he had stayed in a handful of luxury hotels. But for all of that, Tim never loved their bells and whistles. He was a simple man with simple tastes. Give him a no-frills B&B and a decent cooked breakfast any day. Alas, ever mindful of squeezing work opportunities into their forays, Piper had booked them into what could only be described as a juiced up 'Instagram hotel' for their wedding planning spree. After posing next to the reception desk's giant gold pineapple for a flurry of pictures with their complementary mojitos, Tim and Piper were whisked away to an equally bling lift. This was encrusted with Swarovski crystals, and would naturally beg for myriad selfies as the days flew by.

"Ohemgee!" Piper squealed, abandoning her mammoth case and flinging open the door to their penthouse once Tim had generously tipped the porter so they could have a bit of privacy. "They really do have the actual Smeg fridges here!" As Tim hauled their joint luggage into the room, Piper darted to the kitchen area of their suite. A limited edition bottle of champagne was inside the fridge, its protective gold mesh twinkling next to a bowl of strawberries and what looked like a can of aerosol cream, leading him to wonder if the late Hugh Hefner had designed the interior. "I mean, I spotted the pics on Sophia and Talia's Insta galleries a couple of weeks ago, but seeing it here in the flesh is just incredible," Piper carried blithely on.

"I'm not being funny, Sweet P, but you could walk into any branch of Currys back in England to get your high-end white goods fix." Overlooking the fact that this one was candy pink and the bottle inside it would probably cost as much as the fridge…

"Not even remotely the same." Piper's scowl belied the floral nickname Tim had given her once they'd officially become a couple. "Okay, no unpacking. I don't have time to set up the light ring and tripod so I'm going to need you to get a few shots of me discovering the fridge for the first time. It's not every day you come across this little peach, even in a luxury hotel." Piper stroked the fridge as if it were a fluffy kitten.

"But you have already discovered it?"

"Honestly, Timothy! How many times have I tried to explain how much effort I've put into authentically curating my accounts? Seven seconds of this and some clever editing and upbeat music will get me on the For You Page on TikTok and semi-viral at the very least." Piper fished her latest mobile phone out of the back pocket of her black leather trousers, pressed a few buttons, lost herself in a frenzy of screen tapping, and tossed the phone to Tim, instructing him:

"Angle it slightly from above to get the most flattering

footage. The last thing I want is a double chin. And don't shake! You'll probably need to stand on your case. Quickly! I'll need you to be my cameraman for at least the next half hour to capture all of the goodies here. I'm definitely getting my money's worth when it's costing me eight hundred euros a night."

Tim gulped, dreading to think how much an entire week's holiday in this place would cost in August. He did as he was told. He was more than familiar with the basic requirements of the video recording process on TikTok – unfortunately – and he was keen to get the faff over with as soon as possible. He clambered onto his case as if he were Piper's assistant, pushed his fringe out of his face, and dutifully captured the moment that his giddy girlfriend 'chanced upon' the fancy pastel mini appliance for the second time.

Like what was this supposed to do for the world, other than depress or bankrupt people? Tim was a sensitive soul and it churned his stomach to think that his involvement in this little reel/story/whatever-the-current-social-media-terminology-was could end up leaving some impressionable teen, twenty-something, or midlife crisis sufferer stone broke.

Tim had been looking forward to quality time together as a couple, enjoying the simple pleasures of the Med in between wedding appointments. Sipping cool drinks on the terrace, taking romantic strolls around the marina, relaxing in cafés overlooking the beach and basking in shorts and T-shirts in the winter sun, if they got lucky and it hit over twenty degrees. In other words, living in the moment. Savouring the build-up to their big day. Not a chance! By the time they'd finished filming this, it would be midnight and then he could psyche himself up for more of the same over coffee and croissants the next morning. Well, croissants for him, Piper would be hunting out the soya yoghurt and goji berries.

"You really are one in a million. You do know that, don't you?" said Piper, snapping him out of his thoughts. She reached for the bottle opener and glasses next to the fridge to pour them both some bubbles. "Not a single one of my exes understood or supported my career path the way you do. They weren't able to handle my social media success. You're a breath of fresh air, Mr. Nutkins." She blew Tim a kiss and lifted her glass.

Tim accepted his own glass with a forced grin and swallowed guiltily. Suddenly he felt he'd been unfair, judging the ripple effects of Piper's job. Who was to say that those who attended his classes didn't have an unhealthy addiction to exercise? He didn't know their backstories any more than Piper knew those of her viewers. He had no right to jump to conclusions. He was tired, that was all. It had been an early start to get to the airport and he should've allowed himself that extra coffee when they were in the air.

"Look, babe! GHD straighteners!" Piper crooned. "Do you realise how *extra* it is to find these in a hotel room?"

Tim couldn't help but chew back a laugh. There was something so David Attenborough about Piper's mannerisms as she made that statement. As if they were trekking through the Ugandan jungle and after hours of exhaustion she'd finally spotted a gorilla. Besides which, his girlfriend liked to put waves in her hair, so why would she even need to make it poker straight? And, if you were desperate, surely an iron would do?

That had been the hack his older sister, Brittany, had used back in the day before she went on a night out. Not that you'd catch her being quite so maverick now in her role as health and safety director for a large American corporation. Brittany had flown the nest not long after their mam's fall from the top of the stairs in their home, which had left her paralysed from the waist down. Whilst the tragic accident had ignited a passion in his sister for ensuring others were looked after, unfortunately that didn't seem to extend to her mother. Brittany had passed her occupational health qualifications, fled the country, reinvented the definition of career driven as she'd progressively climbed the ranks, and left Tim and their father to care for Cathy Nutkins.

Tim's younger brother, Andy, might have helped his family had he not got himself tangled up in drugs aged not-so-sweet sixteen. Andy was *somewhere in London* and doing 'a bit of DJing for a club in Soho' the last time he'd bothered to get in contact with his parents and older brother. Admittedly, Brittany might find time in her busy schedule to fly to Spain for the wedding, but Tim couldn't imagine Andy making any effort. He'd have to track him down for starters.

Tim could hardly begrudge his sister for snapping up the opportunities in her path; Brittany had regularly sent money to his parents to help supplement Cathy's lost income and help with her care needs, topping up his father's factory wages. He felt less empathetic towards his brother, who had only added to the knots in everybody's stomachs. Tim had tried hard to help Andy reorient his compass a number of times but his virtually-teetotal-by-comparison lifestyle didn't hold the same allure as Andy's friends' tempting ways. It was just a shame that Brittany's success and Andy's going AWOL had happened so quickly after their mam's accident, derailing Tim's own education and career whilst he played teenage carer and frantically tried to search for his delinquent brother.

Dim Tim, some of his younger peers had loved to dub him in reference to his seniority, once he'd finally got himself to uni. The little shits didn't know the half of it. He'd never bothered to fill them in on his backstory. They didn't deserve the time of day. Still, he'd got there in the end. Look at him now. He wasn't doing too badly for himself, all things considered…

Tim shook himself out of his deep thoughts, unsure quite how a humble household iron could take him so far away from the present. He got snap happy all over again, framing his subject and the next object of five minutes of her desire. He couldn't help but wonder how he would fare if the boot (or trainer) was on the other foot and he asked Piper to dole out watermelon wedges to the clients at one of his classes in the hall. Again, he quickly realised he was being unreasonable. Piper's work earned more money for their collective pot. It was as simple as that. Especially with a lavish wedding to pay for.

"Chupa Chup lollipops!" Now Piper was gliding over to the bedroom area, Tim trailing after her like an oversized puppy, mobile phone still in his hand as he awaited his next assignment. "Oh, I really need to get a saucy shot of me with one of these in my mouth, lounging on the bed." His magpie girlfriend clutched the candy as if it were a precious posy of jewels. "Something suggestive, an arched brow, stripped down to my underwear but maybe wearing one of your shirts. Did you bring that white one I mentioned?"

"Well, yes. But I ironed all the creases out of it before packing. You wanted me to wear it for dinner at that Nobu restaurant you'd booked for tonight?"

Tim didn't want to come across as needy or old-fashioned, much less a controlling boyfriend, but why did Piper's shots increasingly lead to her showing so much flesh and shedding so many clothes? Why couldn't she hold up the candy fully dressed? She looked perfect as she was. Less is more and all that. Besides, she never touched sugar.

"Don't be a spoilsport. That's what hotel housekeeping is for," his girlfriend quipped. "C'mon, get it out!"

Okay, he vowed to stop questioning everything. The sooner he cooperated, the sooner he'd have Piper back to himself, her mind off her career and back into couple mode, when perhaps – not to be crude – he could get something else out instead. Things in that department definitely hadn't come to a standstill but Piper was nowhere near as up for action as she used to be. Wedding stress had a lot to answer for. Tim opened his case and fumbled around for the shirt, handing it to a beaming Piper who ran to the bathroom to 'get dressed'.

"I'll be five minutes tops." Tim doubled that and added on ten, sipping at his champagne to pass the time. He wished he could appreciate the stuff a little more, but it tasted like paracetamol dissolved in water to him. He'd much rather unwind with a beer. "Be a love and bring me my makeup trolley, would you?" Piper demanded within seconds.

Tim put his glass aside and walked back to the cabin bag full of cosmetics (the one that never travelled in the hold of the aircraft, just in case it never made it to Piper's destination and said destination didn't have a Sephora store), knocked on the bathroom door, handed Piper the goods and flopped onto the bed, checking himself out in the giant mirrored wardrobe. He thought those had gone out of fashion in the eighties? Who needed to gawp at themselves at all angles while they did the deed?

Yes, he was an attractive guy but he didn't need to see himself starkers while he was otherwise engaged, although he couldn't deny it wasn't a turn on to watch his girlfriend in the reverse cowgirl position.

"She's a lovely lass. Absolutely gorgeous."

For some reason his mother's recent comments flew into his head then. Ew, not the right moment. That flurry of thoughts did not go together at all.

"Ambitious like you are." But Cathy's words of twelve

weeks ago continued to circle Tim's mind regardless as he unintentionally dredged up her reaction to his speedy proposal (and Piper's acceptance). "It's just that¾"

Then his mother had stopped, yanking the rest of her sentence back from the tip of her tongue just before the point of no return, as if she'd managed to restrain herself in the nick of time. She'd pasted on a hasty smile instead.

"*What?* What is it, Mam?"

"Nothing." Her eyes had glassed over. "It's the emotion, that's all. Be-because you're the first. Your dad and I are made up that you've found somebody you want to spend your life with. What with Brittany vowing never to wed and that younger brother of yours unlikely to even contact us if a miracle should happen and he ends up on the straight and narrow. Y-you know me. I've never been much good with words. But we're happy for you. As long as you're happy, then we're happy."

Something about that conversation had felt askew, the last bit in particular, as if his parents were making a statement for him to ponder, sandwiching it with that layer about his siblings. But Tim had pushed it to the back of his mind. *He was happy.* How could he not be? Piper was the dream fiancée: gorgeous and ambitious, just as his mam had said, but kind-hearted and super thoughtful at times too. Like he'd said before, she was forever splashing out on him.

Tim reached for his champers again and polished it off, wincing at the bitter, dry and citrusy mouthfeel. That little dialogue could toddle right off, as his mam would also say.

Eventually, Piper emerged, her makeup as flawless as ever. Tim ran in for a kiss and was rewarded with a tiny peck on the cheek.

"I can't smudge my lippy, babe. I promise I'll be all yours later." She trailed her hand down his back and squeezed his buttocks enticingly. Tim felt himself grow frustratingly stiff. "But work first. Now then, where were we?"

Tim stifled his sigh and steeled himself for at least another hour of videography.

∽

Dozens of heart-shaped inflatables floated irritatingly around the heated outdoor pool. Tim couldn't even pack a few lengths into his first morning swim without interruption. Apparently they were a permanent feature, not just a run up to Valentine's Day. Uber-enthusiastic, uber-groomed females – and the occasional male – dotted themselves around the pool's edge, intent on capturing the early morning sun on their plethora of gadgets as it hit the pool's surface, and lit up their immaculately contoured faces. Even the goddamn DJ was in place for the first breakfast sitting, making Tim wonder if he was in Ibiza.

Eventually he gave up on his attempt to exercise and returned to the room to grab a shower – in between Piper stencilling on her brows and affixing her lashes – and the two of them made it just in time for the second breakfast sitting in the dining-room-stroke-pool-area. Although Tim couldn't see the DJ's deck from his spot at the table, he could certainly hear his terrible remix of Ed Sheeran's songs. Tim might as well have been at a nightclub, because virtually nobody was eating. From left to right, the diners at every table were either chair dancing and filming the moment as they lip synced, or embroiled in the very serious business of setting up selfie sticks and perfecting breakfast platters. Most of the latter consisted of trendy bowls of dark purple açaí berries, scattered with a rainbow of fruit and nut toppings. You couldn't make it up. Yes, Tim looked after his physique and his fitness, but moderation was key, and when he was on

THE WEDDING CAKE

holiday he wanted to eat something a little more filling and a lot more riveting. Preferably without recording the event on camera.

Alas, he couldn't complain too much. Piper had, indeed, made it up to him beneath, and on top of the sheets last night... not to mention the balcony's silk hammock swing in the early hours of the morning. Tim would be lying to say he wasn't up for a bit of risqué love-making, but here in Puerto Banus, once Piper had returned her attention to being a couple, for some strange reason he'd found it harder than usual to relax. Not so much because his limbs had turned into pretzels, and not for fear of the hotel's video surveillance capturing their moves – but the guests and their glut of gadgets. The hotel's semi-circular structure meant that many of the terraces overlooked one another, and he'd yet to walk past a couple, singleton, or group in the hotel who weren't intent on either photographing or videoing everything moving AND everything static.

With the sun trying its best to peep through the approaching clouds and the thermometer managing a moderate eighteen degrees, Tim and Piper skipped lunch and headed straight to the beach. Unfortunately, ninety-nine per cent of the hotel's clients had had the same idea. What should have been an afternoon of wedding chatter, paddling in the sea, ice creams, and cocktails felt more choreographed than the ballet. The Instagram warriors and TikTok tribe were glued to their sleek mobile phones and iPads; pointing, clicking, and making trout- and duck-pout selfies of themselves and their surroundings at every angle imaginable.

For the love of God, was nothing sacred anymore?

And then Tim properly gasped (and not in a good way) as Piper shed all of her clothes, right down to a tiny bright red thong and a teeny weeny matching bikini top, whose triangular 'cups' reminded him of children's birthday party sandwiches. Then she unpacked the lousy light ring and tripod from her rucksack, setting her mobile phone up to her exacting requirements at the water's edge, to boogie in front, side and back profile as she dipped her toes in the sea. And then she returned to her sunlounger and whipped off her bikini top, too. Piper lay beneath the steadily mounting clouds flashing her perky attributes to all and sundry, flipping through a stash of ¡Hola! magazines, which Tim supposed was Spain's equivalent to the infamous Hello! magazine (and its less prestigious rival, OK!). She had stripped off before, and Tim wasn't a prude who had issues with nudity or semi-nudity on a beach. Each to their own. Piper was, indeed, a fully grown adult who could make her own decisions. But this was a rather public stretch of sand, where most visitors were fully dressed – given it was winter, and the current slate-grey shade of the sky suggested imminent rain.

In other words, no matter how delightful his fiancée's figure (and blimey, at the moment, didn't she know it?) there was a time and a place… and he couldn't help noticing the holidaymaking Flash Harrys knocking back the bottles of Estrella Damm on the promenade wall over there were getting quite an eyeful.

He ran his hands through his hair.

"Sweet P, I know you're keen to get an all-over tan but I'm not sure this level of exposure is appropriate. At least not at this time of year."

"Oh, Timothy! That's not what you were saying last night. Don't be such an old maid." Piper giggled.

"But you're covered in goosebumps." Tim couldn't bring himself to appraise Piper's nipples. "Never mind going back to Manchester with a tan, you'll be fighting off pneumonia at this rate."

"I'm enjoying myself, babe. Why don't you relax and take

your T-shirt off too? I haven't seen those lush rippling abs of yours in several hours. I'm getting withdrawal symptoms."

"It's not just the risk of getting a serious chill!" Tim tried to stop himself from shouting back. "Have you seen how many mobile phones and iPads are out in action? You've no idea where all those images are being posted!"

"And I have absolutely no problem with that. You saw me in action down by the sea. I love my body. I thought you did too? I keep myself in peak physical condition, I'm young and I'm beautiful. In other words, I am offending no-one. Quite the opposite. I know it sounds boastful, but I'm the walking, talking advertisement for the rewards you reap when you watch what you eat, work out, and look after your appearance. I have every right to wear as much or as little as I like to the beach to soak up the rays. You can still catch them through the cloud cover, you know!"

Tim took a deep breath. He needed time out. Like yesterday.

"Right, that's it. I'm going for a walk. I'll see you in an hour or so when I hope you'll have come to your senses."

"Suit yourself, party pooper."

Tim couldn't stay there for a moment longer listening to Piper's bizarre justifications. He'd either shapeshifted into an antique since they'd landed in Spain, or his partner had decided to become a full-on exhibitionist. Piper had never taken things to quite this level of vanity before. Either way, he needed to clear his head. He marched towards the promenade and didn't look back.

~

ONE HOUR (and a restorative cuppa and chunk of disappointingly dry chocolate cake) later, Tim returned to a scene that he tried not to find alarming. Piper might now be back in her denim hot pants and T-shirt, having finally acknowledged the light drizzle, but from an unobserved distance, Tim could also see she was animatedly chatting to a male; a male who couldn't seem to stop pressing his hand to the small of her back or tilting his pelvis her way. Was he one of that group of lads who'd been eyeing Piper up earlier? Tim hadn't thought to itemise them. They'd all been wearing designer shades at the time, merging into one giant headache, so it was impossible to say.

Just as Tim's foot connected with the sand again to make his way to the pair of them, the man leaned in and kissed Piper on the cheek. For a fraction too long in Tim's humble opinion. The man leaned in again, this time apparently to whisper something in Piper's ear. As if sixth-sensing her boyfriend's unease, Piper turned on cue to dazzle Tim with a brilliant smile.

Okay, it was weird, but Tim refused to let it sidetrack him. This was not the general order of play when you went for a walk and returned to the woman you were due to marry in a matter of months, especially when you were two days into your wedding planning trip.

"Erm, what's going on?"

Tim liked the authority in his voice. It wasn't a vibe he was familiar with but he felt he could carry it off and make this chancer vanish into the ether.

"Hey," said the man, holding a solitary hand up as if in surrender.

Tim planted his hands on his hips and narrowed his eyes before letting them dart from the handsome brown-haired man with the Gucci shades pushed up onto his head, with his preppy blazer, nautical jumper and skinny jeans, to Piper. But already he felt like a fool and could detect no wrongdoing, no matter how hard he glared.

"Noah was just telling me about his influencer career over

here. He's from Manchester too, but he's lived in Puerto Banus for the past twelve months and he's making a killing! How awesome is that?"

Tim nodded, quickly processing these facts. The man seemed kosher, he supposed.

"Respect," Tim found himself replying calmly as he swiftly downgraded his emotions.

"Back atcha," Noah replied, then strode off across the sand in his baseball boots, the ghost of a smirk on his face. Tim berated himself. He was being judgemental again.

"Okay," said Tim once he was sure Noah was out of earshot. "What kind of man approaches a solitary sunbathing woman without an ulterior motive?"

"What?" Piper screamed. "You can't honestly think he was chatting me up, babe!" She put one hand to her washboard stomach in a fit of laughter, and grabbed her bag with the other hand as they made their own exit from the beach. "He's gay," Piper added after a few beats. "I mean he's gorgeous, and I can't deny it. But he came over to chat because he recognised me from one of my posts from this morning, that's all. It's a savvy thing to do if you're an influencer. You make an inventory of the biggest hashtags connected to your current location and scroll through those posts. Tah-da: there I was. You never know what kind of money-making opportunities you could be missing if you don't take the time to check out your local competition. There are amazing collabs just waiting to be discovered."

"So would that be before or after you shed your—"

"That would be the moment I realised you were right and I put my clothes back on." Piper kissed Tim on the cheek. "Not that Noah would have batted an eyelid. Like I said, he's not interested in women in that way. In any case… I was wearing this top and shorts when we were at breakfast.

Don't you remember? Noah must have seen some of the turmeric latte-sipping poses I posted."

That was strange. Tim could have sworn Piper had been dressed in one of those floaty kaftan numbers when he was sitting opposite her drinking his own (proper) coffee at breakfast. Then again, maybe not. She'd recorded a quick video on the balcony while he was in the shower this morning, too. Maybe she'd been wearing the shorts then? He could hardly keep up with her changes of outfit.

Now Tim felt like a sap. If you didn't have trust in a relationship, you didn't have anything. Piper was constantly on the go, out and about. She'd doubtless had a flurry of dating opportunities since they'd got together and never once had she given him reason to doubt her loyalty. But then Tim had batted away a few close encounters too. Such was the way if you had a good physique, above average looks, and an amiable personality. Not that he had ever contemplated anything more than the return of a smile. He knew how blessed he was to be in this relationship and he would do everything he could to make it last forever.

∾

BY NIGHT, the boutique hotel's facade and its palm trees were illuminated in neon pink. It was a bit in your face, but Tim supposed there was a certain romance about it. Piper looked a million dollars. There was nothing new about that, but she was more in her element here in Puerto Banus than anywhere he'd ever stepped out with her before. Everything about his girlfriend glowed. Tim noticed the number of males eyeing her up, like he was, but none of them were here to plan their nuptials to this beautiful woman, were they? Therein lay the difference. The fusion of booze, sea air and the seductive setting made him want to pin Piper against the nearest and most secluded palm tree, planting a trail of kisses across her decolletage and along the tender side of her neck, leaving her under no illusion that he was going to show her a very good time behind closed doors.

"Pinch me! I'm in a dream!" Piper twirled around, whisking her damned mobile phone out again, filming every second of her rapture, creating an instant barrier to what could have been a cosy moment.

"Do you really need to document so much of our trip?" he found himself wailing. "Can't we keep some memories private, just for the two of us? I mean, we are here to plan the wedding, so it's a bit different from all the other breaks we've had."

Even their intimate dinner for two had been gatecrashed by a couple of Piper's fans. Stuff like that never happened back in Manchester. It seemed she had a captive audience here on the Costa del Sol. First Noah on the beach, then the Canadian girls in the Argentinian restaurant, who had descended upon their table for group selfies without an invite – much to Piper's delight.

"Chill out, babe! My Instagram posts have had a record number of impressions today, one of my TikTok videos has gone properly viral with almost a million views, and my follower growth is up ten percent in the past twenty-four hours. That's *massive*! I'd be a tool not to capitalise on all the interest while I'm here. Manchester's not quite as exotic as Puerto Banus, is it?"

For the first time since they'd met, Tim wondered if *he* would always be exotic enough for Piper? He quickly dismissed the thought. It was ridiculous to pit himself against a holiday destination.

Still, something about Puerto Banus, the hotel, and its vibe smothered Tim. So much so that, in the middle of that night, he woke up gasping for breath, as if the air had been sucked out of the room and somebody was trying to suffocate him. Thankfully, Piper had her eye mask on and her ear plugs in so was none-the-wiser about those traumatic and embarrassing few seconds.

The next day, Piper flitted about town for various photo-shoots and recces about future potential endorsement opportunities in cafés, clubs, bars, and hotel rooms/balconies/pools, and Tim double-checked their agenda for the next few days over room service cocktails on the terrace. Then it was time to reunite, to head to Marbella. Tim swallowed his nerves as best he could. It wasn't every day that you took a tour of the place where you would profess your eternal love.

The villa was out of this world. It oozed elegance and seduction; the epitome of a fairy-tale venue. His father would hate it, was his first thought. Perched on Marbella's Golden Mile, it even commanded its own private beach! As for Tim's mam, well, she wouldn't know what to make of it. And she would need a team to lift her and her wheelchair down those higgledy-piggledy stone steps from the villa's gigantic garden to the sea. Rumour had it that the villa had formerly been owned by someone high profile from the British-American music and TV industry. It was definitely the sort of pad that would come with a troop of housekeepers, cooks, cleaners, chauffeurs, and bodyguards. The kind of place where you'd need a map just to locate your bedroom. Why spend all that money on gold-plated alarm systems, remote control blinds and an infinity pool, when you hadn't even thought to provide a simple ramp for a wheelchair? Admittedly, there were two lifts in the villa. That was something. But Piper was adamant that she wanted their ceremony to take place on the beach, which kind of eradicated the venue's interior user-friendliness.

"I want to be able to hear the sea when we say our vows, babe. There's something so poetic about the Mediterranean."

"Maybe we can play some wave music in the background? We'd lose the stunning backdrop of the villa otherwise. You heard what the wedding planner dude said; the bougainvillea will be a riot of colour set against the luscious green lawns and the swaying palm fronds, all further contrasting with the aquamarine of the pool and the virginal white of the villa." Tim imitated the elderly gent's sales pitch, omitting his irritating 'chippety-chop, off we pop' catchphrase. "What could be better? It'll also mean my mam can see us say I do... without any of the ushers breaking their backs. Which would be nice."

"I'll have a think about it but I've always dreamed of being barefoot on the sand as we declare our love. And it is my special day – well, *our special day* – but the bride always comes first. It's tradition. Anyway, your mum can have all of this to herself, can't she?" Piper opened her arms out wide, gesturing at the dripping-with-luxury venue. "She'll enjoy dipping her feet in the pool."

Tim bit his tongue at Piper's lack of tact. She truly hadn't a clue how difficult even something as seemingly simple as that would be, despite having met his mother a handful of times since his swift proposal. He could only hope and pray that his words – and Mervyn Meehan's – had planted a seed which would grow sunflower-style fast.

After leaving them to have a brief wander around the spacious gardens while he prepped some drinks with the kitchen staff who'd been drafted in for the day from the catering company, Mervyn returned to talk business. He was as much of a sight to behold as the villa. Sort of like an elderly Nicolas Cage with his puppet eyes and long, grey hair. He'd definitely had some work done on the jowls. They were non-existent, a fact which didn't quite tally with his paunch. Tim didn't mean to be unkind. This was just his opinion as a fitness instructor.

Contracts were signed and, keen as ever to flash her cash, Piper couldn't wait to settle the bill already.

And that was when the penny dropped: there was no way anywhere else would beat this drop-dead gorgeous venue. It was everything Piper could dream of and everything she deserved. When Tim had popped the question a few months ago, he hadn't done so with a list of conditions, had he? He was sure Piper would see reason eventually about not dragging his mum down to the sea and holding the ceremony in the gardens. Perhaps he didn't care if he married Piper on a mountain or in the grounds of a mansion. But if this swish villa was what his girlfriend wanted, then this was what she'd have.

FREYA

With the new timetables drawn up for the cakery, Freya's first free morning in a decade arrived before she knew it. She had booked herself onto a sailing course running from January into early February. It felt like the perfect way to start broadening her horizons – literally gazing out at the skyline when time allowed – and the ruggedly handsome crew that would be surrounding her wasn't a bad prospect either.

Freya might not look very different outwardly, since that fateful date with Lars before Christmas. But inwardly she was filled with effervescence, like the champagne she'd knocked back slightly too much of that night on the beach. Ricky was the first to notice the change, when he'd got the paracetamol and water out the moment she walked through the shop door that very next December morning.

"Spill!" he'd commanded.

"Oh, Ricky! It was wonderful," Freya had said with a tired smile. "Everything you could wish for in an evening, and so much more."

She patted her temple and accepted Ricky's offering, nodding a resolute yes to his offer of breakfast. He kept the kitchen door open so he could talk as he popped bread in the toaster and filled the ancient chrome cafetière with ground coffee, adding milk to a tiny saucepan.

Freya had only managed a couple of dreary shop-bought biscuits last night before passing out on the couch with the throw over her, Tiddles on the opposite armchair. Having accidentally set her alarm half an hour late, she'd had no time to bolster herself with carbs before heading to work.

"And when are you seeing Luscious Lars again?" asked Ricky, dancing a merry jig at this most promising piece of news.

Lizard Lars more like.

"Well, it'll go one of two ways," Freya replied in matter of fact style, despite wanting to dissolve in a fit of giggles. "He'll either come to the cakery and go ballistic because he can no longer walk around Marbs without being a Pied Piper for all the gold diggers in town, since I put a pic of him on my socials… or he'll thank me profusely for ditching him quickly so he could get it on with the honey at the bar whose legs and cleavage he couldn't stop dribbling over."

"*Ohh*," Ricky froze mid coffee-pour, and Freya had to scoot very quickly to his aid before the mug overflowed. She made a mental note to buy a Nespresso machine. Every part of her lifestyle needed updating, and they'd burnt their fingers on the leaky old cafetière for way too long. "This I had not expected to hear. And now I feel terrible for encouraging you to go out with the scabby roaster." God, you had to love Ricky's regional insults. "Tell me more."

"There's nothing much to say." Freya smiled as she took her mug from him and helped herself to a topping of steaming hot milk. "But while it was the usual waste of space of an evening in one respect, it was life-affirming in another. I'm going to be making a few changes around here."

"Don't take it out on us minions!"

Now Freya laughed.

"Relax, Ricky. I want you to be in charge on a Monday from this moment onwards – occasionally a Tuesday too. If that's okay with you? Obviously the weekends are our busiest time so I can't abandon ship then, but for too many years I've only allowed myself a Sunday off and that has to stop: I've decided I need to carve out time for living."

"Say that again?" Freya had never seen Ricky looking so alarmed, except perhaps when she'd sent him off on his first and last wedding cake delivery involving a hairpin bend. Oh, and then there was the time when the guy he was two timing had popped his head around the cakery's door. "I'm not sure I'm ready for this! Monday is the first working day after the majority of our wedding bookings. W-what if we get customer complaints?"

"What complaints, Ricky?" Freya looked from left to right as if searching for any quibbles that might be hiding on the shelves beneath the pots and pans. "We are FOM! No, we aren't infallible but we always make sure everything is perfect before it leaves the premises *and* when it's laid out at the venue. Not a corner cut. We're the very best at what we do. Every single one of us. If this step up the career ladder and the extra responsibility isn't for you, then I'll offer it, and the extra money, to Nicola or Jimena. I'm sure they'll bite my hand off for the opportunity."

"*No*, I mean, *yes*, I could potentially do it... I mean—"

"Come on. You know the business inside out and you're my longest serving member of staff. I wouldn't ask you if I didn't think you were capable." Freya folded her arms. "Why not give it a go and if it doesn't work out, perhaps we can devise a rota so that you share the role with one of the ladies."

"I'll make it work!" cried a suddenly animated and wholly convinced Ricky. "Freya, you're a stoater!"

Luckily, Freya knew the latter word to be the Glaswegian for a brilliant person and she was only too happy to accept Ricky's hug

"And what is madam going to be doing with all of this free time on her hands anyway?" her second in command asked her, once he'd let her come up for air.

Freya didn't need any encouragement to share her exciting plans. Her list of potential pursuits was so long that the question was, *what wasn't she going to be doing?*

"Hiking, paintballing, canyoning, white water rafting, jet skiing, horse riding on the beach, paraglid…"

"Stop! That little lot's enough to make me faint." Ricky covered his ears.

Whereas it was enough to make Freya happy dance on the cake turntable. But she brought herself back to present day February: The Goldsmith-Jackson taste test had gone brilliantly yesterday – overlooking the slight price shock hiccup and Merv's annoying behaviour. The team had also received phenomenal feedback on all their recent cakes; a scrumptious medley ranging from towering croquembouches to the perennially popular naked cakes, botanical cakes decorated with foliage and ferns (Ricky's favourite since the decor was a breeze) to a crowd-pleasing giant cupcake – all featuring FOM's characteristic elegant aesthetic and laidback design. Ricky was relishing his new role and the others were responding to his promotion positively. Freya had another taste test booked in for next week (she loved those afternoons, it was always so fascinating to meet her clients in the flesh and it was often the only time it happened during the entire wedding process), and last but definitely not least, she'd just heard on the grapevine that Lars had moved back to Norway, his lucrative business deal with the golf course having fallen flat on its face.

Wasn't that the cherry on the cake?

Things could only get better and better.

ALICE

The invitations had been sent out, most of the replies had already winged their merry way back to Alice and River's cottage at the edge of the stables, and the wedding guest list was shaping up nicely. Their taxi driving friend, Hayley had even offered to lay on a minibus to Spain to take those who weren't keen on flying.

"I'll cover all the local excursions as a wedding present too. It'll save you both forking out on hire costs while we're in Spain. I'm thinking of a day trip to Gibraltar," she added. This totally wouldn't have anything to do with Hayley stocking up on tax free goods she could flog at a profit back in the UK... "And a tour of the second homes of the rich and famous in Marbella." Hayley was incorrigible – she claimed she never got starstruck, then name-dropped lists of all the minor celebrities she'd had in the back of her cab and the intimate details of their conversations. "*And* a visit to that gert lush chocolate factory in Mijas.... They make ice cream there too."

"That's very kind of you," Alice jumped in before Hayley became even more of a runaway train (or taxi or minibus).

"But it's still early days and we ought to take everybody's tastes into consideration." In other words, there was so much more to the Costa del Sol and Andalucía. Like culture!

After their cake tasting with Freya, Mervyn had driven Alice and River all over the coast and then inland, to visit the key suppliers on their list. Although it felt as if they were on a conveyor belt at times, Alice had to admit that the man was efficient and extremely knowledgeable about all aspects of the wedding industry. Age was definitely no barrier for him – even if he was an oddball. Finca Preciosa was breathtaking. Alice had goosebumps from the moment they arrived to the moment River had to drag her back into Mervyn's convertible Jaguar. Everything was exactly as she'd imagined it would be… and so much more.

Even before Mervyn had properly shown them around, Alice had her heart set on getting a collection of wedding pictures taken in the hacienda's rustic tower. Flanked by mountains, green pastures and plantations of olive trees, the place was heavenly. A little swimming pool glimmered temptingly and she just knew that around its inviting blue edge was where they'd congregate the guests for the traditional wedding breakfast. All in all, it was a magical backdrop, and in the evening the lush carpet of the lawn would transform itself into nature's dance floor beneath the canopy of stars. Add a Spanish guitarist and a churros cart to the mix and you had a swoonworthy setting.

They reluctantly made their way back to the coast, with Mervyn factoring in a speedy pit stop at a vineyard. Unable to choose between the delicious varieties on offer, Alice and River opted for a medley of bottles.

"My wedding cocktail menu needs to take pride of place though," said River. "Wine is good but nothing beats my blueberry lavender sangria."

"Except maybe your rhubarb Bellini," Alice reminded him.

Fortunately, the first catering company on the agenda was also located close by, and its sample wedding menu was so delectable – roasted red peppers with cod, avocado tartare with shrimp and crab, chorizo from acorn-fed pigs, the amusingly breast-shaped Tetilla cheese, gourmet tortilla, vegetarian paella and barbecued *everything imaginable* – that Alice and River unanimously agreed they didn't need to test anywhere else. To keep the rest of the wedding's costs as low as possible –something of a necessity after the colossal amount being spent on the finca and the cake! – Mervyn suggested that they serve the eight-tier showstopper as their dessert, which pleased River immensely, totally defrosting his initial reaction to their wedding planner. And it would only make a small dent in the amount of cake left to divvy up to the Spanish villages on their honeymoon.

The florist, photographer, and churros vendor were visited in snappy succession – all of them Marbella-based businesses. Sadly they ran out of time to fit in the makeup artist and hairdresser but Alice had since experimented by asking her friend Zara if she'd have a go at popping her tresses in two French plaits with flowers woven through the braids, figuring that if Zara's artisan chocolate handiwork was anything to go by, she'd likely be just as creative in the beauty stakes. Mercifully she'd been proven right, and Zara – and her boyfriend, Bruno – had RSVP'd to say they were flying over to Spain for the big day.

On Friday afternoon Alice and River ran through the figures in Malaga with Mervyn, who took them to a 'cereal café' in the city, right opposite Hollywood star and local legend Antonio Banderas' theatre. Which was rather exciting because the man himself was currently producing and starring in a musical there, and tickets were still available for the evening performance. *When in Rome...* But funnily enough, Alice hadn't been so thrilled at the prospect of eating cereal for a late lunch and plumped for a baguette. River had been a kid in a sweetshop though. He and Mervyn (who was clearly a regular at the café) scanned the shelves trying to find the most unusual packets of cereal to devour – with imports from America and Australia, as well as some of stranger British prospects, the choice was seemingly endless. River got himself in such a kerfuffle that he ended up settling for a brand that he was already very familiar with: Kellogg's Crunchy Nut Cornflakes. Meanwhile, Mervyn asked the waiter for a bowl of Post's Fruity Pebbles... topped with Smurf-blue milk. Alice could barely look.

There were still a few things to drill down into on the supplier side. They hadn't been able to squeeze in a visit to the Marbella stylist who was kitting them out with mini-Cath Kidston style teepees for the children who would be in attendance, and reams of bunting to be draped artfully all over the garden, but those finishing touches could be arranged from afar to avoid another trip to Spain during such a busy period.

Now they were back in freezing cold Somerset, Alice knew that the time would fly. That's the way it always went when life was already busy. February and March would soon merge into one. By April, the stables would be completed and the first two of Alice's horses – Cotton Candy and Applejack – would have arrived, with the rest of the gang (who were also named after the original My Little Ponies) trotting along behind them in May and June. Meanwhile, River contemplated the café side of the business, setting up meetings with local farm and cider suppliers so he could showcase the very best organic produce in both the little eatery and the shop.

"Jimmy's Farm comes to Glastonbury!" their friend, Hayley had quipped. Her comparison with Jamie Oliver's

bestie's set-up, on Channel 4 in the early 2000s, had irked River good and proper.

He didn't 'do' mainstream TV.

Alice could see Hayley meant well – but she didn't know River like Alice did. Her husband-to-be put his own stamp on everything. From music to cocktails to food, he always had a unique vision. Besides, this was hardly a working farm, but a horseriding business; a stables with a charitable mission. The café wouldn't only be used by locals paying them a visit to buy top quality products. Alice and River intended to work with state schools and underprivileged kids as well – particularly those from cities, who rarely got a glimpse of rural life. Their lessons and lunches would be funded by wealthy business sponsors, as well as their own profit. The two ventures couldn't be more different.

Alice couldn't wait until her wedding, her honeymoon, and her return to her forever home with her best friend.

TIM

"But I don't get it." Tim scratched his head. "You loved the roller coasters when we went to Blackpool and Disneyland Paris! I thought you were a thrill-seeker? I booked this as a romantic Valentine's surprise the moment you mentioned the wedding planning trip and I realised we'd be in Spain on Feb the fourteenth. I thought it would be something special for our last day here together. It's always you choosing the restaurants and footing the bill so I wanted to do my bit for once. The paragliding wasn't cheap, Piper. I'll lose the money if you don't go."

Tim never called his girlfriend Piper. Now she would know he was miffed.

"Oh, babe!" Piper glanced at him over the top of yet another copy of *¡Hola!* and he wondered when exactly she'd become so fluent in Spanish. "I'm so sorry. I love everything inside a theme park, yes. But extreme sports are a tad different, aren't they?"

Tim didn't think so. A roller coaster travelled faster than a glider on a parachute, and it definitely churned your stomach more efficiently than a tumble dryer.

"I couldn't go even if I wanted to." Piper pouted.

FFS, what now?

"I've had another last-minute invite and I'd be a numpty to turn it down."

Surprise, surprise. Why hadn't he seen that one coming?

"And what about us?"

Tim hated sounding so needy but this was getting ridiculous. They'd hardly seen one another and, when they had, Piper had been consumed with airbrushing her photos before posting them on her various accounts. Or she had been accosted by yet more Instagram, YouTube and TikTok groupies, as he sat across the table, keen for some kind of conversation – for *any* kind of conversation – with the woman who was soon to become his wife.

"Believe me, I know how rubbish it must look, and I'm sorry. But doing coupled-up things on 14th February is *so* commercialised," she said. Tim reeled. It was almost a slap in the face. "We'll arrange something else when we get back home, yeah? Maybe we can go back to Blackpool! It's not every day that Sophia and Talia just happen to be in the same town, and they've organised a massive Valentine's-inspired social media shoot at one of Marb's top beach clubs." So suddenly Cupid commercialism *was* okay. Go figure. "It's opening exclusively for us, out of season, which is unheard of unless you're an A-lister or royalty. It's going to be an epic opportunity for some dreamy pics and vids. *I smell video virality!*"

Piper flicked her hair over her shoulder as if she was already there. Tim remained silent, sad to see that she was engrossed in her magazine again, although he supposed it made a refreshing change from the screens.

"You should totally keep your booking though," she said as an afterthought without even looking at him. "We'll meet up in the evening for dinner instead and then you can tell me all about it."

"Great," Tim muttered under his breath. "Remind me again why I bother?"

"Don't be like that. It doesn't suit you." Piper paused and exhaled deeply, reluctantly casting the magazine to one side but resting a protective hand on it. "I really thought you weren't like the others. I hope that's not going to change… especially not once we're husband and wife." Her sigh turned to a frown. "I promise I'll make it up to you. I bought some gorgeous new underwear in the erotic boutique here in PB." Piper's lazy smile followed a long and leisurely wink.

But neither had cut it. He needed more than the carrot-dangle of sex. And so Tim had spent the rest of the day sorrowful at his girlfriend's constant flurry of 'last minute' work opportunities. The next morning and lunchtime too. Until he'd got a taxi to Marbella's old town on his tod and trudged his heavy footsteps to FOM, the bakery that called itself a cakery – where he'd met one Freya Ashcroft.

Present day (or night) Tim pulled the shutter down on the aircraft window, determined not to travel down recent memory lane. He tried to relax into the flight back to Manchester, shutting his eyes, determined to count sheep. But his mind wouldn't let him go anywhere but back to the cake tasting he'd attended alone in Freya's courtyard.

He'd been beyond embarrassed for turning up so early – as mortified as Freya had been, when she'd let slip that he was the first groom in a decade who'd arrived solo for a wedding cake tasting. Mervyn had been due to accompany Tim and Piper, but he'd got caught up in traffic in Malaga. And yeah – sigh – Piper had prioritised a 'last minute' invite to a champagne yacht party in Puerto Banus. It would 'dent her career' if she didn't put in an appearance.

Tim knew it was wrong. Really wrong. Scumbag wrong. But try as he might, he couldn't quell the warm feeling that swelled in his chest in Freya's company. How immediate and effortless their rapport had been. It was self-indulgent, and yet it felt so refreshingly different to his usual initial response to an attractive woman. Chiefly because it didn't come from his boxer shorts. Which was weird (and sounded more than sordid) and certainly wasn't to say that Freya was ugly. Quite the opposite. Her beauty was understated and natural. People often talked about beauty shining from the inside out. Somehow Freya embodied that. Her soft brown curls framed her pretty face, she owned her freckles – unlike Piper, who covered hers up with foundation the moment the sun kissed her skin – and her hazel eyes seemed to light up the entire room. Or maybe it was just that Freya gave Tim her undivided attention? He wasn't used to that. It was shameful to compare Freya's complexion or her conversation with Piper's. But when it came to the latter, the analogy of a seesaw explained it best: any interaction with Piper raised his girlfriend high in the air, with Tim struggling to meet her halfway, often finding himself grounded. But with Freya, everything was on an even keel. Like for like. Which probably sounded extremely delusional. He was, after all, a client. Of course Freya would appear interested in what he had to say. And yet, Tim just knew Freya would be the same in or out of a professional situation.

Tim cursed himself, breaking from his foolish reverie to twiddle the cabin's aircon nozzle. It was just as well that Piper had her pink sleep mask on so she couldn't detect the hot flush that had crept over his face. He carefully reached for the Pringles carton in the netted pocket of the seatback, conveniently shielded by his tray table, and popped a mini stack of potato chips in his mouth, munching as quietly as possible, chasing them down with a swig of his prosecco.

Luckily, Piper hadn't detected a thing when he'd silently

THE WEDDING CAKE

pointed at his order on the laminated menu to the male cabin crew member, who'd smiled soppily in return and silently 'awwed' at Tim's devotion to his Sleeping Beauty girlfriend. But Tim hadn't kept his bar order under wraps for the benefit of Piper's sleep; he was petrified she'd hear he was eating junk food and ruining his pre-wedding diet!

Lately it felt like Piper was stage managing every aspect of his life. Obviously she had the best of intentions, wanting both of them to be in peak condition for their big day, ensuring suits and dresses fit, but there were still five months to go until the wedding. A few crisps wouldn't make any difference. Tim would burn the excess calories off during his first night back in the hall teaching the trampoliners.

He fidgeted in his seat, unable to get comfortable. Piper would have booked them in business or first class with British Airways, but alas there were no direct flights. There just wasn't enough leg room on these budget airlines when you were well above average height, and his niggles were swooping like vultures, picking every aspect of his relationship apart.

Now his bugbear was Piper's career. Again. But blimey, it had deviated from the original plan when Tim had met her! Still, that was her prerogative and Tim could hardly speak; he'd set out on a sports management degree harbouring dreams of becoming an outdoor activities manager... and all he could seem to pull off was indoor aerobics (plus a part-time job that Piper had more or less cold-shouldered from their dialogue: working as a porter for the NHS). Still, it was a marathon not a sprint – ha! – and as soon as they were back home he intended to put his heart and soul into some Pennines and Peak District pursuits, which would hopefully set him on the right track to full-time work in his beloved field of study. His trampoline class would be a great place to put the feelers out for that – as would some of the notice boards around the hospital, which were often dotted with exercise and nutrition information.

Piper, on the other hand, had gained her NVQs in beauty therapy at college, with original aspirations to get into theatre and TV makeup, but never found the motivation to follow through when she finished her course. She'd worked as an assistant at a local salon instead. Then not long after Tim met her, she'd got a tip-off from a former student friend who had seen her own hair and makeup demos explode all over TikTok, YouTube and Instagram. Naturally, Piper decided to dabble... and *kerching*, everything changed overnight.

There was so much Tim loved about his girl, and yet, those qualities seemed to have faded as time had gone by. He didn't want to liken Piper to a chameleon, but the analogy was spot on at the moment. Hopefully it would be nothing more than a passing phase. Oh! Tim had a sudden thought: maybe she was nervous about the wedding? Maybe the way Piper constantly threw herself into work was a coping mechanism? Now he felt guilty. And yet, despite regretting his doubts and gripes, he was compelled once again to replay his visit to Freya's.

Piper's decision to pull out of the cake tasting had grated on Tim. This rendez-vous was the best of the bunch, when you scanned the long list of time-consuming visits they had to get through. But Piper had been so apologetic and had promised to make herself available on FaceTime from the yacht's deck, 'multi-tasking' so they could 'enjoy the experience together'.

He couldn't say she wasn't making an effort, could he? Freya had snorted when he'd said that – and then all of a sudden he had her apologising to him too. "*Oh, my God!* That was the height of unprofessionalism. Please excuse me," she'd said. "I... erm... I wasn't insinuating for one moment that

THE WEDDING CAKE

your significant other has you under the thumb. In fact, let's be honest... it makes quite a change to see a man single-handedly taking on the wedding plans, and stepping up to the plate." Freya screwed her features up at her awful pun.

Tim couldn't help but belly laugh. Her attempt to cover the sizable hole she had dug was super cringeworthy, yet there was something so adorable about Freya's innocence in trying – and failing abysmally.

"No, really. It's not funny at all. I'm mortified. Let's rewind," Freya implored, her bright eyes on stalks. "Thank goodness the rest of the staff are still on their lunch breaks. I'd never live down such a faux-pas."

This woman was fabulous. Salt of the earth. Fortifying.

"You're all right, relax!" Tim tried to reassure her. "I've caught you off guard by arriving so early for starters, and Piper *is* taking unconventional to new levels. She's probably downloaded a scratch, sniff and taste app on her phone... It wouldn't surprise me." He rolled his eyes. "That blessed device of hers has everything on it, bar the kitchen sink."

Tim shook his head. He sounded as fuddy-duddy as his dad. A right technophobe. But he couldn't stop himself laughing. He needed the release. "I've had a full-on week of it, to be honest. If I don't laugh I'll cry, so you're doing me a favour. I can't think of anything better than stuffing my face with cake to ease my woes."

"Oh, heck," said Freya. She looked cute. Cute enough to eat. Tim immediately erased the image from his head. "I'm so sorry to hear it. I know these wedding planning trips can be full on."

Freya's face was a picture of concern now and Tim batted a hand to suggest she ignore his embarrassing vent.

"No pity required. I've lived with the demands of my fianceé's influencer career for a while. Mervyn's itinerary is a walk in the park in comparison. Still, this was never going to be a holiday. It is what it is. Business with minimal pleasure. Present company excepted, of course." *Shit*. Tim realised how inappropriate that must have sounded. He was here to sort out the wedding cake of Piper's dreams, not to enjoy himself with another woman. "I'll just… ah… set my phone up here so that Piper can see as much of the table top as possible, I guess." Tim pulled his phone out of his pocket. He had no idea how much of the pomp and ceremony the camera lens would capture, but it would have to do.

"Right, yes. Good idea," said Freya. "And I'll just… erm… go and fix us some hot drinks and bring the wedding cake samples out to the courtyard then you can dig in. Normally my assistant, Hannah would take care of the refreshments but she's on her break like everyone else, as it's kind of Spanish lunchtime." Freya pasted on a harried smile. Tim couldn't blame her. Why hadn't he been more considerate? The appointment was for three-thirty and he was a whopping fifty minutes early. But that was how keen he was to feel like he was doing something, like he'd not been abandoned by his bride-to-be. "I do make a mean Nespresso though. Unless you'd prefer tea?" Freya added.

"Nespresso's grand. If it's good enough for George Clooney…"

Tim carefully rested his mobile against the least expensive-looking vase on the table ready for Piper's call and admired the handiwork that had gone into decorating the courtyard. It was all things twee and romantic. Beautiful flowers, little fairy lights, candles and petals. There was even harp music playing softly in the background. You couldn't help but imagine a bride and groom standing in a similar setting for an intimate ceremony. Something like this would be so much more relaxed for everyone – him and his parents, his mates, even the humanist minister who they'd just hired for the day. Oh, and Piper. Even if she

THE WEDDING CAKE

couldn't see it. Okay, his girlfriend had collated a massive wedding guest list (and on that note, Tim really should insist he be allowed to take a look at it, she'd been ridiculously cagey when he'd last attempted) but even in the majestic villa, everyone would roll around like marbles and you'd be hard pressed to find the person you wanted to talk to, constantly panning the vista for a familiar face. In a small and friendly venue everyone could come together so much more easily.

"Here we go," said Freya, jolting Tim from his thoughts as she returned with two mugs of coffee. "I sensed you'd be a mug man and I couldn't resist joining you."

Ha, the irony. Tim was certainly beginning to feel like a mug. The kind who had no say in anything.

"I'm guessing you usually have to do the whole teacups and saucers thing with your pinky pointing out, then?" he deadpanned, desperate to change the course of his thoughts.

"Yep, we do." Freya sighed. "Especially when Meticulous Merv is in attendance. Seeing as I've already lost all of my dignity, airs and graces with you, I'll just carry on in that vein. *This is me.*"

Freya hopped out of her seat to turn the music off, but something about the sudden silence made her flush and she tried to mask her discomfort with a cough.

"What am I like? We are not here to talk about me!" Now she threw in a giddy laugh. "We're here to talk about you and that gorgeous bride of yours." Tim gulped at the shocking thought that flew into his head then. Put it this way: he was sitting in front of a woman he'd known for all of ten minutes; a woman who was having such an unquantifiable effect on him, that if he had a wedding ring on his finger already, he'd have removed it and wedged it deep inside his pocket. Like he said, shameful behaviour. He was king of the scumbags. And then some. He reached for his coffee and took a long sip, immediately regretting it when he burnt his tongue.

"Shi... sugar... *bollocks!*"

Well, that had totally broken the ice, that kept melting and freezing around them. What a bizarre afternoon.

"Oh, my God. I take full responsibility." Freya stood and covered her face in panic. "I shouldn't have boiled the milk to such a volcanic temperature, but I find there's nothing worse than cold milk added to hot coffee, except maybe black coffee... or... erm..."

"Cold black coffee," Tim finished her sentence but because of the scald he sounded like he'd just returned from the dentist after a root canal.

"Yes, that. Exactly. *Just no.*" Freya shook her head and Tim sensed she was trying like mad to ward off her own laughter.

"Or cold black coffee without sugar in it to take the edge off." Tim partially recovered his standard voice.

"Now you're a mind reader!" cried Freya, pointing at him animatedly.

Tim wasn't sure why this particular exchange of words or actions was so funny, but it was as if the pair of them had gotten tipsy on caffeine fumes. He could tell that Freya was waiting for him to explode in a fit of giggles, her eyes twinkling expectantly, and he felt his eyes crinkle and his mouth contort in response. Damn, he could never pull off a classic Bruce Willis smirk. Once his lips twitched he was a goner. And now the two of them were both done for; hopeless cases laughing so hard they were practically crying. Tim had to reach for a serviette to dab at the corners of his eyes. What a prat!

Eventually they straightened themselves up and got back to business. Tim felt like a new man. Like somebody had given him a hardcore Swedish massage. All of the tension in his shoulders had melted away. Freya nipped into the cakery

THE WEDDING CAKE

and returned with a green book full of wedding cake orders, a blunt pencil attached to its cover with Sellotape. It had definitely seen better days and looked totally out of place with the rest of her sleek business. She put it on the table and went to return to the kitchen for plates, forks, napkins and cake samples but Tim found he couldn't let her. It was ridiculous when he was technically her client, but for some reason they felt more like friends than supplier and customer. He felt lazy sitting around while this dynamic woman waited on him hand and foot. He'd made himself a right burden turning up so early, the least he could do was earn his keep.

"Oh, all right then," Freya relented after Tim's third plea to help. "I could use an extra pair of hands. But we'd better be quick. I can't risk any of my staff seeing me breaking all my own rules. We would never usually show our brides or grooms around any part of the kitchen. It's top secret! But just for today I'll let you have a sneak peek at the decorating room."

Tim followed Freya into the cakery and up the stairs, once again berating himself for wishing they could get off the subject of his nuptials (and for admiring Freya's peach of a derriere). The decorating room was incredible. He'd seen a few of those *Amazing Wedding Cakes* episodes on TV. Piper had cooed at the beautiful works of art and he'd found it all a bit over the top. But now he was in a similar kitchen, he found he had to agree with her assessment. Impressively complex cake designs decorated the walls on pin boards, and three wedding cakes in various stages of construction lay waiting for their grand finales. The colours were an assault on the senses: a four-tier marbled rainbow cake, a cake dotted with sprigs of lavender that looked in need of a little more frosting on its surface – Tim supposed it was one of those 'naked' layer cakes he'd heard Piper talking about – and a square triple-tier Battenburg wedding cake with a giant pink bow on top. That one really made his mouth water. His gran often served shop-bought Battenburg when he went to her house for Saturday tea.

"We wouldn't leave anything standing about like this for long, I assure you. The staff are on staggered lunch breaks and the first will return in about fifteen minutes." Freya checked her watch. "The moment the cakes need chilling, they are taken next door to the giant walk-in fridge. Oh, and we'll deliver your cake chilled all the way to the villa too. We have two refrigerated vans and we time the delivery just right so the cake has thirty minutes to reach room temperature once it's at the venue. That way the filling has softened and it's perfect to eat. We normally do all of this behind the scenes while the bride and groom are having their photos taken, so you won't even know we're there." Freya winked.

Tim let her words go in one ear and out the other. Except the last few. *He wanted to know Freya was there!* And right now all he wanted to do was get back to the courtyard and eat cake with her: carrot cake, white chocolate champagne cake, lemon drizzle cake, coconut lime cake, vanilla cake. Drip cakes streaked with glossy chocolate sauce, naked layer cakes decorated with daisies and buttercups, metallic cakes, marble cakes, vegan and gluten-free cakes. *All the cakes and all the conversation.* Tim didn't want this afternoon to end.

It wasn't that he thought Freya was one to overindulge in the sweet stuff, but yet again he felt curiously compelled to compare her to Piper. Freya was blatantly an everything-in-moderation kind of woman, whilst his fiancée pecked at her food like a bird or pushed it around her plate ungratefully. Tim missed the simple pleasure of enjoying food together in a relationship. It reminded him of the no-frills dates with his teenage love interests. Shared fish and chips smothered in salt and vinegar on the seafront in Southport. Giggles and banter as the seagulls swooped. It was back to that seesaw analogy again. Although none of his week- or month-long 'relationships' had been the building blocks of future marriage material, he'd been on equal terms with the girls he'd dated back in his teens. The many posh meals he'd eaten out with Piper, on the other hand, always resulted in him feeling like a porker as he savoured all three of his courses and she either tapped away at her phone after eating just half of her mains, sank too many bubbles, or looked at him (and his appetite) as if he was a three-headed alien.

"Of course, the pastry kitchen is air conditioned too," Freya continued, and Tim thought better of himself, vowing to transform back to the groom-to-be that he should be.

"That's really cool." Tim could have slapped his forehead at his lame pun. "I mean it's an inspiring thing you've got going here. The creativity is amazing."

"Yes and no. I mean – yes." Freya quickly fired out the latter.

"But you said *no?*" Tim knitted his brow and found himself planting his hands on his hips.

Freya sighed deeply and his heart nipped; he just wanted to pull her into his arms for a giant hug. She looked like she needed it.

"Like everything, there's always a trade-off. At least as far as I am concerned; let's just say I haven't had much free time over the past few years. But you can't have it all, as the saying goes."

"Why not?" It was none of his business and yet he couldn't help but probe – anything to tease out the conversation.

"Well... I... erm... I just don't think that anyone can have their cake and eat it – for want of a better cliché." Freya folded her arms and gazed at the ceiling. "I am comfortable, even by Marbella's standards. But I have little time to enjoy it."

"I can kind of see what you mean. Piper's bank balance seems to multiply overnight." *Why did he have to bring his girlfriend into this?* And what a cringey thing to say. "But there's never any time off to just, you know... *be*."

"That's a hard relate."

Time seemed to stand still between them and Tim's mind went blank. He had no idea how to fill the silence. His mind was a mess, flitting from hope to betrayal to guilt to lust in a vicious circle of frivolity. After a beat, Freya blinked rapidly, snapping herself back to the moment. She set a thick round cake smothered in peaks of frosting before him. Returning with a large cake knife, she instructed Tim to cut an eighth of the cake into even-sized cubes. Then she returned with a posh cake stand. "If you can add the pieces to this, that would be great."

But Tim hadn't racked up a great deal of experience cutting cakes. He wasn't sure whether he should go straight down the middle of the cake or hack off some of the sponge at the sides. *Freya had said 'pieces', hadn't she?* And a piece was a slice. He'd best cut this like a regular cake then; the way he'd seen his mam and gran do it.

He made a tentative dent in the snow-white covering and gently eased his way into the soft beetroot-red sponge with the knife... but then a movie reel flashed through his mind and he couldn't help but imagine Piper's hands beneath his, just as they would be on the wedding day with the camera, a drone, a video recorder (and a glut of mobile phones) pointed at them, everyone watching expectantly. Tim's breath hitched in his throat and he panicked, completely losing his focus. The knife plunged into the red velvet sponge cake at an angle and he tried to pull it out gently to maintain a straight line without causing any damage, but it was stuck, despite all his efforts... which was pathetic, and beyond humiliating. If he was a contestant on one of those reality TV baking programmes, he'd be sent home in the first round. He exhaled slowly and had another go with a little more force, willing the beautiful cake not to collapse on him, but of course that's exactly what happened, and now he had a mini avalanche on his hands.

"Freya, I'm so sorry. I've made a total hash of cutting this sponge!"

Freya left her own caramel-hued cake and walked over to assess the damage. Tim was hyper-aware of her, now they were standing so close together. The clean, zesty and intoxicating smell of her perfume (so different from the overpowering one Piper doused herself in), her body heat, the brush of their arms as she stepped forward to inspect the disaster…

"Well… How to say this kindly, bearing in mind you are a client?" she laughed. "It might not have style anymore, but my cakes always have substance." Tim couldn't help but nudge Freya playfully, catching a definite blush as he peeped at her through his fringe. "Besides, nothing will go to waste. Just cube up the rubble as best you can and plonk a few bits on the cake stand." *Cube!* That's what she had asked him to do in the first place. What a muppet he was. He turned his head to see Freya's own perfect specimens on the work surface behind him. He'd only ever had to emulate her style, chopping a wedge off the side of the cake's circumference instead of going all in as if he were at his own wedding. A chill ran through him then and he wasn't sure if the sensation came from the W word or the fact that Freya had disappointingly walked out of his orbit. "I work with a charity that distributes food to the homeless, families who have lost their jobs due to the pandemic, and Ukrainian refugees," Freya added. "So all of today's leftovers and trimmings will be recycled – so to speak."

There was no showing off in that statement. Freya only mentioned it in passing, and doubtless wouldn't have at all, if

Tim hadn't cut the cake so messily. But the words rooted him to the spot. *Why hadn't that occurred to him before?* Piper earned huge sums of money and, as far as he knew, she didn't give anything to charity. Not a penny. Okay, he knew he shouldn't jump to conclusions, he was only ninety-nine percent certain this was the truth. There was always a one percent chance that she did, in fact, throw herself into philanthropy while nobody was looking. But this was Piper. Everything was for show. Everything was a profile raiser. No, Tim would lower the philanthropic endeavours stats to 0.01%. That felt more realistic.

"What's up?" asked Freya, and Tim couldn't help but marvel at the way they were constantly concerned for each other's wellbeing. "You look like you've seen a ghost."

"I-I… no, I'm fine. It's just been a tiring trip, that's all. And phew… I'm glad that the remainder of these cakes are going to a good home. That's heartwarming. Tell me more about it."

"It's nothing. I just like to do my bit. The staff help out as much as they can, too. There's so much wealth all around us in Marbella and, when you live in a place like this, it's easy not to see the plight of those in need. Anyway, I think we're all done here and the last thing we want to do is get caught in the act by one of the bakers." That made their kitchen interaction sound well dodgy, but Freya didn't seem alarmed by her choice of words. "Shall we?" She gestured for Tim to help carry a tray and they descended the stairs, to take their seats again in the courtyard.

"First things first, Tim," said Freya once they were settled. "Let's reconfirm the wedding date. I've got you down for Saturday the thirteenth of August. We've got three wedding cakes going out that day, but luckily the others are much smaller, so I can assure you there will be no issues."

"Of course," said Tim, still struggling to snap out of his daze at the mention of the month of August.

His stomach churned and he struggled to identify with this morning's version of himself; a man who craved his partner's attention, a man who couldn't wait to put a twinkly wedding ring on her finger and whisk her off into the sunset on honeymoon. Speaking of which, not only was Piper being elusive about the guest list but she was constantly avoiding the subject of said honeymoon. Oh, well. Maybe they'd stay at the villa in Spain. There were far worse places to celebrate your first week or two as a married couple.

Now Tim had resorted to his own spot of rapid blinking as he processed the image of the beautiful baker extraordinaire sitting before him. Freya's words about charity had really struck him, too. Thunderbolt style. Why hadn't he seen the truth before? *Piper was greedy.* Yes, she appeared to share things with others (well, to be honest, just with him), and yes, she was paying for this holiday. But, now he stopped to really think about it, money was only splashed in great amounts when it benefitted her. When being with him enhanced her image, for example. That was as far as her benevolence went.

Tim couldn't claim to be holier than thou about things, but he did what he could every month, and on a considerably smaller pay packet. The Nutkins clan had never been a church-going family, but Tim had been brought up to help others. He tried to give away at least fifty pounds a month to a charity, he waived the fees for his classes when his students were skint and he would always go out of his way to help little old ladies – and men – cross the road. Tim didn't idolise many sports stars, which could be considered surprising given his career, but he was a massive Marcus Rashford fan. The way that guy used his position to raise others up and fight for so many deserving causes was admirable. When he looked at his relationship with Piper from that perspective, was he being a hypocrite to marry someone who didn't 'do' community spirit, let alone any kind of altruistic deeds?

It was definitely food for thought.

"Okay, that's great. Thanks for reconfirming the date." Freya scribbled something in her dilapidated green book and Tim silently pledged he'd stop daydreaming once and for all. This was a business meeting and there was a wedding cake to taste, a girlfriend to call imminently.

He reached for his mobile phone, still resting against the vase, to make the call to Piper, when her incoming call beat him to it. Tim ran a hand through his hair as if to physically erase his recent thoughts about Freya and pressed the answer button.

"Hey babe! How's it going? What's the cake like? Have you met Freya Ashcroft in person? I bet she's super stylish."

Piper sounded as if she'd rehearsed that entire spiel, and Tim couldn't believe she was wearing another miniscule bikini top. This one in shimmering gold. It was even cooler today than the last time she'd paraded about on the beach. Both changes of outfit really were several sizes too small for her recently augmented bust, but he knew that was intentional. Tim couldn't tell if she was wearing a matching thong on her bottom half but he was sure that Freya would never have conducted a wedding cake tasting with a bride wearing so little – not that she was technically in the courtyard.

The internet connection wasn't great, which was unexpected in upmarket Marbella. Then again he was in the old town, maybe fibre optics hadn't reached here yet. He went to answer Piper, keen to savour the cake so he could relax, but she was already talking over him, full of herself after another day of all-expenses-paid luxury. *'She's not being rude,'* said his heart. But his head said, *'Don't fall for the excuse that there's a time lag because of her phone connectivity issues. She bloody well is being rude.'*

"We've just sailed around the coast and now we're moored up in the port for champers and oysters." Piper tossed her hair this way and that and Tim tried to ignore his uncomfortable feeling of sheer embarrassment at this display in front of Freya. At that, Freya appeared at his side to speak to Piper.

"Hi Piper. It's great to meet you. Looks like you're having a fabulous time there. I'll make sure Tim's happy with all the components of the wedding cake, don't worry. This side of the screen is a little fuzzy but hopefully you can see his reactions, and the individual sponges, a little clearer at your end. It's such a shame you can't be here in person but if you ever want to make another appointment to double-check you're happy with everything, just let me know."

"Aw, thanks, Freya. It's good to meet you too. But honestly, there's no need. I pride myself on clean eating, as you can see." Piper winked and Tim cringed. "As long as you can seamlessly add a wedge of healthy Yacon syrup-baked sponge into each layer, as previously briefed, I totally trust my hubby-to-be. He's got great taste, after all." Piper twirled at the ends of her hair.

Tim clenched his teeth and quickly unclenched them to down his cold coffee in one. He wasn't a spirit fan, or a violent man, but he could suddenly murder a double vodka. He'd never known Piper to behave so exasperatingly. And hang on a minute. Tim squinted at the screen.

"I-isn't that the… *Noah* dude with you on the boat?" Tim frowned.

"Oh, ha, yeah. W-well spotted." Piper pulled her shades down over her eyes. "And you can probably also see that he's with his partner… Giles."

Tim narrowed his eyes to scrutinise the figures on the

other side of the yacht, but the solitary pair of males didn't look particularly loved-up, even if they were getting a little pixelated. '*Exactly*,' his head interrupted. He could have decked himself for all the endless internal chatter *and* thrown himself over the deck on the screen. Which would have been quite a feat, but damn, would this second-guessing ever stop?

Freya plated up the first of the samples for him.

"We'll start with the smaller top layers and work our way backwards," she said, and Tim couldn't have been happier for the change of subject.

"Sounds good to me."

He picked up a cake cube and let the zingy aroma of the lemon curd and passionfruit sponge anchor him to the courtyard and the job in hand. It was weird to eat with two pairs of eyes upon him but Tim brought the sample to his lips anyway, hoping he wouldn't have to come out with anything poetic like the food critics on television.

"Phenomenal," he said, after he'd let the flavours meld on his tongue. And it was. The sponge was moist, but there was no way he was using *that word* to describe it, and the burst of fresh lemon and exotic passion fruit cutting through the sweetness of the smooth icing was the perfect antidote.

"It looks great," said Piper, who seemed to be getting merrier by the minute, taking swig after swig from a giant champagne bottle that had been passed to her by a stray hand. "But couldn't you do it with buttercream instead?"

"I'm afraid not. It's impossible for a summer wedding," Freya enlightened her.

"*Really?*" Piper hugged the bottle to her chest, and then evidently thought better of the chill against her skin. "I'm sure I read about a cake of a similar scale made with buttercream at a Spanish model's wedding last year. I'm paying you enough money. Surely you could make an exception."

"Sorry, Piper." Tim marvelled at the steadiness in Freya's

THE WEDDING CAKE

voice and wished he could channel her assertiveness when asked by his girlfriend to do something he didn't want to. "The only way that could happen is if we decorated the naked sponge at the reception and then stood back for your guests to pile in and wolf it down immediately. Trust me, you'd have an awful mess on your hands. Buttercream simply won't withstand the heat. We can only provide buttercream cakes for winter weddings."

Piper pouted. Talk about showing Tim up. Talk about showing herself up. It was a bonkers request when she didn't even eat sugar. The rest of the guests would be over the moon with the eight-tier showstopper in its original frosting.

In the end Tim had no choice but to cut off their call, later blaming it on the poor connection. Freya had looked more than a little alarmed at his action but he'd assured her it was for the best and he'd diligently signed all the paperwork she'd had at the ready so that the bill could be emailed to Piper. He was desperate to get back to the dinky little bite-sized cubes of sponge. Every flavour was heavenly. Every morsel was a distraction. Light, not cloying, delicately flavoured. Extremely moreish. Tim couldn't stop going in for seconds, much to Freya's delight.

That was the moment, the crossing of the line. He should have come to his senses and walked out of the courtyard without looking back. The job had been done, there was nothing to hang around for. But he couldn't bring himself to move. And from thereon everything spiralled quickly and worryingly out of control. Tim fast forwarded some of what happened next, unable to replay the intimate details with his girlfriend sitting next to him on a plane.

Suffice to say that one thing had led to another and before he knew it, Tim had found himself on the subject of paragliding, as he'd poured his heart out to Freya and told her how his romantic surprise for Piper had completely tanked on him.

"Are you sure you're taken? You sound like my dream man!" Freya giggled. "Oh, my God. There I go again. I have no filter! Just what is wrong with me today? Let's rewind yet another thread of conversation and pretend I never said any of that. *Shit*, what a terrible first impression I must be giving you of my business. And now I'm adding swearing into the mix."

"Hey, stop! Not at all," Tim had found himself flirting back unashamedly, his hand touching Freya's arm in a move that was wholly unnecessary, sending sparks flying from his fingers to his arms, down his chest, and way beyond. He'd quickly retracted it. "In fact, if you're free, why not come along? I'm only going to lose the money if I can't find somebody to take Piper's place. As you've probably gathered, she's not up for it at all. Since it sounds like you're an adrenaline junkie who hasn't had the opportunity to get out much lately, it makes perfect sense for you to join me."

"Oh, I couldn't. That would be… I mean, morally and ethically, it's just not the done thing."

"It can be our little secret." Tim had winked. "Oops, I didn't mean to say it like that."

∼

TIM COULDN'T HOLD back any longer. All thoughts of Hannah and the impending coffee – not to mention the return of the rest of Freya's crew – flew out of his head. He had Freya alone now in this beautiful courtyard garden and he intended to get very creative and savour every moment. He stood and lifted his chair, putting it as firmly as he could against the cakery door so they wouldn't be interrupted, then he returned to the table and a dreamily smiling Freya. Oh, she wanted this just as much as he did...

Freya stood too, deftly unbuttoning the crisp white shirt Tim had so wanted to put his hands beneath. He could already smell the stimulating rose, honey and pepper of her perfume as she walked closer and closer to him, revealing little dollops of butter icing strategically lined up just above the cups of her bra. *How had she done that?* Tim couldn't wait to get his mouth on them! *On all of her skin.* And his hands tingled in anticipation of releasing those generously curvy breasts from their confinement so he could cup them in his hands and lose his mind. Just as Tim's gaze flickered in appreciation at the semi see-through white lace of her bra and he thought his erection might burst, she pushed him up against the rough brick wall of the courtyard with both hands on *his* chest now, laughing seductively. Inches apart, their eyes locked and their breathing quickened. They both meant business. And not of the wedding cake kind.

Freya began to tear at Tim's T-shirt, bunching the material up with her fist and pushing it over his head, and Tim couldn't loop his hand around Freya's back to unhook her underwear fast enough. This was a race against time, there wasn't a moment to waste, although Freya had cherrypicked the prime position for them to get down and dirty. Nobody could see them from any of the cakery's windows, at this angle. But frankly Tim didn't care if they could. Overcome with the desire to ravage all of her at once, Tim pressed his mouth to Freya's soft lips urgently as the upper halves of their naked bodies collided. Their tongues flicked intimately at first and then Freya let out a moan that almost tipped him over the edge as the kiss deepened into a routine that felt as if they had polished it for ever. He had to be inside her. Now. They could do this again slowly later. But if he didn't slip himself inside the sweetness of her immediately, well, he'd basically die.

Freya was a mind reader. She undid his flies, pulled down his boxers and ran her tongue over the length of his penis. And now it was Tim who was groaning in ecstasy. He laced his fingers through her hair as her sensuous lips connected with his body. But it was too much. He knew how he wanted to climax: pleasuring Freya like she'd never been pleasured before. Once again, Freya intuited Tim's thoughts and stopped. She slowly lifted her skirt up, centimetre by agonising centimetre, taking Tim's hand to run it along the inside of her thigh, until his fingers reached the damp lace of her panties... before pushing Tim teasingly away, twisting to press herself against the wall so he could ogle the delicious curve of her buttocks, shown off to perfection in that white thong. Tim bent to kiss Freya's neck, parting the scant covering of lace so he could plunge into her...

A sharp dig in the ribs brought Tim back to his current situation once and for all. He made an alarming gasp for air, astonished at how far and how dangerously he'd let his mind drift. Like right into wet dream mode. Instinctively, he crossed his legs and thanked the aviation gods for the invention of seatback trays. His was down, and he couldn't be more relieved, as it was shielding his infidelity. Piper, eye mask and ear buds now removed ready for landing, was staring at him incredulously.

"Tim? *Timothy?*" she cried. "Snap out of it. What the hell's the matter with you? You're in a world of your own!"

"Hey? What? Sorry... I-I must have dozed off."

"And the rest! I thought you were dead, you were in such a trance. *I have been trying to talk to you for the past five minutes, you know?*" Piper swiped for the empty tube of crisps on Tim's tray and shook it dramatically. "Pringles, Timothy? Really!"

FREYA

Freya Ashcroft never crossed the line in the workplace. Thank eff Merv hadn't been able to make it to the Moss-Nutkins cake tasting. Indeed, it was probably a first for the septuagenarian. Presumably the lack of a bride-to-be for his slobbery rounds of cheek kissing had been the deciding factor in Merv giving the session a miss. It was pointless anyway. He really didn't need to be there. Brides and grooms could rely on their own taste buds. Freya had grown tired of many things in her career over the past decade, and Merv's fusspot chaperoning to appointments was definitely high on that list. She was done with making concessions for his Regency period drama ways. It had been so refreshing, not needing Hannah to be hot on his coattails in case he'd knocked something over in the shop as Freya had made her way through to the courtyard... with the lone groom.

Tall, blond Tim had shifted from foot to foot, his floppy fringe covering his left eye; his dark brown right eye meeting her own gaze so hard that she literally felt her chest melt. This could get dangerous. He reminded Freya of a boy she'd had a massive crush on in the first couple of years of secondary school in England before her family had moved to Spain; a boy whose similar features still cropped up in her dreams, just when she thought her subconscious had forgotten him. Finally Tim had taken a seat, looking somewhat bewildered at all the decoration above and below him. Freya had festooned the table in wedding trimmings so you truly did feel it was the big day. She couldn't put her finger on the vibe he was giving off, but something told her he was perplexed about more than his current situation.

She couldn't stop the blush crawling up her cheeks either. Was that out of a sense of shared embarrassment for his early arrival and his other half abandoning him for a yacht trip? Or was it simply because the man was smoking hot. Not that Freya was looking. She *definitely wasn't* looking. Even during her recent sailing course when she'd been surrounded by an extremely fit and muscly (and mostly male) crew, nobody had piqued her curiosity enough that she'd wondered what it might be like to go on a date with them – and the rest. But Tim? She could easily picture herself out and about with him. Far too easily. Piper was one lucky lady. If Freya had a Tim in her life, she wouldn't let him out of her sight!

The last thing she'd wanted or needed was Tim's help in the kitchen, but how many times could she decline his offer? Thankfully, Freya had managed to play it cool, focused on getting him out of her line of vision and her cakery as quickly as possible. She wasn't supposed to fancy her clients and she wasn't about to start. Yes, she had definitely sent a sign to the universe that she was now open to non-stereotypical dating scenarios – but this was not what she'd had in mind. Not that Tim was trying to seduce her, let alone date her. The notion was ludicrous. He was getting married to a successful influencer. A beautiful, successful influencer.

Once they'd navigated the cake-cutting hurdle, Freya had

THE WEDDING CAKE

felt quite self-conscious and amateur, reading out the details of Tim and Piper's order from the shabby green book. Why in the hell hadn't she updated this when she'd treated FOM to a proper coffee machine? Well, she soon would, and she didn't care what Merv thought about them moving onto laptops and spreadsheets. One of these days the old-fashioned note-keeping they'd relied heavily on for too long would bite them in the backside.

Then came the online conversation with Piper. Talk about excruciating. First off, the woman had been barely wearing clothes. Fine if they were FaceTiming on a hot summer's day, but this was, erm, *February*, and massively inappropriate for a meeting. Secondly, Piper liked the sound of her own voice. *A lot.* Poor Tim could barely get a word in. That's why Freya hopped onto the screen prematurely so she could take some of the pressure off him, offer her expert opinion, and get things wrapped up. And even that was undermined! Inserting the Yacon syrup wedges would be labour-intensive enough. There was no way Freya was taking a chance with buttercream in August! Thirdly, no matter how much she annoyed Freya, the woman was absolutely gorgeous. It was impossible not to feel insecure in her presence, and that was just on a fuzzy screen. In real life, Freya would always look like the poor relation standing next to a woman as glam as Piper.

And now here she went again, pitting herself in an imaginary popularity contest against Tim's girlfriend. The man was getting married and had eyes for Piper only. Which was just as it should be. Freya's thoughts today were seriously screwed up. At this rate she'd have to hand her entire business over to Ricky.

But then, quite unexpectedly, Tim had cut Piper's call off. Despite her better judgement, Freya couldn't ignore the butterflies in her stomach at the thought of getting to spend a little more time with him in private while he devoured the rest of her cake samples. His dreamy brown eyes had peeped out from his long side curtain of hair and he'd looked at her and the cake so intently, *so intensely*, that she'd thought she was going to die. She was almost grateful for his mishap with the Victoria sandwich. She'd been scribbling some pretend notes into the order book, also pretending that she couldn't see Tim's enraptured face in her periphery. But she could. And she could also see the cream… which was dotted most hilariously on the end of his nose. Surely he could see it out of the corner of his eye? But oh, apparently not.

Freya had tried to show Tim via hand movements and body language that he'd ended up with a splatter on his nose, but he was swiping at his cheek, then his hair. She could have told him the specific body part that needed his attention. She could have handed him a napkin while she was at it, but no, all common sense abandoned her, and she found herself at Tim's side of the table, tenderly wiping the cream from his nose with her finger! A long mutual look brimming with possibility and every unspoken word imaginable passed between them, the air charged with latent energy. Freya felt as if she was in a snow globe. Cocooned, not trapped. There were no other words to describe the strange sensation. It was as if she had known Tim for lifetimes.

"Hiya, it's only me!" Freya and Tim had jumped in unison at the sudden and very unexpected intrusion. Freya lost her balance and fell straight into Tim's lap, sending cake and plate flying as he wrapped his arms around her waist and held her close (for a few too many seconds) before releasing her. Thankfully, she had managed to hold in the shriek that had been on the tip of her tongue. She jumped to her feet, wiping the cream off her finger with a nearby napkin. "Oh, sorry. I didn't mean to interrupt anything!" said Hannah, eyes flitting between the two of them.

"It's not what it looks like!" Freya had dashed back to her seat, berating herself for her corny statement as she created some distance between herself and the groom, mightily relieved for being saved by the bell of Hannah's voice.

"Well, of course!" Hannah giggled awkwardly, darting over to the mess on the floor to clear it up.

"Leave it! I'll see to that later!" Freya had been unable to contain her shriek any longer. Hannah slowly tiptoed away from the destruction, looking mightily puzzled.

"Oh," Tim had said, suddenly catching on. "No, no, no. It's totally not what it looks like," he'd added awkwardly, holding up his hand as a barrier. Freya didn't know if that made things seem better or worse. It was petty but his reaction felt like flat-out rejection. And that meant she was out of control. Unfit to run any company, let alone a wedding company. She'd turned into a man eater. Quite literally. What had she been intending to do with that cream? Lick it seductively from her finger and invite him back to her apartment?

While she had fretted over her behaviour and willed Tim to leave (strangely, he'd made himself comfortable again and was about to swoop on the salted caramel sponge), Freya couldn't help but spot Hannah eyeing up the screensaver of Piper on Tim's phone. The very screensaver Freya was trying like mad to ignore. Hannah had masked her curiosity quite well, fussing about and tidying up the cake stand and mugs on the table. Nevertheless, Freya was a little astounded at her ogling.

"Anybody for a refill?" Hannah inquired, finally tearing her eyes away.

"No, thanks. You're all right. If you wouldn't mind returning that list of client calls we made between us earlier, I'd be much obliged," Freya insisted, trying belatedly to redeem herself with some professional talk.

"Actually, I'd love another coffee," Tim had said, taking

Freya by surprise. "Thanks very much." Surely he'd want to scarper? Freya's nerves couldn't handle this, even if there was a contract to sign and a stonking great deposit to pay. She needed him to go – like yesterday – so she could dissect her shameful promiscuity and drink several glasses of ice cold water.

Once Hannah had left the courtyard with her drinks order, Freya had begun to twiddle her thumbs, unsure even how to begin to apologise for her recent actions. But she needn't have worried because Tim was full of words. Quite surprising ones:

"Can I ask for your honest female opinion?" he'd begun.

Freya's heart had hammered. She really hadn't wanted to be grilled on her unwarranted, forward and deplorable approach. That said, Tim had hardly pushed her away, had he? In fact, now she briefly relived the moment, she distinctly recalled his thumb intimately stroking the side of her waist. She could still feel the heat of those arms curling around her protectively, as if she was wearing a belt. It didn't make things any better, no – who knew when common sense would have stepped in, had Hannah not done so? But it did make it feel less one-sided, yes.

"Does a paragliding date on Valentine's Day sound unromantic to you?" Tim had continued without waiting for an answer.

And so, after necking his coffee refill, signing the paperwork and sharing Piper's email details for the invoice, Tim had briskly left Freya and the cakery after a quick and platonic (very quick and purely platonic) kiss on the cheek. He had her number. She had his. It wasn't a date. Freya was helping him out of an awkward situation. That was all. Nobody wanted to paraglide alone when they were supposed to be drifting gracefully through the air with the love of their life on what was billed to be the most romantic day of the year. If she could help him feel a little less lonely, ultimately she was doing a good thing. She hadn't gone into any kind of detail with him as to the scarily similar reason she had recently started taking Mondays off – for the thrill of extreme adventures exactly like this! There was no way anyone in Tim's situation would believe her. *It would sound like she was making a play for him.* No. She needed to keep her love of the great outdoors and its activities firmly under wraps. She would show up at the place and the time, once Tim had sent her the details, and go home again, inspired to do more of the same on her own. And that would be that.

Freya couldn't relate to Piper, though she was just one of many 'normal' human beings who couldn't find the joy in flying through the air on an inflatable nylon wing. It was rather hypocritical, though; Freya was a fine one to talk on the phobia front. Until recently, she wouldn't put as much as a little toe on the sand.

Her world was lighting up a little more every day. Soon it would be Technicolour. Bursting with fun. Tim's invitation had arrived at just the right time, reconfirming her new path ahead and giving a thumbs up to the carefree version of herself that she was increasingly determined to present to the world. He was a signpost. Nothing more. A quick paraglide with a newly acquired acquaintance would be a tonic. Yes, he was a client, but sometimes business could safely be mixed with pleasure. One exhilarating ride... *Poor choice of words, Freya.* But really, it was going to be as clear cut as that.

∼

"The funny thing is, I swear I've seen the Moss-Nutkins bride-to-be out and about this week," said Hannah later that afternoon as she helped Freya clean the shop downstairs before locking up. "She looks familiar."

"I'm sure you're confusing her with someone else," said Freya, scrubbing vigorously at the counter with her cloth. "Piper is an influencer. When she's not been working hard looking pretty in hotels and on yachts, she has done her bit and accompanied Tim and Merv to the various supplier meetings, you know."

Hannah stopped her mopping and stared into space as if deliberating a conundrum. "Your enthusiasm for her sounds a bit fake, if you don't mind me saying so, boss."

"Really?" Freya sighed. "Is it that obvious?"

"You're giving those poor worktops quite a bashing with that rag. You must have broken at least one nail." Hannah gestured at Freya's aggressive cleaning technique.

Freya paused too and let out a deep breath. "Oh, great. I'm meant to be setting an example, aren't I? Staying neutral about our couples."

"You're only human. We all are. It's only natural that we'll prefer some people to others, clients or not."

"That makes me feel a bit better... all things considered." Freya sucked in a deep breath now. "*Argh.* Please forget I said that last bit. I'm being such a loose cannon at the moment."

"I don't think so. You're letting your hair down and enjoying some much-needed time off. That's all. Your new approach to life is bound to spill into all areas. It's been a long time since you've granted yourself so much freedom. On the other hand, you can confide in me if there's... erherm... more than meets the eye, about the rather close encounter that I *encountered* earlier. I won't tell a soul. You know me."

"It's pretty bad, Hannah."

"I won't judge. You have my word."

"Oh gawd! I feel like such an immoral trollop."

THE WEDDING CAKE

"A problem halved."

Freya waited several beats and then blurted her secret out, quickly adding: "Not that it's a date or anything. I am merely filling a gap."

"By going paragliding with the groom? *Okaaay then.*"

"And that's exactly how I didn't want you to react. See, I told you it was dreadful." Freya frowned and slumped into the nearest chair.

"Not necessarily," Hannah countered. "Thinking about it, it's probably one of the safest *dates-that's-not-a-date* since it's *highly* unlikely you'd be able to snog the guy mid-air."

"Miss Hannah Barlow!"

"Sorry. I was just trying to reassure you."

"That's the sort of thing I'd expect Ricky to say. And no, I most definitely won't be doing any of that in the air or on the ground with Tim." Although Freya couldn't deny that she wouldn't have minded experiencing a Tim Nutkins kiss, prior to him meeting and falling in love with Piper. He looked more than capable in the snogging department. He looked more than capable in the *everything* department. She shook the thought from her head immediately. Imagining herself with a pre-attached version of her client was still inexcusable. "At least I assume it's not one of those tandem paragliders," she added in panic. "Not that I would attempt such a move even then. He's about to get married and I am baking his cake. I mean, *his and Piper's* cake."

"It can't be a tandem for just the two of you, no. You'd both need to go with an instructor. They'd never let you loose as an uninitiated pair... and I've never seen a threesome flying overhead when I've been soaking up the sun on the beach in Marbella, so I'd say you're safe as houses and the instructor won't be joining in with you for an orgy either."

Hannah chuckled, and if her spiel hadn't been about

Freya, then Freya might have laughed along with her assistant too.

"Shit, shit, shit. This is far from funny, Hannah. What have I got myself into? What a mess." Freya tugged at her curls as if that might unravel the disaster.

"Don't overthink it. Just enjoy the moment. It'll be over before you know it. How did it come about anyway? I guess you got chatting about your Monday pursuits and the challenge to keep them fresh and exciting… and one thing led to another?"

"That's the incredible thing: I didn't say a word, I swear!" Freya cried. "Tim randomly brought it into the conversation after that weird video call with Piper."

"Which would be just after I caught you in the act of sensually removing the cream from his face. Still, what are the chances of discovering you're both passionate about trying out the same extreme sport? If he wasn't getting married, he'd be your soul mate by the sounds of it. And I wouldn't be in a hurry to kick him out of bed in the morning."

"Yes, all right. That thing with the cream shouldn't have happened. It was me, not him. I'm incorrigible and I swear on the life of every member of FOM that I've never done anything like that before in a decade of running the cakery. Nor will I again. I did try to show him where the blob of cream had landed from the other side of the table, if you must know, but he kept touching all the wrong places." Freya put her head in her hands. "Oh, this is hopeless and now I need a Spanish triple measure gin and tonic. Anything to take the edge off my stupidity."

Hannah creased up with laughter and finally put in her tuppence worth. "That sexy and mysterious hair falling across his face wasn't much help to him, was it? A bit like playing charades blindfolded."

Thank goodness Hannah had been working with Freya for a while. Witnessing what looked like blatant and indefensible flirtation with a client would have had most assistants handing in their notice, and taking their account of events to the press while they were at it! This was no way to train the next generation of wedding cake makers.

"That's it,' Hannah said now. "I'm taking it upon myself, as your ever-attentive assistant, to shout you tapas and that triple Larios in the square. Grab your things and let's go."

⁓

Twenty-four hours later, Freya's date-that-wasn't-a-date had been confirmed. Tim had texted her the details. She would make her own way to Duquesa, the small resort half an hour west of Marbella, to meet him and the paragliding instructor. That rendez-vous was nerve-wracking enough, but the next day Freya found herself sitting opposite Hannah again, in the exact same bar in the orange tree square, another heady gin and tonic in hand. She couldn't let this become a habit.

"Okay, I'm sure whatever it is you needed to tell me, you could have done it back in the cakery." Freya gestured in the direction of FOM.

"Not really," said Hannah. "This conversation requires a stiff drink and I didn't want the others to hear."

"Please don't tell me you're resigning." Freya clapped a hand to her head. In ten years of running her business, she had never let herself down so badly. One stupid, slapdash moment and now she'd lost an absolutely priceless member of staff and friend. Well, she deserved it. She had behaved abominably.

"Nooooooo! Oh, my goodness, Freya. I hope you haven't

been worrying that I was building up to something like that all day. I love working at FOM. You know that."

"Phew." Freya gulped at her strong drink in celebration. "What's up, then?"

"I've got it!" Hannah began to drum her fingers slowly on the table.

"Got what?"

"I just knew I'd seen that face and that waterfall hair-do before… and more to the point, I just knew I'd seen them in a juicily compromised position before." Now Hannah's fingers were moving so fast they were playing *Chopsticks* on the table as if it were a piano.

"Hannah, slow down. You're scaring me and people are staring! Take a breath and a sip of your peppermint tea."

"Yes to the first two suggestions. No to number three. I've changed my mind. I need something stronger too."

"Oh, no. This must be bad." Freya bit her lip.

"It is. I can't even begin the story until I've properly soothed my nerves," said Hannah, as she jumped up to accost a waiter and put in her order.

"Have some of this." Freya nudged her mixer to the middle of the table.

"I'm more of a whiskey and Coke girl." As if he'd been stage-directed, a waiter placed Hannah's drink in front of her. She took a mammoth gulp. "I saw Tim's fiancée sucking the face off another man." Hannah blurted her words out and glugged more of her fizzy concoction.

Freya joined her with another generous sip of her own drink, and swiftly wished that she hadn't.

"Woah." She said when she'd stopped choking. "That's quite an announcement. Are you certain it was Piper Moss? I shouldn't say it – regardless of what also shouldn't have happened yesterday in the cakery – but beautiful though she is, her looks are rather two-a-penny in these parts... if you catch my drift."

"Drift well and truly caught and I agree with you, boss. But I one hundred percent know what I saw."

"Okay, rewind." Didn't that seem to be Freya's word of the week? "Where and when did this happen?"

"When I saw Piper on Tim's screensaver, I realised I'd seen her before... She's the total spit of the woman I saw giggling and smooching her way down the corridor towards one of the top-priced bedrooms with the step-son of Aaron Barrington, the owner of the hotel. Huh, the owner of a Monopoly board's worth of hotels. When I saw her on Tim's phone, I didn't put two and two together, but last night it came to me. Mam's car is in the garage, you see, so I've been giving her lifts to and from the hotel in Puerto Banus all week." Hannah let that statement hang there.

"And what does that realistically have to do with Piper? It's like I said earlier, I don't mean to be cruel or to pigeon-hole any of these influencers, but they tend to favour the same look, certainly in Marbs and PB. I should know, I've designed and baked wedding cakes for dozens of them." Freya paused, narrowing her eyes at her assistant. "Hang on a minute. Why would you even be inside the hotel? Hannah, I don't like the sound of this. You work in the bridal industry, not some amateur Scooby Doo detective agency."

But Hannah didn't seem at all perturbed by the grilling. "Mam had a few re-bookings to sort out before she could get away and I needed a pee,' she explained. Her mother had recently changed jobs, taking charge of room service at a brand new, flash and trendy hotel, mostly frequented by the influencer elite. "I couldn't wait in the car any longer so I went to use the loo inside, but the snooty receptionist was looking. So I took the lift to the top floor when her back was turned. Just to have a nose around and see if there was anyone famous lurking. Plus Mam said there are Chanel soap dispensers at all the sinks in the loos up there."

Of course! *Double Tap Towers.* Piper would be staying there (with a rather reluctant Tim trailing along behind her, Freya should imagine). It was the Costa del Sol's first 'social media hotel', its name a play on the way you 'like' something on Instagram. The cogs in Freya's brain began to turn, but she stopped them: even if Piper was a guest at DTT, as it was already known by the locals, it didn't mean she was the woman Hannah had seen with the minted stepson.

As if reading her mind, and determined to prove her version of events, Hannah began to rummage around in the satchel that was permanently welded to her being when she was outdoors. She looked like a postwoman about to deliver some seriously bad news. Patience in tatters, Freya gulped desperately at her drink. This wouldn't do. She pushed it resolutely to one side and began to attack the bowl of peanuts instead. Finally, Hannah pulled out a brown envelope.

"Geez, Hannah. No... I can't sit here and pry like some kind of spy, rifling through dodgy photographs. That's taking sneakiness to a whole new level. I'm done with the dark side for one week!"

"Please take a little peek." Hannah wouldn't take no for an answer and now she'd taken to nudging things across the table, too. "We have a duty to tell Tim the truth."

Freya made a song and dance of looking over both shoulders – then inevitably gave in. She pulled a succession of images from the envelope and let out a gasp, her eyes growing wider by the microsecond. In her heart of hearts, she knew this was actually Piper. This woman emanated the same vibe of entitlement and all things diva that Piper had let off over the airwaves. She wasn't about to tell Hannah that, though. Her assistant needed no further encouragement.

Some of these snaps were X-rated, to say the least; a man and a woman half-naked in the hotel corridor, clearly unable to wait until they'd reached the door of their room, let alone the bed; a man and a woman finding new ways to use the dressing table; a man and a woman in some eye-opening balancing acts on the couch, and a man and a woman intimately entwined in the shower. It was enough to put Freya off staying in a hotel ever again. Granted, the place was big on videos and photography, but this gave the phrase 'the nature of the beast' a whole new meaning.

"Get these destroyed immediately. How did you even capture them?" Freya yelped, making the ears of a nearby duo of pampered poodles prick up. They were tethered to the legs of a table in front of them, and now in danger of tipping its contents over. "Never in my wildest nightmares did I think you were going to show me anything so graphic! I'm speechless." She pushed the envelope so far across the table it landed in Hannah's lap.

"Please don't think badly of me, Freya. It wasn't me who took the photos, it was my mam." Freya couldn't believe what she was hearing. Hannah's mother had done *what*? "I briefed her on my suspicions yesterday and she jumped straight on the fact-finding mission. It came in rather handy that she's room service manager, and well, Noah Barrington did keep calling; strawberries and a chocolate fountain, champagne buckets and oysters. All the aphrodisiacs. Mam's been inundated with errands on the top floor," Hannah paused for a breath. "She soon worked out what was going on... well, Noah and his *lady* made that all too obvious for her with their exhibitionist carry-on while she delivered their food. They even had the door off the catch! But Mam took advantage of their theatrics and supplied me with as much evidence of Piper's betrayal as she could."

"I'll say. And blimey, your mother moves other-worldly

fast. I can't understand how any of this was even possible, though. She must have had a hidden camera on her. There's no way she could've captured all that footage from anything already set up in the bedroom, without its occupants knowing."

"We're big on justice on the female side of our family," Hannah muttered. "And yeah, Mam's always been a bit of a ninja. She's a whizz with modern tech, that's why she wanted the job in such a tech-savvy hotel. She'd give all of today's influencers a run for their money with the gadgets. She's amazing at hide and seek, too."

Freya downed the rest of her drink in a bid to get over the variety of photographic acts she had unwittingly digested. "I'll admit it's almost certainly Piper." Freya thought back to the scantily-clad bride-to-be she'd chatted with on yesterday's video call on the yacht, comparing what she'd seen of her physique with the – bleugh! – vivid images Hannah had now stowed away in her bag. "But we can't get involved. Even if we did have concrete proof. It's out of the question. We have an obligation to operate with complete discretion for our clients. I never want to see these pictures or anything similar to them again. You could get yourself in serious trouble snooping like that. And as for your mother, you hardly need me to tell you she could lose her job."

"But we can't let him marry that tart!" Hannah's eyes were wild and pleading. "This goes above and beyond anybody's career, surely? There must be something we can do. We must warn Tim. The man's entire life and future happiness is at stake. We can't fence-sit on this."

"Fence-sitting is our only option. All those pictures show us is the profile of a woman who looks like Piper, but truthfully, it could be any number of females – locals or tourists alike. It could even be the guy's girlfriend. It's not our job to dig. If Piper is playing around, then Tim will soon work that out for himself."

"It's not as simple as that." Hannah started to protest. "The thing is, I'm just not sure that I can stop myself from taking further action. You don't understand. It's not in my nature—"

"There will be no further words on this subject." Freya finished her drink and banged her glass a little too loudly on the table, setting the nearby poodles off once more. "I know you and your mother mean well but we're professionals at FOM." She felt like the biggest hypocrite, voicing such a flimsy claim aloud. "We can't afford to get ourselves in hot water so we are going to pretend we never had this conversation." Another theme that seemed to be repeating itself this week. "I'm going to walk out of the square right now, take myself home, purge myself of everything we've discussed tonight with a shower, and sleep. I suggest you do the same. When we see each other again at work tomorrow, we'll start with a clean slate."

Freya stood up, and a reluctant Hannah nodded her agreement as she stared into her drink. She looked defeated. Where had the girl's stubborn protest of a moment ago come from? Freya hadn't known Hannah had it in her. Freya was her boss, for goodness sake – Hannah knew that so well, she often threw the fact into their conversational mix. Admittedly, at the beginning of the conversation, Freya had been petrified of losing her assistant for good after her own shambolic behaviour. But the simple truth was that Hannah and her mother were playing with fire. Whether Aaron Barrington's stepson had encouraged a little PR leakage about his current conquest or not, the Barringtons were incredibly wealthy and well-connected. It didn't pay to cross them. And it certainly wouldn't pay for Hannah's mum to go meddling. Quite literally. She'd soon find herself without a salary.

Freya couldn't deal with this for a moment longer. She

ignored the lift of her heart that told her Tim could soon be a free man (her very own man) ... *if* Hannah's discovery was true, *if* Piper confessed to being unfaithful, *if* Tim decided to call off the wedding, and *if* he was even interested in trusting another woman again. That was a heck of a lot of *ifs*.

∽

FREYA HAD BOOKED the hairdressers long before the paragliding offer had come about, she reminded herself. This trip to the salon the day before their meeting was categorically not part of a plan to beautify herself. How could it be when she'd soon have her curls flattened with a helmet? Tim could take her as she was. Grr. Innuendos had crept into her mind chatter as well now.

"*Qué vamos a hacer, guapa?*" her hairdresser asked her. Freya had always been determined not to be a typical expat, so she took her business to one of the cheaper Spanish salons in the east end of Marbella. They cut her hair well for a competitive price – a bonus in these parts – and they always threw in a relaxing Indian head massage at the end of the hair wash, which made up for the pain inflicted by the hairdresser's sink. She was desperate for it today.

"*Solo un corte, por fa, Pepa,*" Freya replied to her customary stylist.

She was lucky enough not to have a single grey hair yet so didn't see the point in foils, caps and God knew what else being plonked upon her head. A simple cut would do.

Her salon didn't go in for serving refreshments but, like most hairdressers, they had magazines by the bucket load. Freya wasn't normally fussed on the celebrity gossip front, but she carefully picked up the copy of *¡Hola!* to her right, mindful that Pepa would go bonkers if she jogged her while she was cutting Freya's hair.

THE WEDDING CAKE

Once the glossy magazine was safely in Freya's lap, she flicked carefully through the pages, skim-reading through adverts for perfume and features on palatial homes. *Blah-blah-blah*. It was always the same old fodder and she didn't know why she bothered, but she flipped through the pages to the society bit at the end on a whim. Wouldn't it be funny if she saw Lars in his best bib and tucker at some fancy black tie event before he'd had to go back to the cold snowy north and into hiding?

But Freya didn't spot the Scandinavian swindler. She spotted somebody else instead...

Noah Barrington.

Of course. *"¡Por supuesto!"* she cried in Spanish, causing Pepa to reprimand her with a massive tut for not staying statue-still.

According to the copy in italics beneath the picture, he was a professional DJ as well as the stepson of the property magnate who owned Double Tap Towers and its sister hotels in Ibiza and Mallorca. Now that Freya looked more closely, she knew she had seen him in this magazine before – not to mention milling about as a guest in the wedding snaps of some of her previous clients. The only major difference this time was that, according to the story, he was with his 'partner', Miss Piper Moss. There couldn't be two women in town with the same name and face. The Piper who smiled serenely from the pages was a dead ringer for the insufferable female Freya had spoken to on video. And the one in the photos.

Oh, crap. Hannah was right.

~

Freya tossed and turned all night. She was going to look a sight for sore eyes tomorrow morning when she went paragliding. All that pampering at the hairdressers had been for nothing. But she didn't care. She resigned herself to the fact that the zeds wouldn't come no matter how much she willed them to, and got up to make a hot chocolate. Tiddles purred contentedly as she stirred the spoon in her *Cola Cao*. It wasn't a patch on *Cadbury's* but hopefully it would make Freya sleepy again.

Despite what she'd said to Hannah, it was hard to see how Freya could continue to ignore the mounting evidence that Piper was having an affair. Tim might well work things out for himself down the line, but he struck Freya as the kind of guy who tried to see the good in everyone. Hannah was right (again). By the time he realised the truth, it would be too late and he'd be married to the woman. His girlfriend's betrayal might be public knowledge in one or two local circles, but Piper was hardly a famous name in the UK. There would be virtually no comeback from her picture appearing in a Spanish magazine whose influence would fly beneath the radar. It wasn't as if Tim would have a burning desire to pick up a copy at a kiosk and flick through it to see which of the Costa's socialites were having a spiffing time at a fiesta. Clearly Piper was playing a very astute game, doing her homework, booking her hotel stay to coincide with 'chance meetings' with wealthy heirs, and weaving her way into the fabric of Puerto Banus society. She was more than a pretty face.

In the end, after a snatched couple of hours of rest, Freya decided she would wing it. Which was a fitting theme for the day, after all. If the situation presented itself, she'd drop Tim a few hints. It was a halfway house of a solution, and would go some way to assuage her guilt. In her professional capacity, there was no way she could tell Tim what she had found out, but she could get him thinking, perhaps enough to pique his curiosity to dig.

And so that's what she did, after their stiff handshakes

(blimey, it was a disappointing downgrade from the warm kiss on the cheeks, and the protective grip of Tim's arm, and the intensity of his eyes burning into hers, and the sexual tension of two days ago) and an exhilarating glide over the terracotta houses, biscuity sand, choppy twinkly waves, and bobbing fishing boats of Duquesa. Freya tentatively mimicked the sentiment of Tim's question to her the other day, and found herself saying:

"Can I ask you something that I totally shouldn't... something that I have no right to know the answer to?"

Freya's own courage startled her. She put it down to today's perfect flight conditions and the laminar air that had made her feel free as a bird. Being so high above the ground, safely strapped to her instructor, she'd quickly let go of her grass roots view of life, trading it in for an immediate and well-overdue eagle-eye perspective. The flight was now over and the instructors had helped them out of their harnesses and sped off to their next bookings, but Freya intended to refer back to that soaring viewpoint as often as she could.

Now she stood facing Tim in the dusty car park, as if the pair of them were in a Spaghetti Western. Tim gripped the handle of his hire car's door as if Freya's words had triggered his reflexes. And now all Freya wanted to do was bomb out of the place and down the road back to her apartment as fast as she could, putting distance between them in her pearlescent blue Fiat 500.

"I think I already know what that something is." He let go of the handle and looked seriously troubled. They stood but a metre apart. "I... I'm not sure how to put into words how differently I've been feeling since... erm... y'know, the other day wh-when we..." But Tim couldn't finish his sentence. "And even if it doesn't make any sense, I don't think it's just because my path crossed yours... confusing the hell out of me, so yeah, thanks for that."

Freya took in a sharp breath and tried to ignore the little sparks dancing in her stomach. Tim didn't half make her think of an adorable Hugh Grant finally declaring himself to his love interest in a movie

"What I'm trying to say, in a very hashed up way," he continued. "Is… it seems I might have previously fallen in love with the idea of being in love... with just superficial feelings for the person I'm supposed to be in love with. I'm pathetic, I know. But there, I've said it." Now it was Tim who inhaled sharply. "If things were different, Freya… It doesn't take a genius to figure out that I'm incredibly attracted to you. Physically and emotionally. I'd have asked you out for dinner in a heartbeat – if only things were different."

Freya smiled sadly at Tim. She wasn't sure what else she could do. He had said it. She'd been told good and proper. There was no chance. Giving thoughts about him even a micro-percentage of her time had been nothing but a frivolous waste of imagination.

"Things are too far down the road. I really don't want to be that bastard who jilts their bride at the altar, leaving them with a crapfest."

Freya slowly walked a few steps towards Tim. She ignored the utter punch to the stomach Tim's words had delivered. She looked into his eyes, gave him her tenderest smile, for she knew it would be the last time she saw him, and kissed him equally tenderly on the lips, The truth was, she'd never be special enough to anyone for them to not leave her in the lurch. Love didn't even come into it.

Tim's eyes remained closed when she stood back. He pressed his lips together as if he wanted to swallow that kiss and bury it deep inside him for future reference. For a moment Freya even wondered if the kiss might have planted a seed, but then she came to her senses. The poor guy was clearly shocked and seriously wondering why he'd been stupid enough to lead her on with the invite to today's activity – not that they had spent a whole lot of time on their own. Freya had been ten minutes late for the flight and Tim had already been in his gear listening to the safety demo. By the time Freya had been given the lowdown herself and their respective instructors had them airborne, all Freya caught was a scant glimpse of Tim and his shadow as he soared through the sky up ahead of her. Now she realised she'd been watching a metaphor. Tim would always live with a shadow, as long as he neglected his heart and married Piper. Reluctantly, Freya got in her car.

"It's been a fun morning," she said as she wound down the window and started up the Fiat's engine. "I'll always be glad that we met. I know it sounds whimsical but you have been the biggest breath of fresh air. I'll make your cake as planned. It will be pure perfection. Ricky and Hannah will deliver it on the day, though. I think it's best that our paths don't cross again."

She turned the car in a circle, put her foot on the accelerator and sped off up the dirt track to the main road, eyes stinging with tears. She left Tim propped against his car in her rearview mirror as if he was posing for an album cover, his feet as rooted to the spot as they had been when she'd first kissed him.

ALICE

"Did she pass?"

Alice burst into the kitchen, her face in her hands. She wanted to know their camper van's service fate, and she didn't want to know their camper van's service fate! They'd left it too late to book Twinkle in at the garage for any major repairs and it just wouldn't feel the same if they hired a brand new camper van for their honeymoon once they were in Spain. One of the charms of such a long trip was taking their racing green Volkswagen overseas for the first time – crossing from Portsmouth to Santander and then wending their leisurely way around the mountains of the north and across the plains of the centre until they reached the vibrant south of Spain.

"With flying colours!"

Alice uncovered her eyes and jumped up and down excitedly – even more so when she saw a happy River standing in front of her with a shiny steel cocktail shaker poised in his hands, ready to make a celebratory drink.

"Ooh! Can you make me a Coco Loco? It's been ages!"

"I was already on it," River laughed. "And while I chop the coconut, you can tell me how the packing is going."

Although there was still a month to go until the wedding, Alice and River needed to pack their cases *yesterday*. They planned to soak up as much of Spain as they could en route, staying a week or more at their favourite places, and, once the final things on their respective to-do lists had been crossed off, they'd be pootling their way off into the sunset.

"Never mind that for the moment," said Alice. "It's Hayley who's giving me a splitting headache."

"She better not have got cold feet about being a bridesmaid."

"Nothing like that." Alice shook her head. "And even though I'd be gutted if she did, that kind of catastrophe would be much easier to remedy even at short notice."

"What is it then?" River gritted his teeth as he hacked into a ripe coconut. "Tell me she's not trying to pair up any of the minibus guests already." Their friend was notorious for playing Cupid. Especially when her services were far from required.

"I'm afraid it's even more worrying. What started out as her driving a minibus full of people over to Spain for the wedding has turned into... wait for it... a *coach* full of people."

"That's ridiculous." River flung the coconut pieces into the blender and gave them a quick blitz. "There won't be enough demand among the guests for an entire coach," he shouted over the top of the white noise. "Most people will prefer to fly, not spend days and nights on the road. Is she even licensed?"

"Oh, yes." Alice yelled back. "She's got her category D and D1 licence. That's not the issue. My beef is, I hadn't envisaged such a stonking great vehicle clogging up the finca's driveway. It's not very idyllic, is it?"

River turned off the machine.

"Leave it to me, sweetheart. I'll have a word with her."

"I don't think you'll get very far. The thing is, Hayley decided to combine the initial minibus trip down to the Costa del Sol with a pitstop at Disneyland Paris on the way over… and Lourdes on the way back, in case anybody needs a miracle – hence the massive uptake. Whether we like it or not, most of the wedding party will now be arriving by coach."

"Bloody hell. I suppose those would be tempting day trips, but both destinations are hardly what you'd call cheap! I take it she's sailing to France then."

"Apparently her boyfriend knows someone who knows someone who knows someone who runs a chain of cheap roadside motels. The kind that are dotted about on the French motorways. He's given her a special discount for the group."

"I'll make it crystal clear that the coach needs to be parked miles down the finca's lane so it doesn't get in the way of any of the amazing drone shots that the photographer is planning to capture."

"Thanks, Riv. I love Hayley to bits. She's been there for us through thick and thin but she's such a loose cannon with her impulses, and the most infuriatingly stubborn person I know."

"She's definitely both of those!"

Somehow River had already added the rum, vodka, tequila and lime to the coconut. The noise of the creamy mixture being poured into a glass soothed Alice. She watched River expertly strain the fusion, turning it into silky liquid goodness. Before she knew it she was taking a restorative sip.

"Wow. That's hit the spot."

"And I'm hoping I might be able to do the same later." River quipped.

Alice slapped her boyfriend on his backside, hinting that his luck might be in.

"So, time's ticking," she said, reminding them both. "My packing is coming along nicely, since you asked, and I've got some last-minute calls to make to the caterers as your mum claims she's only able to eat food cooked in flaxseed oil all of a sudden."

River rolled his eyes.

"Soon there won't be anything left that she *can* eat."

"What's left to do on your list?" Alice ignored yet another tangent to the progress they needed to be making and sipped at her tropical cocktail. It was tempting her dangerously to suggest they make another change to the wedding: destination Antigua. But, no. Focus so close to the big day was key.

Alice and River had divided the remaining tasks equally, as far as wedding and stables preparation was concerned. All bases needed to be covered since they'd be opening their business at the end of September after their month-long honeymoon in Spain and Portugal in the camper van.

"I've just got to pick up my suit and pay the builder. Then we're done."

"Ah, yes." Alice gulped down the rest of her drink for courage. "On the subject of the last thing, you might want to take a seat."

TIM

Tim stuck his Pennines climbing and Peak District wild camping ads on the notice board in the hospital's corridor. He doubted he'd get many takers, as both were slightly hardcore pursuits. But it would make a positive start to married life if he was to be proven wrong and a flurry of fitness fanatics signed up for his mid-August start date. It was a bit late in the season to get the ball rolling as far as his chosen career was concerned, but his mood had plummeted since the trip to Spain back in February and his motivation had deserted him.

His eyes scanned the other posts on the pinboard relating to physiotherapy, meditation and counselling. Checking nobody was looking, Tim carefully removed one of the counselling fliers and stuffed it in his pocket. He had no idea why.

Who was he kidding? He had every idea why. But he doubted anybody could help him. He was beyond rescuing. Especially this close to his nuptials. He had to do something, though. Weeks, and now months, had passed and he still couldn't stop thinking about Freya's brazen kiss... or how he wished he'd reciprocated, taking her in his arms for a fully loaded and passionate encore. And then there was the one hundred euro note she'd tucked in his rucksack to pay her way for the paragliding experience. He'd hardly given her value for money.

Back in the UK, things with Piper hadn't been all that bad, he supposed. Once they'd cleared customs at Manchester airport after the flight from Spain that winter's evening, she'd apologised for having such a monumental go at him during landing. Tim had made life easier for himself by being careful to eat only the most nutritious, low carb food in front of her. He'd actually lost his appetite, so fitting into his suit should be a breeze. And although Piper was tired a lot of the time and less in the mood for bedroom antics – much like himself, because all he could think about was a certain cake maker – she seemed to be happy enough with her lot and all the weekly career goals she was setting and exceeding. She was spending a lot more time on the phone too, dashing off to a quieter area of the apartment to make work calls, but this gave Tim the time and space he needed to contemplate his next career move as the weather turned warmer.

Or rather it gave him the time and space he hadn't wanted (but probably needed) to evaluate his love life.

Tim finally made his way out of the rabbit warren corridors of the hospital and into the car park. This couldn't go on. He needed to take inspired action and call the number on the card immediately, before he found a hundred reasons to procrastinate. Even if the person on the end of the phone couldn't solve his problems, they could listen. Sometimes that was all anybody needed; an impartial stranger to listen to them. If he could get these bottled-up emotions off his chest then he could move forward and feel confident that everything would turn out okay. Maybe not as wonderful as a Disney movie. But good enough.

FREYA

"Freya, can I have a word?"

Hannah did not look like her perky self when she entered the decorating room clutching a piece of paper tightly in her hand. What now? Not that Hannah had been asking for many words with her boss of late. They'd both successfully skirted the subject of Piper's infidelity for five months and counting, which was something of a miracle given Hannah's apparent obsession with the pursuit of justice – and the incessant thoughts of Tim that swirled around Freya's mind, particularly when she tried to sleep. But the way Hannah was asking to take Freya to one side rang alarm bells, of the same decibel level as those February get-togethers in the orange tree square's bar. Whatever was up, Freya could already tell that it didn't bode well for the near future.

"Sure. Shall we pop into the office?" Freya asked without waiting for an answer.

She removed her apron, washed her hands, and stepped away from Ricky and Alejandro, whose amazing artistry she was overseeing as they decorated their first ruffled deckle-edged wedding cake together. It was such a fiddly task, but they'd nailed the brief admirably and she couldn't wait to see the pastel pink masterpiece take pride of place at Saturday's same-sex wedding at the bodega.

Hannah mooched along behind Freya to the small office, her eyes glued to her feet. Once they were inside with the door firmly closed, Freya motioned for Hannah to give her the paper, which she did with a visibly shaking hand.

Freya looked, looked again, and looked a third time. She closed her eyes and screwed up her face. She pinched herself hard on the arm in case she was having a literal nightmare, and then she gingerly opened her eyes to look yet again. She wanted to let out a blood-curdling scream. She was awake, but this could not be right. Merv had only been and double-booked the Goldsmith-Jackson and Moss-Nutkins wedding cakes for August the sixth!

The situation might have been salvageable were both couples opting for small and modest cakes, but no: Merv had basically promised the gargantuan eight-tier showstopper cake would appear at *two weddings* at completely different locations up and down the coast *on the same day*. There was no mistaking the hard facts swimming before Freya's eyes, in Merv's trademark spider-crawl handwriting on the stupid feint ruled page with the paperclip still attached to it; the paper clip that had presumably, at some undefinable point in time, come loose from the order book.

"B-but I don't understand. Where did you find this?" Freya whispered, shock fizzing through her veins. She couldn't even look at Hannah.

"Do you recall hearing the downstairs door slam earlier when that client didn't shut it properly and the wind almost took it off its hinges?" Freya couldn't answer and couldn't see where this small talk was going. Hannah carried on. "A huge gust blew in, and that was when I saw a sheet of paper fly out from beneath the counter display unit. The one where we keep the book in its cubby hole. Well, of course it's a large piece of furniture and regardless of who has been mopping the floors these past few months – you, me or the cleaner – the gap underneath the unit is miniscule. I picked the paper up, scanned it quickly, almost had a heart attack, and brought it straight to you. I'm guessing Merv didn't attach the sheet of paper to the book properly and it fell, then somehow slid underneath the unit and remained there undetected."

"*Gawwwwwwd!*"

Freya pelted downstairs to the shop floor, snatched up the dumb excuse for a professional order system and returned to the office breathless. Throwing the old green book with its cracked spine onto the table, she rifled through its pages to August as fast as her fingers would allow.

"I've been through these orders time and time again," she said in a wobbly high-pitched voice. "Merv added the details of the Goldsmith-Jackson wedding in here himself. See: there they are! August the sixth. Finca Preciosa." Freya gulped for air and wondered if she might start hyperventilating. "When he first started talking about the Moss-Nutkins wedding way back when, and I saw that he hadn't added the details of that cake order to the book, I called him immediately. He made no mention at all of having previously recorded the order in writing, so he simply dictated the information ref Piper and Tim's wedding cake over the phone. Date, August the thirteenth! In other words, an entire week away from Alice and River's wedding." Freya drilled the pencil down into the page until she made a hole. "One: when, in ten years of this business, have we ever tried to squeeze two of our biggest and most expensive cakes into one day? What was Merv thinking? And two, how come he didn't flag this enormous date error up, when we went over every aspect of the Moss-Nutkins order on the phone? Surely he'd made a note of the wedding day being August the sixth at his end? This is an absolute disaster. We've had a few little calamities and mild panics over the years. That's to be expected. But never anything like this!"

It was the last week of July. Every hour in the approaching weeks of the busiest season had already been accounted for, as had every ingredient and kitchen appliance. There was no chance of rearranging anything this close to both monumental orders.

Hannah began to hop about like a hen. "You can't let him get away with this."

"I know I can't," Freya snapped back at Hannah, feeling immediately guilty. "But call me a fool, I care about his feelings. He's not getting any younger and I don't want to lay into him and give him a coronary. This is half my responsibility in any case. I've been a doormat, making too many allowances for his archaic ways. I should've insisted long ago that we record the cake details properly on a computer system. Talk about screwing things up!"

"Point taken. *But I'm not letting you take the blame*, and I won't stand back and listen to Mervyn slating you when he's made such a whopping mistake. He's the wedding planner, Freya. No matter how old he is."

"We're going to have to call the brides." Freya panicked. "I can't bear breaking the news to either of them. Alice, because she's so sweet and deserves better and I loved her music when she was in Avalonia… and Piper because if that call on the yacht was anything to go by, she's not going to take this lying down, and I dread to think of the way she could defame us on social media. We haven't even got time to try to convince one couple to have the cake and the other to go for something a lot smaller. It's August. We're completely booked up!"

"We'll come up with a solution, boss. There's always a

way around these things," Hannah insisted. "And hey, luckily, it's a humdinger of a cake so neither wedding party will go hungry."

"Oh, Hannah." The lump in Freya's throat turned to tears and she dived at the box of tissues on her desk, pulling half of them out and dabbing furiously at her face. "That's a lovely sentiment but it's a tad simplistic," she sniffed. "Can you honestly see Piper Moss accepting half a wedding cake… and even then, which way would we cut it?"

"Well, four tiers each, obviously." Freya couldn't help but belly laugh. "You never know, this might set off a new trend," said Hannah, deadly serious. "You could put it to madam that way. I'm more than happy to make the call for you if that helps. Looking at this logically with a bit of Yorkshire pragmatism, I really can't see a problem. I know it's not so great for us as a business, but each couple will save themselves a small fortune as we'll have to refund them at least half of the cost – and that's another reason you have to tell Merv about his mistake; Weddings in Paradise should take the financial hit. The other thing to remember is there's no way either wedding party will get through all eight layers on the day. And, since the tiers are being repeated, so there are four sponges and fillings times two, by halving the cake, nobody will end up going without their favourite flavour."

"Kind of," Freya had to give Hannah an ounce of credit where it was due. "Slightly overlooking the fact that each repetition of tiers starts off with the scrumptious salted caramel layer, which does tend to be most people's favourite… and totally overlooking the fact that the tiers get smaller as the cake gets taller. In other words, one couple would end up with a giant base tier of the most delicious flavour – as well as generous sized-tiers of the others – and the other couple would get a significantly smaller version of everything."

"Then there's only one thing for it: the cake will have to be split equally down the middle – from top to bottom – and the iced waterfall of roses will have the same treatment too."

"How can we possibly do that? It'll look hideous."

"It'll look avant-garde. How else do some of these weird and wonderful wedding cake trends come to be? Ricky will rise to the challenge and the rest of us will rally around to help him. Piper might not warm to the idea at first but once she's turned it over in her head and thought about how leading edge she'll come across to all her influencer mates, I'm telling you, she'll be converted."

"I admire your confidence. I can't see the wood for the trees, or the dowling rods for the tiers, right now. It's enough to reduce me to this kind of tears all over again." Freya pointed at her panda eyes.

"One step at a time, love." Hannah was perfect. A modern-day walking and talking agony aunt. "How about I take care of breaking the news to Mervyn? Diplomatically, of course, and just as the first point of contact. You can follow up later. Meanwhile, you deal with the brides."

"I've said it before and I'll say it again: you're my rock, Hannah Barlow. I honestly don't know what I would do without you," Freya cried. "If it hadn't been for your eagle eyes, we wouldn't even know there was a problem. Can you imagine how much more of a fiasco this would be on the wedding day?"

ALICE

*T*he sun rose on a brand-new day in Salamanca. Drawn by its rich Celtic history and fabulous architecture, River and Alice had made a beeline for the stunning northern Spanish city as soon as they'd driven off the ferry in a super shiny and polished Twinkle. Today was their third night at the Airbnb located off the central square, and River had driven to the out of town hypermarket to buy yet more delicious Mediterranean provisions, insisting that Alice soak up the early morning rays in a café on the Plaza Mayor before they got too intense and *siesta* time called. Could there exist a better man in this world?

She'd taken a bit of a risk keeping her financial skeleton in the closet for so many months, but she still didn't regret delaying before telling River about the stables benefactor. To throw another cliche into the works, once that horse had bolted, things would have quickly led to a flurry of arguments at a time when there was already plenty of stress over the amount of work to be done. Hopefully, now there would be no more little secrets between bride and groom to be. They had a solid and trusting relationship and loved one another to bits, but their respective upbringings could not have been more different. Occasionally that made it hard for one side of the couple to relate to the other.

River had taken the news of Alice's dad's secret cash injection into the transformation of his late aunt's former caravan park about as well as she thought he would... hence her resorting to alcohol before breaking the news.

"I wish you'd told me before," River had said, when Alice blurted everything out after that delicious Coco Loco. "There's no way I'd have let your dad play knight in shining armour. Only a couple of years ago he strung you along so badly, leading you to believe he'd invest in your dream Cornish stables, then pulling out at the last minute so you had to rent that shabby, rundown place on the edge of a tumbledown farm instead. He can't just flit in and out of your life on a whim. It's so shitty of him."

"I know and I'm sorry I didn't bring up his contribution to the renovations before. But if I'd told you at the start of the project, you'd have said a flat out no," Alice had explained.

"Too right I would. I love you so much, Al. It's been hell seeing you distraught about your father's shoddy behaviour in the past – his favouritism of one daughter over the other. And don't get me started on your mother. I know I have little experience in the parenting department, with no father figure in my own life since day dot, and I know my mum's style of taking care of me has been eccentric over the years, to say the least, but I don't like the way your old man thinks he can buy in or out of your life as he sees fit."

"I understand your reluctance but it felt like a gift I couldn't refuse. The thing is, it didn't come from him directly, but through him... if that makes sense?" Alice had wished River would fix her up with a second cocktail to take the edge off this discussion. "When I moved back to the UK from LA, I think he took it for granted that as I'd chosen to live in Somerset, I'd mould back into the family dynamics and fit in with expectations. My mother didn't even know about us uprooting so quickly and moving yet again, down to Cornwall, until a few weeks after we'd gone. It all happened in quite a rush, didn't it?"

River looked a little sheepish now. It had been the one and only rough patch in their relationship and it had definitely made them think they needed an urgent change of scene. Cutting a very long and complicated story short, River had been completely swindled by the sister of a former childhood friend, who would stop at nothing to drive a wedge between him and Alice. It was no wonder he'd become a lot less trusting of people.

"Yeah," Alice continued. "So she found out about my father's undercover trips down to Cornwall and basically blackmailed him: If he dared to contribute to my dreams – regardless of the fact he was technically squaring up with me and giving me the money I was owed – she would divorce him and take him to the cleaners."

River's jaw dropped.

"Nooooo! I knew your mum could be manipulative but that's just…"

"Awful," Alice finished. "Even as recently as last year I held out hope of us healing our relationship. Now I know better. It's futile. But it really would appear that my father has started to see how devious my mother has been over the years. That's quite a development and the last thing I want to do is shut him out. He might even need us down the line, Riv. Things have become unbearable." Alice sighed. "Anyway, he cashed in some shares without my mother knowing, and he gifted me the money. It's not quite as much as my folks have spent on my sister over the years, but I accepted the token because it was timely, the universe would frown upon me if I didn't… and we all know it's foolish to look a gift horse in the mouth." She giggled at her equestrian pun and even River's mouth began to twitch into a tiny smile. "It's never wise to block your channels to abundance, as *your dear mum* would say."

River cracked and began to laugh and, despite all the unnecessary heartache that her own mother had created, Alice had to join in.

Her relationship with her parents had been rocky for years. You could pinpoint the exact day and hour: the moment she'd walked into the drawing room of the grand family home in the Somerset village of Butleigh, and announced she was joining the rock band, Avalonia (as opposed to pursuing Olympic glory with her horse as per her parents' expectations). She had been cut out of her inheritance, and her mother and father had fawned over her elder sister, Tamara, ever since. But deep down Alice had always known it was her mother who wore the trousers (or jodhpurs). Her father was simply scared of rocking the marital boat and would go along with anything his wife decreed; from the holidays they took to the brand of coffee they drank… and the shade of Farrow & Ball paint that adorned the many rooms in their beautiful country home.

Now Alice's mobile phone began to vibrate on the table, making her jump. That would be River, no doubt deliberating over the Spanish food labels at the hypermarket and needing her to help decipher things with her rusty GCSE Spanish. Alice picked up the phone and looked at the caller ID. But it wasn't River, it was a Spanish number instead.

"Hello. Is that Alice?" said an female English voice which sounded kind of familiar, its tone unmistakably urgent. "It's Freya from FOM."

"Oh! Hi, Freya. What a lovely surprise. How are you? Is everything OK at your end?"

"Well, that's why I'm calling. I really wish I could say that it was, but unfortunately I have some pretty bad news. Can I just check that you're sitting down? I am so very sorry, there's no easy way of saying this." Alice's stomach sank. It sounded like somebody had died. Her hand began to shake so she thought it best to put her coffee down before she spilt it all over her white sundress.

"I'm s-seated," Alice replied with a shaky voice to match the hand.

"Right. Good. Okay, without going into the finer details – because that's something for me to sort out personally to ensure that it never *ever* happens again… it's come to my attention that your gorgeous wedding cake has been double-booked." Freya didn't even stop for air. "Due to this massive oversight, the tight turnaround and lead times required for staff, hours, ovens, and ingredients, unfortunately we are in a situation where just one wedding cake has been booked for your wedding venue *and* that of another couple's on exactly the same day: August the sixth – yours at the finca, and the other bride and groom's at a villa down in Marbella."

"Oh, crumbs." Alice grimaced at her unfortunate choice of reply. "I mean, that's really tricky." Her heart began to race. The news was terrible, there was no denying it… and yet it was nowhere near as life-changing as it had initially sounded. Clearly this wasn't Freya's doing, and from the way she had worded things, it didn't take much imagination to figure out who had fudged up the planning. Still, it totally changed her big surprise. What a bummer so close to the big day, with no time to find a solution! She went silent for several seconds as she let the expletives fly around her head. But there was no point taking this out on Freya. She would have a good old scream on her balcony later before River returned, and preferably without any onlookers on the street below if she timed it just right.

"Obviously I'm devastated to hear this, but..." Alice paused to sigh, thinking how dreadful this call must be for Freya. "I can't even begin to imagine how gutted you guys must be too, what with all the love and skill and hard work goes into making such a large cake. I'm sure it was a genuine mistake. It must be beyond frustrating to have such a conundrum on your hands... but it's not a matter of life or death, is it? We'll cooperate however we can and help solve the issue. It's such a huge cake. There's more than enough for both weddings. Perhaps it could be transported from one venue to the other, sliced up at a location in the middle and shared? The other party may not agree of course, but River and I will be open to pretty much any possibility to salvage the day—"

The line fell silent and Alice stopped waffling, wondering if she'd been cut off, but then Freya began to sob.

"Freya? Are you all right?"

"Y-yes. Just about. But really it should be me asking you that question... and me coming up with a solution. How can you be so kind and understanding? I just don't get it."

"Well, it isn't the best news I've ever received, for sure. But I guess everything in life is about perspective. I'm sitting in one of the most beautiful squares in Europe, sipping coffee in the sunshine, watching the world go by, and about to marry my soulmate. Compared to billions of others on this planet, I am very lucky and I try not to take that for granted. Yes, I had envisaged a huge cake..."

At this point, Alice filled Freya in on her plans to give the cake out to as many Spanish and Portuguese villagers as possible during their honeymoon – which reduced Freya to further tears. Alice wished she could hug her. Then she went on. "But we'll improvise. Hey, maybe you could whip us up some trays of flapjacks or a Bakewell tart or two? Just a handful of quick English classics. If you could get them over to us at the finca by the time we leave for our honeymoon,

THE WEDDING CAKE

I'm more than prepared for you to forget the refund. In fact, I think it might even work out better. It'll be fun to bring some of our sweet English roots and traditions to the locals, and smaller cakes will be a heck of a lot easier to store and distribute. In a roundabout way, you might even be doing us a favour."

"It would be my pleasure, and I will make you a plethora of traybakes and tarts," said Freya, expelling a giant sigh. "But you will still be getting a refund. On that point there is no negotiation."

"If you're sure and that's what you want. Oh," Alice added, feeling the kick of the caffeine acting like a muse. "I've had another idea to solve the issue: Let's just cut the cake in half, straight down the middle – assuming you have a knife that's big enough for the job?"

"It's funny you should say that," Freya replied. "Not in the literal sense, of course…"

At the end of the call Alice felt that at least they'd found a solution that was acceptable to herself and to FOM. On the other hand, Freya hadn't yet made the call to the other couple concerned, and instinct told Alice they might not see the situation in *quite* the same way. One thing was certain, though: River would be elated at the money refunded, even if Alice's surprise cake jaunt in the camper van wouldn't be quite as ostentatious as planned. There was nothing wrong with a good old Bakewell tart, and she could still keep that side of things under wraps. They would have so much fun meeting local people and seeing their reaction to the treats. Perhaps River could make and serve cocktails to pair up with them.

Spain's laidback attitude had properly seeped into Alice's pores and she refused to get upset about what was essentially *just desserts*. These things happened to the best of people and where there was a will, there was a way around them. There was no time to make a different cake from scratch and Freya only had a certain number of expert hands at her disposal. Those were the facts and they could analyse the problem day and night. The only solution was to halve the cake. It would still be tall and it would still be rustically beautiful and delicious.

TIM

"Squirrel, we need to have a serious talk before we set off tomorrow," said Tim's friend, Josh, calling him by the Beatrix Potter nickname he'd never managed to brush off among his school friends.

Josh, Kyle and Nath were heading out on the same midday flight as Tim and Piper, travelling from Manchester to Malaga, although they'd be going their separate ways once they landed in the Costa del Sol – until the stag do. Even Marbella's 'budget' accommodation was too pricey for Tim's friends, so they'd be staying half an hour along the motorway in down-to-earth Torremolinos, and that's exactly where Tim intended to join them for a very laid back evening prior to his wedding. A few pints in a pub, a game of snooker, and a meal in an unpretentious restaurant that didn't require you to eat with umpteen knives, forks and spoons whilst your breath hitched at the thought of the bill. A very laid-back evening that definitely didn't involve getting himself tied to a lamppost… or waking with his eyebrows shaved off. He honestly couldn't remember the last time he'd done anything so normal on a night out and it was the only part of the wedding proceedings he was excited about.

"Yeah," added Kyle, snapping Tim out of his daydream. "We're worried."

"But I thought we'd covered the best man thing? I can't possibly choose between the three of you, and I can't possibly ask all three of you. When I suggested tossing a coin for it, none of you were game. It's too late now. Everything's set in stone with the ceremony and seating. Of course I'd have asked my brother if things were different, but they're not, so it's on with the show."

"No, Squirrel. This hasn't got anything to do with best man duties." Kyle took a swift slurp of his drink.

"Oh, mate, I know you're a nervous flyer," said Tim. It was true. Kyle had never contemplated long haul, and would travel like BA Baracus from the A-Team in the belly of the aircraft, given half the chance – and if it were safe to do so. "But it's only a couple of hours on the plane and then you'll be relaxing in some proper blissed-out surroundings, trust me."

"We have been to Spain before. We do know what to expect." Nath tutted, and Tim acknowledged that he totally deserved the dirty look, given that he and the lads had indeed holidayed in Benidorm, Magaluf and the Canary Islands together over the years. "And it's not Kyle we're concerned about, buddy." Nath folded his arms and looked Tim in the eye. "Take this as a last minute pep talk from the three of us: Piper's got you so firmly under the thumb that you're in danger of losing what little is left of your freedom once you become man and wife." Josh and Kyle, seated either side of Nath at the boys' local pub on the outskirts of Manchester, nodded their heads in unison, grim expressions on their faces, mouths pressed into lines.

"What? Where's all this come from?" Tim laughed

nervously, hugging his pint closer to him. Okay, now he was terrified they would tie him to a lamppost *and* shave his eyebrows off – to prevent him from going through with the wedding. "Listen, I appreciate your concern, lads. But you're so far off the mark," Tim lied. They really weren't. "Everything is sweet between me and Piper. I can't wait to marry her and there's no way she's in charge of every aspect of my life. Can you imagine me letting that happen?"

"C'mon, pal. This is us you're talking to... and yes, we flaming well can imagine it happening, because it already is. You just can't see it." Nath sighed. "You've always been this way with the ladies in your life. You're too kind, that's your trouble. You're like this with *everybody*, putting other people's happiness first and caving in to make life easier for those around you. We've been friends since we were knee-high to grasshoppers, to borrow the phrase your mam always uses, and you haven't changed a bit."

"Or, to throw another idiom into the mix: we can read you like a *Smash Hits* magazine and it's time to look out for *number one* a bit more," Josh chipped in, looking proud of himself for his contribution, a reasonable pun if you were of a certain age and used to read said music magazine.

"Basically, you're a peacemaker," added Kyle. "You always have been. Ever since the day Kirstie Wilkins brought that giant bag of jelly babies into Miss Mitchell's class on her birthday and civil war broke out. You went without your own share back then, as I recall – all to pacify Gary Wheat and to stop him from smacking Pete De Camps in the face for taking too many sweets."

Tim felt like a spectator at a tennis match, watching the banter go back and forth like a ball. The memory rang a brief bell but Tim couldn't believe it was so clear for his friends. Had they been taking notes on his behaviour all his life? Now he was feeling paranoid.

"All right, Josh and all right, Kyle! Did we or did we not agree that *I'd be the one doing the talking* so we could stick to the point?" Nath took command of the conversation once again and cleared his throat to continue.

Josh pretended to pull a zip across his mouth. Kyle went back to slurping at his drink.

"We might have stood by and watched you put your own life on hold in your twenties when Brittany and Andy scarpered, leaving you to care for your mam and help your dad out ... but we'd never forgive ourselves if we didn't speak up before you potentially make the biggest mistake of your life. It's not too late to walk away from Piper. Nip things in the bud now before it gets harder to break it off and she changes you beyond recognition – or worse: before she completely destroys you. She's not the one. You know it and we know it. And there... I've said it on behalf of all of us and you'll probably never speak to me again. But that's the risk I needed to take. That's what friends do."

Nath knocked back a third of his pint in one go and let out a resounding gasp.

Silence fell on the table, nobody knowing quite where to look, until they let the giant TV screen and its current football match reel them back in.

"Cheers for the unsolicited lecture but I've made my bed and now I'm going to have to lie in it." Tim then muttered, flipping one beer mat with another as if he was playing a game of tiddlywinks. "Even if I am sleeping with the enemy."

"What the fuck?" said Nath, in such a loud voice that drinkers' heads turned at other tables, wondering if a goal had been scored by the opposition and they'd somehow missed it. "Has she done the dirty on you or something?" he whispered, eyes wide with disbelief.

Little did they know – and little would they know. If Tim couldn't tell a non-judgemental counsellor what had been

THE WEDDING CAKE

going on, then he sure as hell couldn't tell his opinionated friends.

"Tim?" said Kyle, leaning over the table to give him a much-needed shake.

"Nah, of course not. I'm pulling your leg!"

Tim let out a hearty chuckle, put on his best fake smile and berated himself for letting any of that not-so-little-lot slip out. *What was the matter with him?* He'd already psyched himself up mentally, deciding that the path of action was straight ahead, hoping that things would get better of their own accord once he and Piper had exchanged their vows. Everyone made the mistake of thinking married life would be a bed of roses. At least this way Tim was under no illusion about the thorns that lay in wait. Hopefully this was his and Piper's one rough patch and they'd simply got it out of the way before they had rings on their fingers. He would not be tempted left, right or backwards (to thoughts of Freya).

Which was slightly contrary to the advice the counsellor gave him. But what did she know? Could she look into a crystal ball and tell Tim this wouldn't happen again if he walked away and ended up in another relationship? *Exactly.* And that's why the only walking Tim had done was to take himself *out* of his second counselling session once the seemingly 'trending' theme of people pleasing (oh, and Middle Child Syndrome) came up. He'd not set foot in that supposedly calming blue- and green-painted office since. Obviously he'd done the decent thing and waited until the very end of session two, not wanting to cause a scene as he sat opposite Jacqui on the comfy cream couch behind the shield of the fluffy cushions (well, there were too many on the seat and he could hardly throw them on the floor), patiently biding his time with nods and smiles of agreement as she did most of the talking.

Now his friends, too, were suggesting he was too easy-going for his own good! And what was with the random childhood references from the classroom? Tim didn't like it one bit. Everyone was making him sound like a doormat, the kind of man who'd be knocked down by a gust of wind. It wasn't true. He was realistic, that was all. Especially on the subject of romance. Prior to Piper, every relationship he'd had had felt untenable in the long-term. Mostly the women were too worldly-wise and intelligent for him. Tim might have cleared hurdles faster than all of them on an athletics track but he couldn't keep up with the leaps they'd made in their professional lives – from Penny the hedge fund manager (whose name could not have been more apt), to Beata the digital marketer, and Kim the trainee lawyer. Whilst none of them had voiced their opinions on the slow development of his career path post-uni, he never felt he could hold his own with their lofty goals so he'd let the relationships fizzle out once the honeymoon period was over, and gracefully accepted when his girlfriends had, one by one, called it a day.

"Life's not all fairytales," his granddad had said to him as he lay in bed, dying of Parkinson's, offering up pearls of wisdom to the then twelve-year-old Tim whilst everyone else was out of earshot. It was strange how those words had come to him in a flashback the day he'd started the therapy sessions. "You will never have everything perfect so don't waste your time trying to force anything. Not in work, family or love. Ha, definitely not love." Young Tim had looked on inquisitively at the time, unsure as to whether Grandad Nutkins was talking to him straight, or the morphine had led to delirium. "After your grandma's affair I was tempted to leave her and find myself another woman, but what was the point? It's better the devil you know than getting carried away with fanciful ideas. So long as you can keep up the facade of a happy marriage; there's food on the table, a roof over your heads, clothes on your back, and a little left over to play the lottery and treat yourselves to fish and chips of a weekend, no bugger is ever any the wiser and you rub along okay. It's a lot less hassle that way, son. Take it from me."

Grandma Nutkins playing the field had been news to Tim! Why hadn't his parents told him about this? And how old was she when the hanky panky happened? Maybe they didn't even know because her affair had gone on after Tim's dad had flown the nest? Subconsciously, Tim supposed he had always let his grandad's final piece of advice guide him. How could he not? It seemed pretty significant that he should tell his grandson all of this the day before he passed away. As if the words had come from his soul.

The pub crowd roared, snapping Tim back to his current coordinates. Tim's friends joined in, jumping to their feet since Manchester United had scored the equaliser in their away game. Tim belatedly and half-heartedly joined them, putting on his own facade of happiness. Nath could piss off with his path of least resistance snub and his agony uncle advice. Tim's friend had never made it as far down the relationship path as him. What the hell did he know anyway? In fact, Tim had never met anybody quite so choosy when it came to the opposite sex.

At the end of the day, Tim's friends, and Jacqui the know-it-all counsellor, could think what they liked. Because Tim had done some thinking of his own and his mind was made up. He and Piper would work it out. They had to. Not because he was living in denial, believing she loved him unconditionally and would stay faithful to him until the end of time. He knew the score on that front. Maybe he was doomed from the start and it ran in the blood? Obviously it had skipped a generation with his parents but Brittany and Andy, to the best of his knowledge, had experienced little luck in love. And so it probably was true that Tim's fiancée would constantly be on the lookout for better. But he accepted that. Like his granddad said, you had to know what you were dealing with. That way life couldn't deliver any surprises. His friends were right about one thing: he'd spent his late teens and early twenties in a constant flux of upheaval, waiting for dreaded phone calls about his mam's deteriorating condition in those first few weeks after the fall, frantically trying to get hold of Brittany so he could offload, fruitlessly trying to track down the errant Andy. Everything merging into one. The anxiety had been unbearable at times. But how must his parents have felt?

"You're the only one keeping me going," his mam and his dad had told him over and over – on separate occasions, each oblivious to the other's words.

And that was the reason Tim had to go through with the wedding; to spare his parents the humiliation, to give them something to be proud of, something to look forward to. They'd already lived through two sets of disappointment with Brittany and Andy. Tim couldn't face putting them through it a third time after all their bad luck. They deserved better. His mam deserved better.

So yes, fine. Call him a people pleaser, accuse him of being a pushover, tell him he couldn't handle disapproval. But none of this was for Piper's benefit. His parents had pinned everything on him and they needed him. He had to stay on the straight and narrow, do the honourable thing and commit to this woman 'for better or worse'. And that was that.

He'd figured all this out before his waste of time sessions with Jacqui, in any case. There was no need for him to bring up Piper's infidelity on the two occasions he did go for counselling. Which is why he never returned.

THE WEDDING CAKE

THE PHOTOGRAPHS HAD ARRIVED on a Monday way back in March. They were addressed to him and to him only. In a sense, Tim had been expecting them, although he did wonder who could be so callous as to try to derail him? Surely Freya, for instance, wouldn't do such a thing? When Tim squinted, the gorgeous brunette in the graphic images didn't look like Piper. Besides, he'd never seen any of this underwear before. Tim's initial thoughts were, what a sick stunt for somebody to pull. And that meant it had to be the work of a rival influencer. He'd seen so many of them eyeing Piper up in and around the hotel in Puerto Banus. It wouldn't take much to impersonate her. That's why you couldn't clearly see the face in any of these pictures, even when your eyes were on stalks, taking in all the activity. The male had a whiff of that Noah dude about him, but Tim knew that was impossible given he was gay.

But then Tim had made a cup of tea and come back to the photographs without his rose-tinted glasses, setting aside the incessant internal chatter. Reality had bitten him as he'd tucked into his plate of (secretly stashed) Bourbon biscuits.

It was Piper. Now he could see the beauty spot on her left buttock. And it was Noah too. Evidently, he favoured the same smirk during intercourse as Tim had noted on the beach that day. Tim had been massively in denial. And as for Piper, why would she still want to get married to him when she was mucking about behind his back? For a split second, Tim wondered if she'd been forced into this series of compromising positions? Who was to say that she hadn't been bribed or blackmailed? Like he'd just said, the influencer world was super competitive when you reached the dizzy heights at the top. Tim had chewed on another Bourbon in contemplation. The sugary hit of the no-

nonsense biscuit had brought him back to his senses for once and for all. Piper wanted Noah as much as Noah wanted Piper. Tim hid the pictures in his sock drawer. He needed time to process things. He needed time to decide what he was going to do.

As the weeks and months rolled by and Piper kept up a remarkable act as the quintessentially excited bride, Tim found he couldn't get angry, despite his disappointment – even if he tried. Another realisation: he didn't love Piper at all. How could he? Everything he'd said to Freya that day when she'd sped off from the paragliding session had been true. He was in love with the idea of being in love – but he wasn't in love with the person he was due to marry.

Unfortunately, that hadn't, it seemed, stopped him from falling head over heels for Freya. She was the first thing he thought about when he woke in the morning, and she then filled his head until dusk. She was the last thing he thought about at night when his weary head hit the pillow. Tim's predicament was torture. Another reason he'd decided to keep things simple and go through with the wedding. Nobody needed the drama. It was hard enough for him. How would his parents cope with the cancellations, money lost on flights and accommodation, outfits and hats? His dad had eaten right into his precious savings so they could stay in an all-inclusive beachside hotel in Marbella. This whole trip was a once in a lifetime holiday for them. And so even more weeks and months had passed by, Tim and Piper both faking their love to one another – and doubtless countless orgasms too.

～

Just when Tim hadn't thought his pre-wedding nerves could get any worse, Piper had got a phone call from Spain at the very end of July, mere days before they were due to fly out to the villa.

"What the hell are you talking about?" she'd shrieked into her mobile in the hallway as Tim had dutifully sliced the avocado for her sprouted wholegrain toast at the kitchen worktop. "How can you possibly double-book a wedding cake, you useless cow? *Mine absolutely has to take priority!* I'm a high profile influencer. *Do you realise which magazine is covering my wedding day? Do I need to remind you who used to own the villa we're getting married at?*"

"Shit!" Tim had lost his concentration on the job in hand and cut his finger. He'd quickly swaddled it in the nearest tea towel, torn between the need to seize the phone to rescue whoever at FOM was on the other end of the line (highly likely Freya) and concern about his fingertip. *What was all that about?* It did not sound good. Tim panicked as he took in the bloodstain growing on the cloth. But still he'd cast his mind back to that February afternoon and his conversation with Freya. She'd produced that old-fashioned order book and gone over the finer points with him, hadn't she? But had he been too lost in his deep and immediate attraction to her (and the delicious cake)? What if *he* hadn't picked up on the fact that she'd mentioned the wrong date? What if he'd caused all of this pandemonium? This could not be happening on top of everything else. With one hand, he managed to open the first aid kit and slap a large plaster on the cut. It didn't look like it needed stitches. He'd dress it properly later.

"I was about to call you anyway," Piper had continued in the kitchen doorway. Tim had held his breath for the next instalment, praying he wouldn't get roped into the conversation. He definitely hadn't been up for talking to Freya in front of his bride-to-be. "I want a floating wedding cake table to go with my *fully-formed* eight-tier showstopper." She wanted *what* now? "I don't care how much it costs. There are a couple of perfectly sized palm trees in the villa's garden and it's going to look epic in the middle of them, suspended like something out of a fairy-tale. Mervyn will send you the garden plan and pictures but you'll definitely need to get your team down to the villa – like yesterday – to work out how to put it all together. Basically, the cake needs to be tied securely to the palms with the finest silk you can get your hands on, so that it swings between them on a wooden seat… it also needs to be fixed to the seat very securely."

Tim had heard a frantic voice – *Freya's frantic voice* – on the other end of the line. For sure she'd be protesting about that. It would be impossible this close to the wedding to factor in the time to make such a finicky addition. Meanwhile, Piper cruelly held her hand up in the shape of a beak, to take the mickey out of Freya explaining why she could not drop everything to fulfil this outlandish demand, which sounded acrobatic to say the least. Tim had visions of the cake flying through the air and splatting Piper in the face. On second thoughts…

"No, I am not falling for your tricks," Piper had continued. He wasn't sure he'd ever seen her so worked up. "How would half a cake ever become an influencer trend? You don't even know my business or the things that are currently in hot demand so stop trying to tell me how to run my career. Get me the cake I ordered on the day I ordered it… along with my updated requirements – or else. And I hardly need to spell out what the 'else' part of that sentence implies."

Piper had cut the call and thrown the phone over her shoulder. It landed (somewhere in the hallway) with a clunk. Oh, well. It wasn't like she didn't have any back-ups.

Tim had focused on the here and now with all his brain power. The urge to hop on a flight and check Freya was okay was enormous.

"Erm, everything okay, love?" Tim had asked Piper pointlessly as she walked into the kitchen. "Avocado toast?"

"Are you living on another planet?" she spat. "Of course everything isn't all right. But it will be! You can forget the lunch, though, I've lost my appetite."

Piper had stormed out of the room as quickly as she'd entered it. Tim had binned the toast. He knew avocado was a superfood but he couldn't understand the fascination with its soft, oily texture and would not be partaking. Before he cleared up he had to make fists of his hands and rub at his eyes, like they do in cartoons, to check that he wasn't dreaming. Piper had turned into one giant nightmare of a bridezilla and frankly she petrified him. Besides which, how could anybody be expected to cut a cake while it was swinging? Assuming, of course, that he'd heard that bit of the extremely one-sided conversation correctly.

He'd decided he would need to intervene and call Freya (or whoever he could now speak with at FOM, since Freya had probably headed to the nearest bar to drown her sorrows), ensuring the cake was salvaged in whichever way the professionals thought best, and apologising for Piper's outrageous request. He'd wait until his girlfriend left the apartment, and he'd rehearse something.

∼

"Tim? *Tim!* We're moving on, Squirrel!" Josh nudged him hard in the ribs before he could replay the way he'd attempted to remedy the situation. "The Chinese takeaway calls. Are you coming or what?"

Like so many things that could not continue, Tim's trances and reveries into the past had to stop.

"Not tonight, boys. I'm watching my weight."

Well, damn. There he went, falling into the trap of

making Piper look like she was in control yet again. And on that note he remembered for the gazillionth time that she was still being evasive about the guest list and the honeymoon. He really needed to know who was coming and where he was supposed to be whisking her away to, once she'd thrown the bouquet over her head to the next ignoramus.

"Right, well," said Josh. "I guess the next time we see you will be at the check-in desk at the airport. Unless you cha—"

"That you will," said Tim, determined that nobody or nothing would make him backpedal. "Make sure your shoes are buffed and your suits packed neatly. It's going to be a wedding to remember!"

FREYA

*A*lice was wonderful. If Freya ever had a daughter, then that's what she'd call her: amazing, awesome, admirable Alice.

That was well and good. But Freya couldn't help but think she was about to go from one conversational extreme to another. Which was why (and she hoped this wouldn't become a regular occurrence) she'd treated herself to lunch at one of the orange tree square's bars; lunch with a rather fat G&T.

She didn't drink it all! She wasn't *that* unprofessional, despite having had her moments this year… Still, those few sips helped take the edge off the call that she had to make, because the days were whizzing by and there was no longer anywhere to run or hide. Hannah had flagged the subject up with Merv. He had been incandescent, and Freya realised she should have made the initial call herself. Merv had always been so suspicious of Hannah and was forever making cutting little remarks in her presence. But Freya wasn't going to beat herself up about another faux pas. She would deal with Merv in a couple of days when he was back in the cakery and they had a whole heap of bookings to go through. She would also be introducing him to their brand-new order system, and ripping the damn green book to shreds. It seemed harsh but it was the only way to make it clear that they could no longer accommodate his old-fashioned requirements. He needed to get with the times, else the business would find their clientele from elsewhere. There were plenty of other wedding planners in this part of Spain and Freya could not afford to have FOM's reputation dragged through the mud again.

Once she had trudged with heavy feet back to the office, she perched on the edge of her desk with her mobile phone and made the call. She didn't deviate too much from the opening line she'd used with Alice.

"Hi Piper. It's Freya here at FOM in Spain. I hope all is well... blah-di-blah... *BOOM!*"

Freya broke the news about the cake's double-booking and braced herself for the inevitable outburst, which was pretty hideous to say the least, and yes, who in these parts wasn't aware that the venue had once belonged to that opinionated tosspot of the mainstream music world. Big deal!

"I really am sorry, Piper. It's completely inexcusable but we'll find a solution. That I can promise you."

There then followed a very uncomfortable few minutes of shouting, which Piper finished off with her swing bombshell. "...And the cake also needs to be fixed to the seat very securely."

Freya listened to the idea, and took a deep breath. "It's pretty late notice, Piper. I'm not sure that we'll be able to accommodate this sudden change, although we will try our best, of course. If we could maybe focus on the cake solution for the moment, that would be great. Obviously, it's not ideal for the other bride and groom who find themselves in exactly the same upsetting position as yourself and Tim."

Freya willed the image of a dapper Tim and a svelte and stunning Piper out of her head until she'd reduced them to a couple of stick people. She was going to need to employ this visualisation technique a lot over the coming days. "But they have agreed to us cutting the wedding cake in half – from top to bottom – and actually, by doing so, you'd be at the leading edge of bridal influencer trends, which would be an amazing bonus for you…"

"Get me the cake I ordered on the day I ordered it… along with my updated requirements, or else. And I hardly need to spell out what the 'else' part of that sentence implies."

Freya had known the call to Piper would be challenging but she hadn't been prepared for quite so much confrontation, or such an ostentatious last-minute demand. But, reading between the lines and putting her limited experience of bridezilla behaviour to the test (mercifully, her clients had mostly been positively angelic), there was a small chance that, if she could pull off this pathetic swing requirement, there would be some damage limitation. So she had to try. Her only other hope was to call Tim, which might have been an option had she not deleted his number after the paragliding trip.

"Hannah!" yelled a trembling Freya, before she changed her mind, did a runner, and never came back. "I need you here!"

Freya opened the door, only to discover Hannah was already standing right outside. So close that they almost bumped noses. She must have been passing. Great minds thinking alike and all that.

"Oh, there you are."

"Yes. Haha. Here I am… and here you are too! What can I do for you, Freya?"

Was it Freya's imagination or did Hannah look a little embarrassed?

"Can you go and get Ricky, and can the pair of you work me a miracle?"

ALICE

Alice couldn't believe it. The camper van rambled along the track to the finca after its epic journey through Spain… only to be greeted by a giant coach parked in front of the entrance to the rustic and beautiful wedding venue. Hayley's blimming coach!

"Great! So not only is that monstrosity of a vehicle obscuring the view and any hint of romance, but now most of the wedding party has arrived before us."

Alice was easy-going. Her reaction to the cake calamity was proof enough. Most brides would have completely lost it! But she drew the line at this. Especially when River had supposedly told Hayley not to leave the coach where it would be an eyesore.

"I did make it clear that if Hayley and co decided to arrive the same day as us, then it had to be early evening so we'd have a chance to settle in, I swear. I'm so sorry, Al. I'll get her to move it immediately."

"I'm guessing Mervyn let them all in, when Hayley called him with the contact details he said would be stuck to the front door." Alice tutted. "What's done is done. I refuse to let it ruin things. Let's get out and hug everyone before we check the place is still intact, the vintage wine corked, and that nobody's started skinny dipping in the pool."

She jumped out of the camper van, determined to snap out of her mood. If Hayley didn't reverse the vehicle, then Alice would do it herself. Hayley, clad in a vibrant swimsuit, sarong, sunhat and shades – a giant glass of wine in hand – must have heard Twinkle's wheels crunching on the gravel, and came running out to greet the bride and groom within seconds. She'd certainly made herself at home.

"That had better be the Spanish vineyard house red she's necking." River grimaced, striding over to greet their friend too.

"I'm on it, guys!" Hayley waved her arms, quite forgetting her drink, red liquid splashing all over the ground. "I've only had a couple of sips, don't fret. The thing is, I had to drop everyone and their luggage off and I couldn't expect them to haul it up the long driveway in this heat. Your mum made a beeline for the vino, Riv. I was powerless to stop her."

Alice supposed Hayley had a point. It might only have been midday but the sun was relentless already, and due to hit thirty-eight degrees later. Hardly the best idea to start partying already. They'd have to keep an eye on River's mum. She was such a twig that it wouldn't take much to get her trolleyed.

"Erm, Hayley?" River tapped at an imaginary watch on his wrist.

"Oh, right. That, yes." Hayley laughed nervously, which was quite unusual for their friend, who firmly believed she was in the right 99.99% of the time. "The last motel we were meant to be staying at was fully booked... so on the subject of lasts, that's the last time I trust a friend of a friend of my boyfriend's. We've had to drive ten hours straight... hence cramping your style and arriving a tad early, like." The

THE WEDDING CAKE

sunshine brought out Hayley's Somerset twang and her favourite filler word at the end of her sentences. "But three quarters of this lot," Hayley gestured at the finca and the guests who were no doubt already milling around inside it, "will be out of your hair in a jiffy and I'll arrange taxis to their accommodation in Mijas village as soon as they can check in, like."

And just *like* that, Alice's heart went out to everyone. It was impossible not to feel sorry for her friend and her passengers after such a long stretch of time on the road. It was no wonder Hayley had resorted to daytime drinking. Let them enjoy the finca's facilities for a few hours. If she and River had been let down by their hotels, at least they would have been able to kip in their mode of transport.

To give Hayley her due, she could have been a travel agent in a previous life. Despite the fact she was exhausted, she shepherded everybody together marvellously over the next couple of days, taking them out on all the excursions she'd promised them, and more. This made the atmosphere at the finca as chilled as could be during the days building up to the wedding. Alice and River were able to sunbathe, swim, and read their books, soaking up the paradise of the venue's surroundings.

Zara and Bruno arrived three days before the wedding to learn some basic mixology and help River set up his cocktail bar, so his beloved blueberry lavender sangria and rhubarb Bellinis could be served as planned. Alice's cousins descended with their offspring the same day – the village tailor running around the lawns after them, when she wasn't beckoning for them to get out of the finca's swimming pool for last minute flower girl and bridesmaid dress adjustments. Rio and Justin, the couple's newly acquired friends from their stint in Cornwall, showed up the following morning. They'd become so thoroughly enamoured with Glastonbury, after taking a sabbatical to hang on Twinkle's coattails when Alice and River had spent the festive season travelling in her, that they'd quit their scriptwriting jobs at the BBC and secured premises to set up a Keanu Reeves-themed 'Kindness Cafe' in the town (as one did). Alice and River were overjoyed to learn the news. It was better than any wedding present! Which was just as well because Rio and Justin forgot to bring one.

In a move that surprised everyone, Lee and Jonie had closed Glastonbury's cocktail bar on the high street for a few days, since most of their regulars were River's old customers and they would be travelling to Spain courtesy of Hayley's coach, so it wasn't worth staying open. River would have asked Lee and Jonie to run the wedding cocktail bar, but they deserved some time off – even if super-pale, easily burnt Lee would be spending most of it in the shade.

Heather and Terry, River's mum and stepdad, had decided to travel the long way down with Hayley and co. Alice held her breath as to whether Blake (River's school friend-turned nemesis-turned step-brother... who'd had a bit of a thing for Alice all through high school) had been able to make the trip with Ali, his girlfriend. But thankfully, the couple were now running a cat sanctuary on a Greek island, after their stint on the school reunion reality TV show, *Bubblegum and Blazers*. Which had worked out pretty well for them, all things considered.

"I'm so relieved Blake won't be here to see us get *meow-rried*," River had quipped, which was almost enough to give Alice second thoughts about getting hitched at all.

On the subject of felines, Alice couldn't deny she was having kittens about Georgina putting in an appearance. She had tried to create a rift between River and Alice, prior to moving to Spain. But she was supposedly on the way to being happily married herself, now. Alice was also fretting about her parents finding out she and River had 'eloped', via the extended family grapevine. But ultimately it was hard to get too stressed in such a relaxing place.

Although the guest list was small, owing to a distinct lack of family on either side, it was full of friends and love. Even Alice and River's former Avalonia bandmates, Alex and Bear, were putting in an appearance – although thankfully the band's former manager, Lennie (who had also, to cut a *very* long story short, turned out to be River's father), didn't dare show his face.

Now it was time to savour every moment with all these wonderful, quirky people who had flown for hours – or endured Hayley's cheesy CD collection and non-stop karaoke for several days on the motorways of Europe. Alice intended to give them a wedding to remember!

TIM

Tim waited until the next day, and then he woke like a man possessed (in a good way). First off, he sent an apologetic text message to Freya, instructing her to do what she thought was best with the cake. It was greeted with no reply, just as he expected. But hopefully it would take the pressure off. He was the groom, after all, and he should have a say in something regarding his own wedding.

And then he did something he hadn't done for a very long time: he took himself to Manchester Central Library. It wasn't the most obvious choice of venue for someone who was about to get married, but most men in Tim's position didn't have a Ferris wheel of questions rotating through their heads. The counselling hadn't worked, and after the get-together with his friends, the last thing Tim wanted or needed, in the days running up to his departure to Spain, was to be accosted with yet more do-gooder opinions. He needed to work things out for himself using his own guidance system... and the wisdom of a good old book – or a dozen.

He'd always taken his time to grasp new concepts and ideas when he was at uni, hence the Dim Tim moniker. The library had been his refuge then, away from the chatter of the smart arses who could magic up their essays two hours before deadline on their bed, coffee on tap, music blasting, and still end up with a 2:1 or higher. Once Tim had discovered the haven of the library, he could see clearly and make headway with his own assignments. It had been a game-changer. Now he took a seat at the large table nearest the psychology section, drew a timeline of his life on a piece of paper, and headed off to the rows of books, letting his inner compass do the navigation. Today he would work the answers out for himself, learn who he was, and how he had become that person.

The more Tim read – well, to be precise, the more he dipped in and out of books, letting his intuition open a hardback at a random page, flicking through a paperback and innately sensing when to stop and soak up the ink on its paper – the more a solid and cyclical pattern began to emerge.

Conflict (and compromise). The turning of his mind mirrored the many diagrams in the books he pored over, which brought him back to the seesaw analogy again. Wasn't this the constant illustration to Tim's life? The image in his head since forever. He could have worked this out for himself a long time ago, if he'd only listened to his inner monologue! Which wasn't to discount or discredit the brilliant work of counsellors (other than Jacqui) and the words of good friends. Both had their place. But everyone's style of learning is different. The student was ready now and the teacher (or tomes) had appeared. In the end, a few days of reading was all it took, as Tim reflected on his timeline. At long last he could see everything plainly for himself:

- **The nursery incident.** This had long been Tim's first vivid memory. Now he started to sense its relevance, and the message it had probably always been trying to impart. Three boys at his nursery had simultaneously scrabbled to get onto the bright orange rocking horse. The one with the swishy woollen tail. Tim had panicked when little hands had started to push and shove so much that one of the kids toppled off, snotty tears falling down his little face. Tim had pulled him into a hug to help calm him down, scouring the room for a nursery assistant to sort the other boys out. But nobody was available, so Tim had returned to the rocking horse with the traumatised kid, gently taken hold of each of the four-year-old lads and lined them up, explaining that they could *all* have rides on the horse, one after the other. He decided it was best to forgo his own fun since that would only make the queue longer for all concerned and possibly reignite the friction.

- **The school incident.** No, not the one his friends had mentioned in the pub. This memory came to him in flashes. Jigsaw puzzle pieces which he could now put into a whole. Winter in the school playground. A snowball fight. Bullies pushing a girl into the muddy slush and soaking her coat. Tim, unable to ignore her plight and, yet again, unable to find a teacher, whose job it surely was to mediate and discipline. Tim helping the girl out of her coat and giving her his own to wear. Tim walking home after school as fast as he could in his thin grey Asda school jumper and cardboard-collar shirt. His teeth still chattering after his mam had fixed him a hot chocolate – and given him a clip around the ear for being so careless and 'losing' his

black Adidas puffer jacket that had cost a small fortune.
- **The blackmail incident.** "If you don't take the blame for the Easter eggs going missing, we're going to tell Mam it was you who stole them". Andy had discovered the Easter eggs hidden under their parents' double bed, so naturally, he and Brittany had worked their way through them until they were sick. They blamed him anyway, the rotters. Before Tim could even pluck up the courage to lie to cover their fat arses.
- **The spying incident.** Brian needed to know that Cathy wasn't having crafty cigarettes on the back porch while he was grafting at the factory. They couldn't afford the dirty habit now her assistant role in the shoe shop had been reduced to part-time hours, and her blood pressure had been through the roof at her last GP check up. Tim had felt uneasy about this request, especially as he knew the answer already. Yes, Cathy was puffing away several times a day out back, in between washing and cooking and cleaning (pre-accident days). She always scrubbed her hands with soap and scoffed mint humbugs to ward off the eau de nicotine. Tim had felt like such a snitch, but he couldn't let his dad down since he'd been entrusted with this mission. It felt like he'd let his mam down, though. She was an adult and deserved to be treated as such. Smoking was bad, but she needed a release and that choice was hers to make. Tim wasn't her parent.
- **The favouritism incidents.** Tim's grandparents never had much money and on the rare occasions the siblings went to them for tea, Brittany and

Andy would get all the best biscuits in the Family Circle tin (when Grandad wasn't looking); Brittany because she was a girl and deserved the 'pretty red Jammy Dodgers', Andy because he was the youngest and 'hadn't had as many chocolate digestives as Tim over the years'. Tim was left to hoover up the perennially unpopular shortcakes – and usually declined.

And these examples were just the tip of the iceberg. Once Tim got thinking, he couldn't stop listing similar scenarios. He'd never been a martyr, though, huffing and puffing over his saintliness. It was just easier to let everyone else have their way and stop the drama in its tracks. Still, all these key interactions with family, friends, and peers screamed two words: *overly* and *compromising*. Tim constantly gave in. Big time and without a fight. He'd lost not only his sense of self but his sense of justice.

Maybe Jacqui had been right about the middle child syndrome theory? Maybe that had reinforced Tim's need to keep the peace. But his younger brother hadn't come along until Tim was eight years old. Maybe Tim had always known Andy would arrive on the scene, then? Maybe he'd resigned himself to diplomatic duties early. Whatever. The fact was, now Tim had made the links for himself and studied his own concrete examples, the penny had finally dropped and there was no going back. This was no way to live. All he'd done was to create himself a shitshow of inauthenticity.

On the other hand, Tim learned there were merits to being the middle child: savviness, empathy and openness. He needed to start channelling these qualities like his life depended on it. Because it did.

Tim had no choice but to face his fears, dig deep and do what needed to be done. So the moment he and Piper reached the villa in Marbella (and he'd managed to spend most of the flight ignoring Nath's pained expressions across the aisle), Tim cancelled out on his friends and the stag do the next day. He sent them a text to say he'd eaten something dodgy and needed to ensure he was in fine fettle for the sixth of August. He couldn't risk them swaying his decision at this critical point in time.

"If I could afford two return taxi journeys from Torre to Marbs in a matter of days, I'd be round at that swanky villa of yours now, Squirrel, knocking at the door like Fred fucking Flintstone to drag you out!!! But fine, have it your way. We'll see you Saturday. And don't worry: we won't do anything daft and interrupt when the registrar asks if anyone knows of any lawful impediment as to why you shouldn't be wed. Final reminder: there is still time to change your mind..."

Shit. Tim hadn't been worried about interruptions at all… until Nath had mentioned this. Surely his friends wouldn't dare pull such a stunt?

He chose to spend the night before the wedding alone in the sprawling villa. Piper's newest VIP influencer friends, who had taken priority as far as the spare bedrooms were concerned, had headed into Marbella for dinner. Meanwhile, Piper had gone to Puerto Banus to meet up with the legendary Sophia and Talia. In other words, she was squeezing in 'one last night' with Noah. The villa's chef didn't know what to make of Tim, having clearly waited on grooms who tended to be surrounded by family and friends in the run up to their wedding day. Especially when he asked if they could knock him up a plate of egg and chips. Tim had long ago decided it would be his last meal if the BBC announced the world was ending tomorrow. Which was somewhat symbolic. The chef rose to the occasion, and Tim let the no-fuss nourishment fortify his soul.

He could have invited his parents to a slap-up meal tonight, but they'd know something was up. In any case, the all-inclusive accommodation they were currently enjoying further along the coast looked amazing, and they deserved an evening of pure pampering and zero worries the night before their middle child tied the knot.

Tim slept surprisingly well until four am, when he was woken by the flurry of partygoers heading back to their various rooms; more than a couple of male voices now thrown in the mix. He hoped he'd be spared any orchestral manoeuvres in the dark. Piper's room was next to his. She was determined to play things traditionally, and Tim was under strict instruction not to go in her room before the ceremony, lest he catch a glimpse of her dress.

But rules were there to be broken. Especially when you strongly suspected your betrothed had brought the guy she was sleeping with back to your wedding villa, on the very eve of your special day, intending to let him conveniently merge into the crowd the next morning, along with the rest of the star guests who Tim mainly didn't know. But Tim hadn't needed to break and enter Piper's room for a look. That old chestnut, the glass pressed against the wall, had done the trick, and the guttural noises would haunt him forever. Besides which, Tim had indulged in a little detective work after taking receipt of those dodgy photos. Every 'influencer trip' Piper had made since they'd gotten back from the wedding supplier's visit had coincided with Noah Barrington's movements – from London nightclub foam parties to a networking event in Reykjavik, and a digital marketing conference in Amsterdam. These little excursions always seemed to tally with a grand new hotel opening in the same city. Influencer hotels in the ever-expanding Barrington portfolio. Whatever the deal was with Piper and Noah, Tim wasn't as dim as his contemporaries from the past had dubbed him. Noah, on the other hand, was a braggart and a fool. He couldn't resist any opportunity to grace the pages of local and regional newspapers, society chat magazines, and the end of a Getty photographer's lens. Piper trailed along behind him like a lovesick puppy. It was insane, the way that Tim and Piper had traded places. He shuddered in the realisation that this was exactly how he used to be with his girlfriend in the early days. Up until the two Fs: February and Freya.

Tim knew Freya would stay true to her word, organising for another member of her team to drop the cake off tomorrow so they could avoid one another. He wanted Freya to stick to her promise – and he also didn't want her to. The need to see her again was indescribable.

Before common sense could get a look in, Tim found himself in Piper's unlocked quarters next door. Nobody was in the main room or on the lavish balcony, but he could hear the shower running in the bathroom. Now Tim could take in every scrap of evidence of Piper's blatant betrayal with his own two eyes: there was stooping low and there was scraping the bottom of the barrel. Sex toys and flimsy feather, silk, and lace costumes lay strewn across the massive bed; the reek of aftershave was intoxicating. How could she do this to him so openly? Had she no shame? He was a laughing stock to everybody in this villa!

All right, it was bad luck for the bride to see the groom on the morning of their wedding day – but now Tim knew this was just a convenient excuse for Piper to hide behind and take diabolical liberties.

Tim pulled his mobile phone from his pocket. After his message to his friend, pleading with him not to cock up the ceremony, Tim needed to be certain that Nath, Josh and Kyle knew the drill. The last thing he wanted was any unexpected surprises. So he banged out a quick text reminding the boys to respect his wishes.

The door swung open then, snapping Tim from his worries. A naked Piper paraded into the room, steam trailing behind her like a ghostly wedding veil. Tim wondered if Noah would appear as well, a bit like those cabaret stage acts from the eighties that were all smoke and drama as you waited for the artist to reveal themselves. Mercifully, she was alone. She gasped when she saw her groom, and grabbed the nearest towel on the bed to preserve her modesty. Tim had never felt more like howling with laughter at the ironic ways of his exhibitionist bride, but he needed to keep it together. This wedding simply had to go ahead. There were far too many people depending on it, depending on Tim. And Piper herself was top of that list.

"I..." she began.

"Don't even think about saying it's not what it looks like." Tim filled in the gaps for her, eyes scanning the disgraceful scene laid out between them.

"You really wouldn't buy it if I explained that I just wanted to imagine how great *sex* would be on our wedding night?" She whispered the S-word as if she'd morphed into a nun. "Hence all the accessories and um, well, roleplay... with... um... myself?"

"Give me some credit. Since when did roleplay extend to using Chanel Allure Homme?" Tim sniffed at the air, recognising the fragrance he'd been lambasted with at the airport perfume concession. It was so pungent he almost choked.

"Imagining how great your husband is going to smell, when you finally get down and dirty after a day mollycoddling the wedding guests, is always going to help turn you on." Piper crooned after several beats.

Mollycoddling *others*? Tim wasn't sure the concept existed in Piper's world.

"Oh, all right," she snapped. "It's no use trying to pretend this is anything other than it is." Piper held her hands up in surrender and the towel she'd draped around herself dropped to the floor. She stooped to mummify herself in it again. "You were my project, Tim. That's how it started. That's how I intended for it to stay. Don't get me wrong, I'm as physically attracted to you now as I was back then, I just wish you had a wind-up key in your back so I could make you more dynamic. I out-pace you at everything. I'm so weary of it!"

Piper made it sound like she'd put in an overtime shift at his dad's factory. Tim couldn't speak. Evidently his thoroughly active life as a spring-jumping fitness instructor – and part-time hospital porter – rendered him a couch potato.

"I-I didn't mean to take things so far, and I should never have let you move in with me, or accepted your proposal, but you were good for me." Piper pursed her lips and fluttered her eyelashes. "You tamed my wild ways... *for a bit*. But then the ambition thing took over. You looked great on my arm. The Influencer and the Fitness Instructor." She gazed out at the horizon through the balcony's floor-to-ceiling glass doors. Christ. The way the woman said it made their union sound like the title of one of those Ladybird pocket books that had been handed to Tim as a child. "There's something so Hollywood about us. That's why it doesn't really matter what goes on behind closed doors. As long as we give everyone that *illusion* of togetherness. We could both live separate lives in separate houses if we wanted to. You could only ever get me so far in the career stakes, you see. Noah's super-connected. Not just here but all over the world. Plus I've developed feelings for him. But there's no chance of him marrying me. I don't have the elite family connections. So I'll give him up if you want me to. You only have to say the word." Piper went quiet. Tim felt like a fly trapped in a sticky spider's web. "But then we could also be smart about this, babe, couldn't we?" she finally added, twisting her long rope of dark hair. "You must have watched the film *Indecent Proposal*?"

"You what?" Did she honestly just spout that uncoordinated lot out? Tim felt like he was in a seriously warped nightmare. Any minute now his alarm would wake him up. He'd jump out of bed (and back in time) to eighteen months ago, and the day he should have been on a boys' holiday to Mallorca with his friends (when he would kindly ask the cabin crew to ask the pilot to divert to Malaga so he could walk into Freya's cakery) instead of meeting Piper at his gym class.

"I have indeed seen the movie," he answered, with a heavy bump back down to earth and his actual life circumstances. "But clearly I'm the only one who's watched it to the end." Tim furrowed his brow. "Spoiler alert: Demi goes back to Woody and decides the money wasn't worth it!"

"But we can make our own choices, can't we?" Piper put a manicured finger in the air as if she'd had a Eureka moment. "Do it a little differently. At least for a while, until there's more money in the bank. I could keep seeing Noah. Milk the opportunity for all its worth."

"Please!" Tim covered his ears at Piper's turn of phrase.

"And we could still go through with the wedding," she continued, still in her clouds of deception. "You could forgive me. Have a little fling of your own if it makes you feel better. Settle the score. Or not. All of this has happened before we've said our vows, after all. I mean, who doesn't have one last little night of freedom before they settle down?"

Tim brought his fist to his chin and posed in contemplation. She couldn't even offer him half a commitment. One minute all was apparently over with Noah. The next she was trying to prolong her affair. He eyed her through his side curtain of hair. It came in handy at times like this. A shield from life's curveballs. But then he remembered he was a brand-new Tim. Physically and mentally, he knew what to do to bat those pesky curveballs away now.

"That would be most people, Piper. Yeah, funnily enough, most people who are about to get married, they generally love one another and are committed from the get-go," he finally replied. "But this situation," Tim pointed at the exhibits scattered across the bed and floor, "is something else! How did we even get here?"

"Oh, Tim. You are too trusting. That's what I love about you."

Tim said nothing. Let Piper think what she wanted.

"Okay, then," she relented, as if she'd been silently turning everything over in her head, working out the pros versus the cons of all her future potential love stories. "Let's start over. No more naughtiness." *Oh, was that all it was?* "Just you and me. Forever. In harmony."

Tentatively, Tim reached out his hand to shake Piper's. He felt like the world's weakest man. But what choice did he have? He might not buy a word of this laughable turning over a new leaf claim, but how could he let his family down? Especially when Brittany had flown in from the States that morning. The answer was, he couldn't disappoint them.

But he could do something else.

FREYA

It took Freya a while to fathom who the text message was from, but then her heart skipped several beats. It was Tim. He must have changed phones since that day when she'd blocked him. She held her breath as she read his words.

Mortified by Piper's behaviour on the phone with you y'day! I can only apologise. Sooooo embarrassed :-(Feel free to carry on with your suggestion for the cake. It's no big deal XX

He had left her not one kiss, but two…

Why would he do that when they had agreed to forget everything? Was this a suggestion? An ember of hope that a miracle might change their tragic circumstances? It was pathetic and morally wrong to go back there. But Freya wasn't Buddha. She was a human being full of flaws, faults, and fancy.

Before her head hit the pillow after yet another hectic day at the cakery, Freya deleted the text. She would – as Tim had instructed, and as she'd already decided – go ahead with

THE WEDDING CAKE

cutting the cake straight down the middle. Fortunately, Ricky and Hannah were pulling out all the stops with the ludicrous swing. FOM was meeting the bitter bride halfway and that would have to do. Maybe this didn't sound like the right attitude, coming from a high-end wedding cake baker, but it was all Freya had left to give. The season had wiped her out before it had got started, and by June she'd found herself turning her back on those precious self-care Mondays, coming to work instead, forgoing her salary so that Ricky still got his for the extra hours and responsibility. Between him and Hannah (and Nicola, Jimena, Alejandro and the part-time staff, of course) every other wedding had run like clockwork. If they'd just scaled down the bookings by twenty percent, and gotten more selective with their clientele, Freya estimated that they wouldn't even have needed her there to oversee things. Between them, her team knew the business inside out. And that got her thinking.

But for now she had bigger fish (cakes) to fry (or bake). The first days of August were sweltering. A high of forty-five point six degrees centigrade saw the month in, and even with the luxury of aircon, everyone was struggling to keep their shit together. Merv was no exception. His visit shortly after the discovery of the double-booking had been what could only be described as *volcanic*.

"Freya, darling," he'd wafted through the downstairs shop door to the cakery like a bad smell on the humid breeze. "What's all this nonsense about abandoning our precious green order book? I never thought you had this kind of rebellion in you." Merv had stood there in the middle of the room, hand on the top of his cane, moving it this way and that as if it were a gear stick in a racing car and he was about to press his foot to the accelerator to mow her down. He pinned Freya with angry blue eyes.

Freya, caught off-guard, was too weary to reply. She'd

been making last-minute adjustments to the basic product range on the ground floor. In all the years she'd been working in the wedding cake business, it never ceased to amaze her how much trade Marbella wedding parties and hen and stag celebrations would bring FOM's way. They always needed to be stocked up with meringues, cupcakes, macarons and small layer cakes. Basically everything except cake pops. Oh, and cakes on swings. Whether that became a fad or not, as long as Freya was running FOM, she would never agree to her team making and installing another one of those. The business was a cakery, not a playground.

"I put it down to that assistant of yours," Merv snarled, thoroughly disgruntled at Freya for continuing to straighten out her wares when she evidently should have been jumping through hoops to apologise. "Such a strange woman, such a bad influence. Why on earth did you hire her? You'd never have entertained the notion of using a computer for the bookings before Hannah came on the scene!"

"What a nerve, Merv… *yn*," Freya finally straightened herself up to look the doddery old fool in the eye, adding the last bit once she realised her statement sounded like the title for a children's book. Plus he had riled her so this was no time for terms of endearment. She'd pick the audacious specimen up and put him on the adult equivalent of the naughty step if she could. "You're nowhere near as long in the tooth with technology as you make out." She let out a sarcastic laugh. "What about all the garbled WhatsApp messages you leave me in the run up to our clients' weddings? Utterly unprofessional and confusing. Every last one of them. But that's by the by. My point is this. You seem to think you can pick and choose which bits of tech you want to engage with, forgetting we work *with* you, not *for* you… It has left us with a wedding disaster big enough to sink both of our companies, and," Freya stuck her finger in the air, halting Merv's comeback. "You also seem to think you have the authority to bad-mouth my staff as you see fit. Well, not for a second longer." Freya put both hands in the air now, blocking Merv's face. "If you want to continue to work with FOM then it's my way or the highway. There are plenty of other wedding planners on the Costa del Sol and I am more than happy to work with them."

Freya then glared at Merv. She should have done this years ago. Any notion of friendship between them was pure fakery. All the man cared about was himself. Merv was just an older version of Sid. But he hid it better by working in the bridal industry.

"Well, well, well," he chuckled irritatingly. "Your true colours have come out at last, my dear. How ungrateful. I invested time and patience in you when you were nothing. A minnow in a sea full of competition. Now you've apparently got so big for your boots you can talk to me as if I'm a turd stuck to the bottom of them. Do you realise there are umpteen wedding cake makers that I could also take my business to? I shall go away and have a jolly good think about doing so." He tapped his cane on the floor tiles.

"Fine by me. And good luck with that... I'm not sure that anybody else would put up with you falling asleep at the table after pigging your way through the clients' wedding cake samples."

"How very dare you. I've never been so insulted in my life!"

Oh, Freya! She cursed herself inwardly. *He'll never leave the bloody shop now. Some things are better left unsaid, even if they are true.*

Merv seemed to read her mind. He brandished his cane in the air, then hooked it onto the glass cabinet's handle to their right. It was a move that looked worryingly rehearsed and made Freya question her past stock-taking ability and the sweet treats he'd evidently snuck out of her business before. Next he opened up the case and seized a large triple chocolate tiered 'off-the-shelf' wedding cake, hugging it to himself and making for the shop door. Freya could only blink repeatedly, until a fuming Ricky appeared from nowhere, blocking the impertinent wedding planner's exit. Freya had to do several double takes. What the eff?

"Going somewhere without paying, were we?" Ricky looked Merv up and down, utter disdain etched across his face. Merv morphed from monster to mouse.

"Just let him have it, Ricky. It can be his leaving present."

"I will not!" Ricky's tone was insistent. "I've never liked the whalloper as much as a cake crumb and he must be oot his nut if he thinks he's walking out of these premises with that beauty."

Merv, perplexed at Ricky's Glaswegian patter, lost his grip on the cake so Ricky took advantage, pulling it firmly into his orbit.

"Merv won't be taking a euro cent more from this business." Ricky headed for the counter without seeing Merv toss his cane to the side, rub his hands together and propel himself forward. "Not now that I've discovered who his stepson is."

That stopped Merv in his tracks and tipped him off balance. He flew headlong at Ricky, face-planting himself with a mammoth splat into the cake.

"Don't you dare tell Freya!" Merv muttered into his just desserts.

ALICE

*A*lice walked down the aisle, hardly able to believe that her twisty will-they-won't-they relationship with River had brought her to this precious moment. The many hints she had dropped, the years she had secretly pined for him when they'd both been in separate relationships in the band, all seemed like tiny stitches in the rich tapestry of life now.

Her groom looked dapper in his suit, standing just in front of the eucalyptus and olive leaf archway where their civil ceremony would be conducted. Judging by the twinkle in his eye as he awaited Alice, and the grin plastered across his face, she hadn't scrubbed up too badly either. Tears pricked at her lids and she silently berated herself, determined not to look at their guests on either side of the aisle as she walked down it. The absence of her parents and her failed attempts to mend that broken relationship meant there was nobody to give her away, but she vowed she wouldn't get all emosh. The last thing she wanted was anybody's pity. She was her own person and she was the one granting River permission to marry her. Sod tradition! So Alice thought about her dress, hair and make-up instead. And okay, yes, she did look gorgeous. Zara's hairstyling skills had created the most breathtaking French plaits, intertwined with orchid blooms that made for a stunning contrast with the gypsophila in her bouquet. It was a bit of an extravagance, and a bit of a hotchpotch of flora and foliage – then again she was wearing that plain Etsy wedding gown she'd snapped up, plus her baseball boots. And then again, you hopefully only walked down the aisle once, so why not do it differently? Besides, River had bucked convention himself by opting not to have a best man.

The ceremony was as moving as Alice knew it would be, and thankfully free of any unwanted interruptions. Well, aside from Hayley whooping when she and River shared their first kiss. Which started everyone off, the laidback officiator included. Plus there were a couple of little hitches when some of the guests had to be asked to remove their giant Mickey Mouse ear headbands, bought fresh from Disneyland Paris, for the ceremony photos.

Once they'd exchanged their vows and pledged to love one another eternally in this lifetime – River whispering in Alice's ear, "you're stuck with me eternally in every lifetime," making goosebumps ricochet all over her body – they turned to face their guests and walk back down the aisle as newlyweds. The sea of happy faces was a moment Alice would cherish forever. It had been her focus in bringing this day to life, and here it was, manifesting perfectly before her.

"We didn't expect to see you in person, Freya!" Alice made a beeline for their cake maker as soon as etiquette permitted her to tear herself away from the friends and family who were vying to catch her attention and congratulate her in person; making the photographer wait before he whisked her and River to the little tower at the top of the finca for their drone shots. "How did the other couple take the ahem… cake situ?"

Alice couldn't help but notice that Freya had tears in her eyes, which were already puffy and bloodshot. Enough said.

"Oh, you know… we made it work… just about."

"In other words you had a complete diva on your hands," River hazarded a guess as he freed himself from his mother's hugs and joined in their conversation.

"I couldn't possibly say." Freya winked, adding, "anyway, I must be off. I'm heading to the mountains later this afternoon for a hiking retreat, but I'll be back in four days' time with the you-know-whats." No sooner had she said those last three words, than Freya's face fell. She'd evidently remembered that River hadn't a clue as to the cake distribution side of the honeymoon, and she made a grab for Alejandro, the cake maker who had helped her with the delivery, scuttling away to her car before Alice could run after her. Alice thought something seemed very off. She didn't know Freya well enough to call her a friend but she sensed she needed a shoulder to cry on. She'd check in with her tomorrow. But she owed it to herself, River and their guests to fully focus on their special day.

"What's a *you-know-what*, when it's at home… or in a Spanish finca?" River whispered.

"Oh… well, that would be telling." Alice thought on her feet… or, in this case, her thigh. "Something borrowed, something blue, you know the old saying? Freya meant she'd be back in four days' time to pick up the you-know-what she lent me… don't make me spell it out and ruin tonight's surprise." Alice ran her hand down her upper leg and alluded to the garter she was currently wearing, although it had been borrowed from another friend, not Freya. River just looked at her blankly. Evidently his unconventional upbringing with

Heather meant he'd never even heard of the tradition of wedding good luck charms.

Just as they were about to trail off with their patient photographer, a medley of guest screams rang out across the lawn, making everyone jump out of their skin. Alice turned to take in the sight of a cocksure male stranger stalking across the lush velvet grass. Even the Spanish guitarist stopped playing his rendition of the Bruno Mars hit '*Marry You*'.

"Where's the cake?" the man shouted, arms open wide, as if insinuating that one of the guests was hiding it. "I am here on behalf of Miss Piper Moss, soon to be Nutkins, to return it to its rightful owner... and I'm not leaving without it. Every last crumb *and* fondant rose! We can do this the easy way – which would be advisable – or we can do it the hard way. The choice is yours but I will be taking the other half of the eight-tier showstopper my lady paid for and that is that."

What the hell?

Some of the guests were off their heads already on River's free cocktail bar – like the couple's annoying former band members, Alex and Bear. No doubt their pockets were also full of grass. And not the stuff on the lawn. Alice had known they'd be trouble. They hadn't changed their wild ways enough to be included in the celebrations. River was too flipping soft, inviting them at all. They proved her fears right within moments, pointing the man in the cake's direction, as if he was doing nothing more sinister than asking for a slice.

Alice and River stood stock-still and watched on in horror as the Harvey Keitel look alike (think Reservoir Dogs era, complete with the jet black suit that meant business) bulldozed through their paradise to the precious dessert table.

"Shit! Do you think he's the groom from the other wedding?" River finally yelled, dashing past the revellers now he'd processed the situation and realised somebody needed to act. "Come on guys," he said to no one and everyone, "let's pin him down!"

"I don't know who he thinks he is," Alice shouted as she began to sprint across the lawn after her husband, glad she'd had the sense to wear such suitable footwear. "But there's no way he's taking our beloved cake!" Alice tried to ignore the highly worrying sight of Hayley in her periphery, chest puffed out, as if she'd always known her muscle power would be required at some point during the wedding. Meanwhile a pack of males including Lee, Bruno and Terry charged after the intruder ahead of River, intent on reliving the glorious summer field fights of their school days. Even the waiting staff abandoned their cocktail trays by the side of the pool, crisp white shirt sleeves rolled up and ready for action.

"*¡Vamos, qué tontería!*" the booming Somerset-infused Spanish words assaulted everyone's eardrums through a loudspeaker. Hayley must have been playing her language-learning App during that mammoth coach journey. "Lay a finger on that work of art and you'll live to regret it." Hayley's warning stopped everyone, Alice included. She pivoted gingerly to take in the full and rather sparkling vision of her friend in her bridesmaid dress. Hayley clutched the loudspeaker that Bruno, their unofficial toastmaster, had brought with him to help gather everyone up throughout the day. The finca wasn't vast, but it wasn't tiny either, and there were so many nooks and crannies –particularly where children or those seeking an undercover wedding party kiss might chance to hide. It had been a necessary but intrusive prop.

The Harvey lookalike turned to take in the vision of Hayley, too, and merely hooted with laughter, attention back on his destination within moments, upping his pace as he headed directly for the towering half-cake and its delicate waterfall of iced flowers. How he thought he would succeed in transporting the masterpiece without a truck to do the heavy lifting, Alice had no idea. It might only be half its intended size but it had taken both Freya and Alejandro, and bags of energy, to deliver and assemble it. He'd have a fair few people to get past first. Now Alice had visions of her gorgeous cake in smithereens all over the garden.

"I'll say it one last time since you don't seem to be getting the message, *hombre*: are you seriously stupid enough to think you can get away with this?" Hayley bellowed through the loudspeaker once more and turned to the Spanish guitarist. "Oh, and strike up the band again. Black Eyed Peas *'I've Got a Feeling'* would go well with what's about to come."

Alice, still rooted to the spot, pinched herself hard on the arm and noticed River doing the same. Even in the craziest of situations they were soul mates, and this one was up there with some of the strangest things they'd encountered together. Unfortunately she wasn't in a bad dream, but witnessing her previously textbook wedding going more pear-shaped by the second.

River began a slow jog over to the others who had circled Harvey, but it soon turned out to be in vain. Harvey sniggered and pulled a pistol from his pocket, a move which elicited a new succession of screams from the guests, most of them cowering to take cover, children shielded by grown-ups and taken to the relative safety of the teepees in the courtyard's chill-out area. How on earth had their wedding day turned into this? It was, indeed, like something out of a Quentin Tarantino movie, and categorically not what Alice had signed up for when she'd paid good money to have a wedding at this finca. Mervyn hadn't said anything about needing security staff on the doors. How had this idiot got in? And as for the so-called *wedding planner*, where was he? She didn't care how many ceremonies the guy had

THE WEDDING CAKE

crammed into his prime Saturday in August so he could line his pockets, he should have put in an appearance at their special day by now to check everything was running smoothly.

The guitarist's music really didn't suit the tableau unfolding before their eyes, but Alice supposed it was a positive number. He carried on anyway, Hayley's glare telling him this was non-negotiable.

"Hayley," River chanced, shouting across the lawn at their friend. The guitarist played a little quieter and Alice willed her husband to follow suit with his voice in case the maniac fired. "Put that loudspeaker down. Our guest can have his cake and eat it. It's not worth the risk to any of us," his voice began to quiver. "Put that contraption on the ground and we'll co-operate our way out of this."

Alice could tell Hayley was baring her teeth even from afar. Reluctantly, she did as River asked and Alice let out a tiny sigh of relief. It was rare for Hayley to give in. Thankfully, today was just such a moment. "I know you love to jump to the defence of others," River continued, feeling that he needed to keep pacifying her in case she got a second wind. "And Lord knows we have wound up in some weird situations with you doing that over the years. There's no doubt that you possess the stealth of a f-fox." He began to stutter now, sensing Harvey's impatience. "But in this extremely delicate scenario, I think it's best for all concerned if we ease our way out of this quickly so we can continue with the celebrations. Let the other couple have what they want. We don't need the cake. Nobody's future happiness depends on it."

Now Alice was asking herself why she'd had to be so extravagant in the first place. This was all her fault. She should have gone for a cupcake wedding cake stand and then none of this would have happened.

Hayley squinted into the distance. Alice tentatively followed her line of vision. She was staring at Harvey.

"Ha. It's a toy!" Hayley cried.

Before anybody could try to stop her, she hurtled towards him, parting the circle of men surrounding him by the force of her shoulders alone. Onlookers held their collective breath as the pair of them danced around each other, Hayley unable to ruffle Harvey with whatever move she'd envisioned. This was not good. And it had always been sure to happen one day by virtue of the law of averages. Hayley couldn't win every battle in the pursuit of justice. The next thing everyone knew, Harvey had managed to dart behind her, jabbing the pistol into Hayley's back in a swift ninja-like move. Alice's pulse rocketed. *All this over flour, eggs, butter, and sugar?* She couldn't begin to imagine how Hayley felt, but while Alice should have gone for a simpler wedding cake, Hayley should never have put everyone in danger like this. Several of the men who had previously encircled Harvey began to walk cautiously towards him. And now the madness stepped up a gear. Surely the guy would shoot in a minute? Everything was happening in slow motion now. Alice didn't want to look, and yet she couldn't tear her eyes away from the terrifying scene.

"All right. Now I've taken care of the woman who got above her station, everybody else needs to stay still so that nobody, and no cake, will get hurt," yelled Harvey, pressing the weapon firmly into Hayley's back. "Then very slowly, I'm going to ask two of you men to carry the cake with me to my van at the farm down the road – I've changed the number plates, by the way, so no funny business thinking you can take pictures," he tilted his head at the photographer. "Or call the cops—"

Even as Harvey focused on sweet victory, Hayley dodged to the side, taking him by surprise. She twisted her torso, swung her right arm and dug it sharply into Harvey's face, stunning him and buying herself microseconds with which to slide her hand down to the gun, directing its barrel at the ground and away from the guests and the finca. She finished him off with a powerful knee to the groin, at which point she was able to snatch and secure the weapon, pointing it at the wedding crasher himself instead. Then Hayley opened the gun, to reveal it was empty of cartridges.

"I stand corrected. It was real, but he was still having us on. Weren't you, *Rob?*" she cried at the man face down on the lawn. "Got above my station, did I? The mere female taxi driver. Ha. I'm smarter than you realise, mate. Not only have I got a bit of an obsession with the minor celebs who sit in the back of my cab, but I know who *you* are, too... and I know exactly what you did last summer, Mr Senior Influencer." Hayley made a sneery face. "Glastonbury festival. 30th June. I never forget a face, date, or a conversation. Even if you are out of your wellies and beanie hat and in your tux today."

Hayley shook her head at the recollection and Alice couldn't believe the serendipitous turn of events. "You and your braggy mates gave me a right migraine that evening, wittering on about your viral TikTok videos and Instagram posts backstage when you watched Kylie Minogue, thinking that each of you stood a chance with her. You should be so fricking lucky." Hayley guffawed. "And now let me guess what's going down *here.*" Hayley gestured at the finca. "The bride at that upmarket Marbs wedding is an influencer pal, she's well miffed that the cake got double-booked and cut in half, and she thinks it's her prerogative to send you down here to nick it. Do you not realise whose wedding you've invaded? Do I really need to spell it out that the bride and groom at this far more tasteful establishment are one Alice Goldsmith and River Jackson from the band Avalonia!"

"Erm, that would be Alice Jackson, now," said Alice with a giant beam.

"Anyway, enough of the backstory as to how this idiot and my good self are already acquainted. I could use some help over here, guys. What are you waiting for?" Hayley shouted to everyone within arm's length.

Now the guests were giddy with emotion. Oohs, ahhs, thank yous, and several stronger words flew around the finca's parameters as a pile of men fell on Rob from all angles, ensuring he stayed pinned to the ground.

River and Alice quickly directed everyone to the chill-out area with its beanbags and teepees. The Spanish guitarist followed them, switching songs to D:Ream's *Things Can Only Get Better*, as he led a procession of gobsmacked and shaking guests away from the main lawn and over to the courtyard so that Hayley and co could sort out the mess. Meanwhile, Zara and the waiters fixed everyone up with much-needed cocktails, and the photographer trailed behind them all, tearing his hair out, although thankfully he had managed to hide behind a bush and snap some essential footage of the afternoon's proceedings, which Alice would be sending to the police and Mervyn.

"Al, I think we should cut the cake and hand it out before anybody else is tempted to pull a similar stunt. I know it's doing everything backwards and we should all be sitting down to the wedding breakfast first, but now we've ascertained that the jumped-up shit over there isn't the other groom, the last thing we want is anyone else turning up laying claim to our wedding cake," said River.

"And then it might be an idea to get your official couple photos done!" The photographer nudged his way between them. "We are way off schedule after all of that."

Once Alice had seen that everyone was settled, relaxed and sipping at something suitably fizzy, she followed River to the cake table, gesturing at Hayley, Lee and Terry to ensure Rob wasn't in their eyeline. Their friends were only too happy to oblige. Lee had found some strong twine in one of the kitchen cupboards, and he deftly bound Rob's wrists together. Hayley nudged Rob to get up, and the man, knowing he'd been defeated, followed them all to the side of the finca with his head down.

In a funny kind of way, the half cake looked even more stunning than its fully-fledged original. Taking pride of place on a plank of wood resting on top of two giant sherry barrels, its pastel pink and white waterfall of sugar roses seemed more dramatic like this, and the one-off (though duplicate) work of art suited the rustic setting of the wedding perfectly. As for the taste – although Alice had only sampled the bottom salted caramel layer – it was even more out of this world than she recalled from their afternoon with Freya back in February. As the waiting staff handed out plates to the revellers, Alice panned the clusters of guests to give Freya her verdict. But then she remembered all over again that the cake maker had disappointingly vanished.

"Yeah, it's nice," said Hayley interrupting her thoughts and appearing from nowhere, quite as if nothing had happened. She crammed a chunk of salted caramel sponge in her mouth, eyes glazing over, and Alice guessed she deserved this treat after playing heroine yet again. "But I can't believe you haven't put chocolate in any of the layers. That's just a travesty."

"There's always one." River rolled his eyes.

"It's phenomenal," said Heather, River's mum, as she tucked into the lemon curd and passionfruit layer. "The flavours meld so fluidly. I'll have to get Terry to whip me up a smaller version at home."

"Hang on a minute. I thought you were only eating things cooked in flaxseed," River joked, although Alice knew he was overjoyed that his mum had started eating properly again. Not so very long ago, her sister Sheba's death had knocked her for six and she had barely touched her food.

"Ah, well, this is a wedding… and when in Spain," Heather replied.

"It *is* a wedding," said the photographer for the hundredth time. "And if you please, some of us have a living to make out of it. Now, let's get the happy couple positioned in the finca's tower so we can get those wow factor shots at long last."

Finally, obediently, Mr Jackson took Mrs Jackson's hand and they carefully climbed the winding staircase to the roof and the ornate hacienda tower, where they had a hilarious view of the drama unfolding beneath them as the photographer briefed them on the poses he'd like them to adopt for the drone, which he would be flying by remote control in a few minutes.

As Alice snuggled up to her husband, the pair of them giggled at Lee and Bruno below. They were keeping guard over Rob, but intermittently finding their human side and holding him up a cocktail to sip. Intruder apart, Alice realised the day had been everything she could have wished for. And the best thing was, they still had four more nights at the finca to spend quality time with their family and friends, before heading off on another amazing adventure on wheels. Life didn't get better than this.

TIM

Tim's bride looked as pretty as any in a glossy wedding magazine – or an edition of *Sleb Magazine!*, whose photographers and journos, it quickly emerged, were part of the hush-hush guest list. Tim might have known. It totally explained Piper's caginess. Once again, she was putting herself and her work at the top of the seesaw. His thoughts about her appearance said it all. Her outer beauty was indisputable, but there was nothing beneath it. She was perfectly hollow.

Many would call Tim delusional for standing here today at the gigantic floral beach altar with its virginal silk curtains, waiting eagerly for Piper to join him in her Vera Wang wedding dress. He might not have seen the gown before today, but he had certainly seen the price on the receipt that Piper had carelessly left on the dining table. But Tim had weighed up all his options and decided to go through with the ceremony. Yes, just a handful of hours after Piper had confessed her betrayal, Tim was determined to forgive and forget, despite the fact that his love rival was currently watching on, sandwiched between who knew who from the social media world, his arse firmly planted on a silk ribbon-backed chair to match the draping of the beautiful altar. And so it was that Tim took a deep breath, looked earnestly out to sea, then back into his fiancée's eyes as she made her dramatic and fluid entrance down the aisle to Coldplay's *'Paradise'*; the fantastical, dark, rich notes coming from a baby grand piano, as a pair of doves were released from an ornate cage and a hidden bubble machine added another level of intrigue to the proceedings.

Tim thought he would be more nervous. But that trio of Buck's Fizzes had hit the sweet spot, bestowing him with just the right measure of cheerful confidence to get through this. Everything would be okay. In the end. Piper smiled serenely at him when she reached the altar with her dad. Her hair looked exquisite, trailing down her back in those waves that had first caught his eye, a sparkling tiara loaded with gems resting on her head, the fragrance of peonies from her bouquet tickling his nose. For a moment, Tim might have believed they were in a different reality.

Piper's father took his seat, and Tim thought of his own parents sitting proudly behind him on his side of the aisle, the moment of truth playing out imminently, with nowhere to run or hide. Still, the fizz warmed his belly and Tim knew this was the right path to take. It was a very different HEA to the one he'd envisaged, but somehow he just knew it would deliver, and then everyone could get on with the party and enjoy themselves.

He went through the motions, listening as Piper recited the words she had written for the both of them (or, more likely, grabbed from the Internet). It was best to let her parrot them off and get this bit over with: *I love you completely, wholly and unreservedly, and I give you my heart to hold until my dying day... blah-blah-blah.* Just as the officiator prompted Tim to spew the first words of his vows aloud, he gave a little cough to clear his throat.

"Enough." He held his hand aloft to signal his intent. "I think we both know that in light of recent events, you can't truly mean a word of that." The wide-eyed wedding guests gasped, the officiator expelled a nervous giggle, and Piper winced, emitting a pained sound. Her bouquet dropped to the floor, but Tim would not be deterred. "I think we also both know that somebody else should be standing here today, don't we, darling?" He looked Piper in the eye, watching the flash of crimson slowly make its way up her neck and across both cheeks, until it painted her forehead. At which point Tim couldn't look for a second longer, especially now the guests were beginning to murmur, big and little conversations sparking up everywhere. He put a hand to his own forehead, shielding his eyes from the shards of sunlight sneaking their way across the gathering, as he scoured the wedding party behind him for the person in question.

"Not Noah, Tim. *Please* don't say his name," Piper let out a crackled whisper. "I told you there's nothing more between us."

Their (well, mostly her) 'friends' and family fell silent again, waiting for the climax of this unexpected turn of events, eyes also panning the sea of people for any errant body language that might give the third person in this love triangle away. Sensing his duty at last, a man several rows back on Tim's side of the guests (Piper had insisted on inserting various top influencers closer to the front on both sides of the aisle) got to his feet. But it wasn't Noah who shuffled out of his row to walk down the aisle.

It was Nath.

All the years Tim had known this guy. All those seasons of friendship and support and laughter and tears had culminated in this. Who'd have thought it? Nath and his ill-fitting grey suit meandered towards the altar looking every inch the guilty party. Head slumped, hands in pockets. Hundreds of pairs of eyes cast their aspersions, burning holes in his back, banking up the tidbits of conversation for when they could let their hair down at the reception, bitching and laughing about his betrayal as they wolfed down the lobster and necked the vintage Dom Perignon.

"Hang on, mate! What are you like? You've forgotten this," Josh and Kyle both cried out to the lone figure, Kyle tagging on an ear-splitting finger whistle.

A mass of hats and heads turned at once to the two Northern lads and their announcement. Tim let out a sigh of relief that everything was going to plan.

"Oh, yeah. So I did," said Nath, suddenly straightening himself up and jumping into his role as if he was centre stage in a theatre. He paced back to his friends. "I couldn't wait to do the honours. Got a bit ahead of myself there."

Josh and Kyle lifted a long, flat object, covered in the same snow white as the drapes and chair bows decorating the beach set-up. They eased it up, one of them holding each end, faces more serious than Tim could ever recall. Like… not even after a Man United home defeat.

"What's going on, Tim?" asked Piper at his side, unable to keep her voice to a whisper now, fidgeting in her heels. "Talk to me, please! I'm *almost* your wife!" She began to tug on the sleeves of his white linen jacket.

Tim shrugged, a beam working its way across his lips. He kept his eye on his friends, patiently waiting for all to be revealed. It was tricky to overlook the astonished faces of his parents and sister, trickier still to ignore the muttering of the celebrant and the perplexed expression of the photographer, who did what he could to capture a handful of appropriate happy wedding day shots, but Tim had resolved to stay focused, no matter what. Finally his friends edged their way along their row among the guests so they could pass the item to Nath. It was nearly the same height as him and he seized it triumphantly, tucking it under his arm, making his way back down the aisle to the bride and groom.

"Do you want to do the honours, my friend?" Nath asked when he reached Tim. "Or shall I?"

Tim weighed up the offer as he admired his friends' handiwork, the afternoon sunbeams revealing the gift hidden beneath the layers of material. Nath, Josh and Kyle had excelled themselves.

"I can't deny that it's you and the boys' persistent nagging that made me realise something wasn't right," said Tim, waving a hand in Josh and Kyle's direction. They grinned self-consciously back, unfamiliar with being in the limelight among such a large group of people. People who mostly hogged it for themselves. "But I think you've done more than enough." Tim returned his attention to Nath. "How you sourced a shop that could make you one of these," he nodded at the object, "with little more than twelve hours' notice, I will never know. You can relax now, guys. I will take over from here."

Nath passed him the shrouded item and walked back to his seat. Now the hullabaloo really got going, and Tim knew he needed to act fast. Some might judge his next moves as malicious – and perhaps they were right. Maybe he should have taken the moral high ground, discreetly walking away before things had gotten this far, but for one, Tim found he couldn't resist and secondly, when it came to counselling and matters of psychology, maybe a statement such as this was the only way to help Piper reassess her life?

By trading places today, he could save Piper and her new beau the added expense and hassle of planning their own wedding. They had everything in place, after all; the press, the influencers, the ridiculous cake on its swing seat. Not that the cake itself was a joke. Nothing and nobody who came out of FOM could ever be that…

Tim was contemplating all these things, and about to unveil his grand surprise to a statue-like Piper and their audience, who were literally on the edge of their seats. Then Mervyn took to the aisle with his sparkly walking stick, just as Piper's dad got up too. Both looked the other up and down and hovered, waiting to make their move should Tim's next actions require intervention. Of course, Tim's parents had already looked askance at him once or twice but they weren't the kind of people to cause a scene. And as for Brittany, well, she just looked jetlagged.

Tim composed himself. He could either do this slowly and tantalisingly… or he could do it like a plaster ripped off a hairy leg. He opted for the latter. Somehow it felt more in keeping with the theatrical venue. Tim, Piper, and the officiator would be the first people to take in the vision. He felt it was only fair since he was, in a sense, giving his bride away. Tim held his breath, and ripped away the material from the life-size cardboard cut-out.

"Ta-dah!" he announced, impressed with the vision that stood before him.

Piper Mark Two was identical to the real Piper in every way, even down to today's hairstyle. Constructed from a photograph, she might have been wearing a vest top and hot pants, but from a distance the effect would be mesmerisingly realistic for the guests – and the press. This bonkers scene really did make it look as if they were all gathered today to watch Piper marry herself.

"What the actual fuck? Is this some kind of practical joke?" Piper stammered her words out, twisting and turning in all directions as if seeking out undercover TV cameras.

"Not at all," said Tim. "It's the only way you'll ever truly

THE WEDDING CAKE

be happy. I'm just saving you the time and effort of working through more men."

Perhaps Tim shouldn't have said that bit aloud. It was the trigger for Piper's dad to edge forward, fists at his chin, challenging Tim to a fight. "This isn't a hen or stag party, lad! Stop this bullshit immediately, get your arse back under that arch of peonies, man up and marry my daughter... or else!"

It was only the third time Tim had met Fergus Moss. And it had been three times too many.

"I'm inclined to agree." Mervyn said, looking absolutely petrified of the bride's father. "I've invested time and energy into putting on the most incredible day for you both. This is Weddings in Paradise's reputation you're putting on the line, Tim. Tie the knot, and keep your nearest and dearest happy." Mervyn waggled his cane at the guests. "As, erm... as well as your beautiful bride."

"Trust you to think of number one," a Yorkshire accent came from the back of the crowd before Tim could muster up his next move. "May I put in my tuppence worth, Tim?" Hannah stepped forward without waiting for him to reply. She waved to the guests. Some gingerly lifted their hands to be friendly in return, completely lost as to what in the hell was going on.

"Tim's being a gentleman," Hannah directed her statement to the groom's dad. "It's clear to see that the wedding is doomed to fail. Why should either party put themselves through all that heartache? Besides, they're all the rage now, these sologamy ceremonies," she announced. "And they're a refreshing idea to boot." Hannah went on to explain to her captive audience – Tim guessed they hadn't come across the self-marriage concept before. It had certainly been a new one on him mere days ago. "Basically, it's far from being self-indulgent." Okay, Tim stood corrected by Hannah and probably shouldn't have portrayed Piper marrying herself as utter vanity. "Self-marriage is an act of self-compassion; a declaration to honour oneself. Tim here," Hannah pointed him out in case anybody was in any doubt as to his identity, "is offering Piper a fresh start." Hannah turned to Mervyn now. "I'm not suggesting that a sologamy ceremony should be conducted at the drop of a hat. Self-marriage should be taken as seriously as any conventional ceremony, but I'm surprised you haven't got your finger on the pulse, Mervyn. You're missing a trick and overlooking a lucrative niche in the market."

Oh, how Tim loved this woman. In the platonic sense. No wonder Freya had snapped her up.

"You really think you have the answer to everything, don't you?" Mervyn snarled. "What would you even know about my clients, you silly, not-so-little," he looked the stocky Hannah up and down, and it was all Tim could do not to smack him, "woman?"

"A darn sight more than a man like you," Hannah replied. "Unfortunately."

She flicked her eyes at Tim and one of her brows shot up. In that split-second he understood *everything*. So it was Hannah who had sent him the photos. Highly unprofessionally and wholly inappropriately. And yet, she had basically saved his life and he couldn't be more thankful for her rebellion.

"Nonsense," countered Mervyn. "You're nothing but trouble. Stirring things up, just like you do with those icky witchy herbal brews you're constantly trying to shove down my clients' necks."

"I wouldn't push your luck with the compliments, Mr. Meehan. There are plenty of people here today who'd be *very interested* to learn of your recent shenanigans at our beloved cakery," Hannah retorted.

She stuck out her tongue at the wedding planner, clearly

knowing she had the upper hand. What was all that about, Tim wondered? He had never particularly gelled with the dude himself. Something didn't sit quite right.

Tim peeped through his side-swept fringe to give his mam a quick smile for reassurance purposes, trying not to falter when he spotted her eyes were full of tears. She looked amazing today in her shiny blue dress and fascinator, and he was grateful to the villa's muscly security team who had kindly carried her down the steep cliff steps to the beach. Not that she was looking particularly proud of the mess he'd made of his life right now. But then his mam was just one of many confused faces. How exactly was a guest supposed to react when a wedding bombed? It wasn't something anybody got taught at school. That didn't stop the usual suspects taking advantage of the fiasco. Tim couldn't help but notice the not-so-discreet mobile phones that were now being brandished by their well-wishers. Piper's friends would have her very personal dirty linen airing all over social media within seconds, amassing millions of new followers. *Shit.* And Tim's name would be mud across gyms and town hall fitness classes all over the UK, what with the footage being taken out of context. He hadn't mulled that part over at all.

Now his thoughts turned back to Piper. Had he been too cruel? No sooner had he pondered the notion than his ex-fiancée morphed before his eyes. It never took long for her to add up the dollar sign opportunities in any given scenario, as Tim knew well.

"Piper, love," Fergus Moss pleaded in desperation, still pacing the aisle. "Work your magic on Tim. Flutter your eyelashes, remind him of the day you first met… Try *something*! You can't let him publicly humiliate you like this. We've all spent a shit ton of money to be here. Your mum and I don't need the stress at our time of life."

Was that seriously the best Fergus had?

"I've got this, Dad." Piper shook her head at her father's attempts and smiled knowingly. "Tim's right. *You're bloody right, Tim! He's bloody right, everyone!*" She took off her heels and began to jump up and down excitedly, punching the air. "I *am* going to marry myself today. It's a genius idea." By now she had obviously totted up just how much extra publicity this ritual could potentially bring her and her precious career.

"Hannah," Piper beckoned Freya's assistant. Hannah tentatively walked to the altar. "Can I just check that I'd legally be allowed to get married for real at a later date… should the right man eventually come along?" she whispered.

"I think so, yes. A self-marriage is gestural as far as I know. Erm, perhaps you ought to check with the officiator though?" Hannah cocked her head to the spare wheel in their discussions.

Piper turned to their celebrant and smiled radiantly. "Do you think you could marry us *now*? Me and my better half, that is?" Piper stroked the cheek of her cardboard cut-out and Tim didn't know whether to laugh or cry, despite the fact it was he who had played matchmaker.

"I… it's not exactly in my repertoire."

Piper gave her a death stare.

"B-but since you're all gathered here today – and since so much money has been spent on the celebration, as your father rightfully points out – it would be a shame to waste the moment. Oh, and yes, to reiterate what Hannah has just said, since there are no legal documents accompanying a self-marriage, you can definitely do things in the usual way in the future."

"That's settled then," said Piper, rapture all over her face.

"Piper, are you sure about this?" Fergus quizzed, face scrunched up into an impressive monobrow.

"The girl knows her own mind, Ferg!" Piper's mum piped

up at long last, waving an emery board in the air now she'd finished buffing her nails. Evidently, she had also had time to process what this could mean for *her*: getting those talons professionally manicured at least once a week, for starters.

"I've never been more certain about anything in my life." Piper put her hands on her hips to back up her statement. "Relax, Dad. You just close your eyes and think of all the Formula One merch and VIP tickets to the race tracks I'll be able to buy you."

Oh, yes. One of the few facts Tim had learned about his ex-partner's father during their sixteen months together was his penchant for fast cars.

"Okay then, everybody." The officiator reminded Tim of an auctioneer waiting to seal the deal with a hammer before anybody else could change their mind. "I have another wedding to get to later this afternoon so if we could all take our seats… except for Piper and her bride. The show must go on."

Tim wasn't sure where to put himself now his role in the ceremony had significantly changed, but he passed Piper's wedding ring to the officiator and turned to see Hannah had produced a spare chair from thin air. She coaxed him back to the front row and onto his original seat, setting her own chair next to him. Mervyn, tutting, frowning, and reluctant to let any of this go, grabbed his perch from the end of his row and dragged it along the aisle, crumpling the silk runner, and rendering his walking stick charade pointless, as Tim had noted so often seemed to be the case, depending on circumstances. He too bagged himself a front row view, amidst the background tittle-tattle of the guests. Once again, Tim couldn't look at his family sitting behind him, although he did feel the reassuring pat of his mam's hand on his shoulder. He'd doubtless disappointed them all but he couldn't go on disappointing himself. He deserved better.

This was his life and they'd just have to deal with his choices.

The celebrant married Piper and her cardboard cut-out, in what Tim could only describe as the most bizarre experience of his life; Piper putting words into her double's mouth and looking deeply into her eyes as they prepared for their future together. The guests couldn't get enough of the happy occasion; snapping and filming and whooping away. Especially when Piper kissed herself. The bevvy of photographers, which ranged from their officially chosen Spanish one via Weddings in Paradise to *Sleb! Magazine*'s crew, had a field day with the imagery and poses. And Piper Moss was in her element.

When the clamour finally died down, Tim went over to Piper to hug her and wish her and her double well.

"I've said it before and I'll say it again, you're a breath of fresh air, Tim Nutkins. You understand me better than any other man ever has or will. I'm sorry it didn't work out for us." Piper sniffed unconvincingly. "And yet I'm not sorry. You deserve better. Now I've had a chance to stand here and think about my recent behaviour, I can see that I've put you through hell."

"It's been a life lesson for both of us," said Tim. Well, it was true. "But what about Noah? I know it's not exactly any of my business anymore, but where does he figure in your future plans?" Tim willed away the eccentric love triangle that had just flickered, quite unnecessarily, through his mind.

"Pfft. I have me and myself now. I don't need *him* anymore. Noah didn't even put up a fight today! Just sat there like lapping everything up like Vince Vaughn and Owen Wilson's characters in *The Wedding Crasher*. A right hanger-on. There's a better man out there. I know it. *We* know it." Piper looked, starry-eyed, at her beloved reflection made of cardboard. "I just need to be patient and wait for him. Until then I am sure we can amuse ourselves." She winked at Piper Version 2.0.

Blimey. Tim needed a drink. This was all too much to process. It had gone down better than he could ever have imagined. With the slight exception of his family's falling faces. He retreated into the background, keen to escape the spotlight.

"Seeing as this wedding is all about breaking from tradition." Piper shouted to the gathering, pausing to pull her mobile phone out from her bust, frowning and eye-rolling as she scanned the screen for updates. "And seeing as some woman called Hayley has informed me on Rob's behalf that he's failed in his mission over at Mijas." She tossed her phone behind her in annoyance. "I'm going to cut my beautiful swing seat wedding showstopper now – with my love – and we're all going to have our cake and eat it."

This put everybody in even higher spirits and the guests began to follow Piper, chatting and laughing – as if she was indeed the Pied Piper.

Rob? Was Tim missing something? Don't tell him… yet another male on Piper's list of conquests to help enhance her career. He didn't want to wonder who on earth Hayley was. Yep, Tim had definitely made the right decision today.

"Tim?" Hannah looked suddenly panic-stricken. "Your ex will remember to stick to her bit of the cake, won't she?"

Sugar-loaded sponge was the last thing Piper would worry about now, surely? Then again, probably not, this was Piper Moss Hannah was talking about…

"Hey!" Hannah rushed over to Piper, without waiting for Tim to reply, intent on ensuring she got her custom-made slices. Well, he supposed that whoever had baked the eight-tier masterpiece would want each couple's half to live up to its expectations. He could only hope that the bride and groom in Mijas were having a smoother experience. "Make sure you eat your designated wedges and leave the rest for the others to enjoy, won't you?" Hannah yelled after the bride at *this* wedding, her words streaming behind her. "I mean… only your taste buds are suited to the acquired taste of Yacon syrup. You've worked so hard to stay trim and preserve that beautiful figure." She laughed nervously at Piper's rapidly disappearing back as the bride paced across the beach and up the cliffside with her lookalike under her wing. "You can't let things slide now you're married!"

"Why would Hannah be so meticulous about that?" Mervyn sidled up and nudged Tim. "And why is she still here, anyway? I swear I've seen that thug of a Ricky character loafing about in the background too, with his lurid green Versailles hair-do. What's going on? Cake makers are never VIP enough to get an invite to the wedding. That's the planner's perk."

"Hannah and Ricky were asked to keep a close watch until the cake got cut. In case there were any issues with it staying on the swing seat," Tim explained, thinking surely Mervyn should be aware of all of this in his capacity as wedding planner. "As you'll probably remember, Piper upgraded her requirements after the disaster with the double-booking."

"Well, that was all Freya's doing," Mervyn shook his head and tutted dramatically. "Weddings in Paradise are punctilious when it comes to detail."

"I know that ridiculous order book could not have been Freya's idea." Tim found himself shouting at the fool. "Everything else about FOM is swish and modern and *reliable*… with the strange exception of that old notebook, which was practically falling apart at the seams when she unveiled it with a grimace and recounted the details of the order to me. You know that book, too: a pencil on a string stuck to its cover in the same way that parents used to tie their kids'

THE WEDDING CAKE

mittens to their coats, the antiquated *spider scrawl handwriting* on its pages assaulting all five of your senses."

"I don't know what you're talking about! And neither do you by all accounts. Stick to your day job, Mr Floppy Fringed Trampoline Fitness Instructor!" Mervyn sneered, getting to his feet and making a sprightly dart across the sand so he didn't miss out on his cake. A startled Tim wondered how he kept in business if this was the way he insulted all his clients.

"Yay, Squirrel! Words cannot express how proud we are of you," said Nath, bounding over to Tim now he, Josh and Kyle could finally get a word in.

Well, at least his friends were elated. He had yet to talk to his parents, but he'd seen that his mam had been lifted back up to the villa's gardens by the security guards, where he would hopefully be able to explain himself to his family.

"I can't thank you enough, lads. That went extremely well." Tim patted each of them on the back. "The Pimm's are on me. Well, on Piper and her wife. But actually, I did pay for the drinks bar, the flowers, and the honeymoon. Not that I'll be jetting off any more, thank God. Neither of the Pipers will miss me. They're staying at another Double Tap Towers."

"Never mind the plonk. I'm just glad you let common sense prevail with that last-minute text message. Even if all four of us will now find ourselves splashed across social media. It was worth it to get the old Tim back."

"I know." Tim pulled all three of his friends toward him for a non-negotiable group hug. He felt the stress of the last sixteen months come crashing down on him again and wondered how he could have been taken for such a ride. "I was pretty lost there for a while," he mumbled into Nathan's shoulder before pushing him back. "But now I can see more clearly than ever before."

Tim removed his expensive loafers and streaked across the sand towards Hannah and Ricky, before they headed home and he lost the chance to talk to Freya's assistants. He'd need to swallow down his nerves but it was now or never.

Alas, the Nutkins clan were waiting for him at the villa's back gates. Cathy dabbed away at her tears with a giant floral handkerchief. There was no escaping the dressing-down he was about to receive.

"Why didn't you tell us?" Tim's dad did the speaking since his mam still couldn't find the words. "We know it's small change compared to the cost of the wedding but we've shelled out a fortune to be here. You should have said something. We're your family. Me and your mam knew Piper wasn't right for you. We did try to tell you a number of times, but, well… you seemed so set on things and you're a fully grown man. We had to let ourselves believe you were caught up in the same kind of whirlwind we found ourselves in back in the day when folk got hitched quickly. An old head on young shoulders. Clearly that wasn't the case." Brian Nutkins' brows furrowed and Tim felt sad when he saw the deep lines this accentuated. It wasn't often they appraised one another in direct sunlight. His father's face was beginning to put him in mind of that antique cake order book.

"And my flights weren't cheap either," Brittany whimpered, without as much as going in for a hug. How long had it been since she'd seen her younger brother? Five years, perhaps even six? And this was the way she greeted him? "Do you realise how little vacation I get working for an American corporation?"

"I'm sorry. I'll reimburse you – and Mam and Dad." Tim flicked his gaze across them all, trying hard not to absorb the guilt now he'd officially changed his M.O. He remembered the Bucks Fizz was still in his system. It was now or never. He looked his sister up and down before he said something he should have said a while ago; something that would get her back right up but something that simply couldn't wait a second longer. "Brittany, it's high time you saw our parents and did your bit. You might live in another country and you might have a busy and successful career, but it shouldn't take the excitement of a wedding for you to come over to see Mam and Dad. I hope this is the start of more effort on your part. Neither of us can count on Andy, so both of us should be doing our bit to check in on them. Not that you're about to go into a retirement home or anything, don't worry," Tim added, glancing sideways at his parents, guilt momentarily licking at him for being so blunt and direct in front of them.

"Flaming cheek," said his mam, half laughing, half snivelling.

"Listen, this is a happy occasion really," Tim tried his best to reassure them. "I want you to stay here for the time being and enjoy the food and the atmosphere. It's not every day any of us get to be in such lavish surroundings."

"Well, I've been to a few posh mansions in the Hamptons…"

"Oh, ay." Brian cut through his daughter's boast. "I've heard the rumours about the music mogul with the high-waisted trousers that this pad used to belong to!" A tiny smile lit up his father's face and Tim tried to tamp down the annoying theme song to the guy's reality TV music shows, which had just struck up in his head.

"All will be fine, I promise. Eat, drink and be merry." Tim hoped they really were coming around and the sparse smiles weren't just the figment of his imagination. "I'll be back to talk to you properly in a while. There's something I have to do right now."

By the time Tim had batted away his family's protests at being told half a story when they deserved the full version of events, and by the time he'd reached the cake-cutting area, Piper was nowhere to be seen. Hannah and Ricky were packing up their bits and pieces to leave, and Ricky's face was thunder as Mervyn continued to hang around Hannah like a bad smell. Surely he should have been overseeing the catering, the photography, or the flower arrangements, in his VIP role of wedding planner?

"Hannah! I'm glad I caught you," said Tim, doubling over to catch his breath, such was the vast extent of the property's gardens. "I take it the cake didn't fly off the swing then?"

"What?" she replied curtly, barely giving him a glance. "No. No, it didn't fly. Although it did go down a storm." Hannah chucked more kitchen paraphernalia in the box that Ricky was currently guarding like a gorilla daddy. Tim wasn't the only one who needed a drink, then. "Piper went for the Yacon syrup wedges, thank goodness," she continued as she rifled through the culinary odds and ends, and Tim marvelled at the sheer amount of equipment needed to fulfil his ex's random wish. "FOM has to think about future potential clients, and, well... erm... can you imagine how off-putting it would be if one of the guests bit into the disappointing Yacon syrup part? We're more than happy to accommodate food intolerances and special requests, but we need to be ever mindful of our mainstream clientele... that's why I might have looked like I was overreacting back then." She laughed nervously. "What I mean to say is, if somebody tasted a piece of the healthy side of the sponge, they'd probably think we'd made it from cardboard... whereas to a clean eater like Piper who has weaned herself off the white stuff, doesn't have a very sweet tooth, and doesn't even allow herself a drop of fizz on her wedding day, it probably tasted like heaven."

"It's okay, Hannah," Tim cut in, "you don't need to explain yourself. I can only imagine what a nightmare it's been. I was there at the taste test when my ex's stipulations were relayed to Freya, remember? Oh, and actually clean eaters can drink alcohol. If there's one thing about Piper, it's that she loves a tipple."

"C-can they really? And does she? W-well, you learn something new every day. Ha, oh, yes, you were there, weren't you?" Hannah replied robotically.

"So where is Piper now? Don't tell me she's comatose from the glycaemic hit?"

"W-why would she be?" Hannah replied anxiously, once again avoiding all eye contact. "Yacon syrup might have a slightly caramel flavour but it's half as sweet as honey and is extremely low on the…"

But she didn't finish her sentence. A massive splash and a scream reverberated throughout the gardens. Everybody's attention turned to the infinity pool, where, like a comet, Tim spotted the tail end of his ex's wedding dress and her long wavy hair in flight, a giant piece of cake held aloft in her hand as if Piper thought that might somehow preserve its structure as she broke the water's surface.

Tim, Ricky, and even Mervyn, rushed across the lawn to the scene. Thankfully Fergus and a couple of the security guards were on top of things already, hauling the soaking-wet bride out of the pool as if they'd just caught a bedraggled mermaid. Piper gulped for air like a fish. What a state. In a sense, Tim couldn't help but feel responsible, until he remembered that he was done with guilt and people-pleasing. She'd created this scene all by herself.

"Shitting hell. This is the last thing Freya needs!" said Hannah, rushing along behind them all. Tim refused to look at the surge of gadgets videoing the situation that she was no doubt referring to.

"Stand back and put those blessed mobile phones and cameras down!" shouted Fergus. "Enough is enough. Is nothing in this world private anymore?"

Wow. Tim might give Fergus the benefit of the doubt

after that retort, which sounded a lot like his own thoughts over the previous months. Perhaps there was hope for his daughter yet. Maybe she would spend some time with her new love reflecting on the importance of keeping something back for herself. Everybody peeled away at the father of the bride's command. Even Mervyn retreated several paces, although unfortunately not into the pool.

Piper was conscious at least, but she didn't half look sleepy. The sudden volume of sugar must have been like a drug. Fergus and one of the security guards carried her into the villa. Tim watched on, stunned that most of the wedding guests (now they'd been told to put their screens away) were completely engrossed in flirting with one another, getting wasted on all the free booze, and generally chomping their way through the beautiful wedding cake, since they were famished and the caterers' plans were now on hold.

"I suppose she's necked a couple of glasses of champagne by now too," he said to himself. "That would only make the sugar hit of the wedding cake worse… and then she'd be buoyed up from the adrenaline of the ceremony… Still, something doesn't quite add up." Tim thought of the chefs, waiters and sommeliers who would be working to a tight deadline, not to mention that photographer they visited in February, who was an absolute pro. He definitely wouldn't be happy about being delayed for the garden shots. Piper might have been frazzled but she was also far too good at donning her business opportunity face and cracking on with things. "Just look at all the people waiting to celebrate with her, and, more to the point, waiting to make her extremely famous," Tim aired his thoughts to one of the villa's naked statues. "Why would she go off for a nana nap at such a crucial moment in time?" He shook his head in disbelief.

"I'm a flaming liability," he swore he heard Hannah whisper behind him.

"*What? What is it?*" He turned in her direction.

"I… I. Nothing. I just need to double-check that I've packed the edible glue." Hannah looked completely dazed. Far too dazed for such a trivial matter. "Freya's not got much of it in stock and I erm… I used quite a bit to secure the cake to the swing at its base."

"Okay, well I guess I ought to make sure Piper's definitely going to be okay before I leave. Now the ceremony is over, and she seems genuinely happy, me and my family and the boys will be moving on. Not that I have much of a Plan B. Just a little hope in my heart." Tim wasn't too enthralled by the prospect of tiptoeing around Fergus to say his farewell – although at least Piper's mum was spellbound in chit-chat with Noah and his friends. Hmm, the apple really didn't fall too far from the tree.

"She's asleep, Tim. It's time to focus on yourself for once," said Hannah with a shaky voice and a mechanical smile.

No, Hannah's reaction wasn't right. It didn't make sense. And another thing was bugging Tim too. But until he knew Piper was physically fine, that concern would have to go on the backburner.

"Tell me about it," Mervyn chanced to interject, just when Tim hoped they'd gotten rid of him. "There's something rather fishy going on here. You know as well as I do, Hannah, Piper went at that cake like a baby at one of those hideous modern day cake smashes. She became sleepy mere minutes after eating it. She was what can only be described as *staggering about*."

He positioned himself before the table, where Hannah was still going like the clappers arranging all her utensils, his hand cupped to his chin, and his sparkly walking stick denting the formerly pristine lawn.

"Oh, piss off you dafty. She was capitalising on the drama, that's all." Ricky spat. "No offence, Tim."

"None taken," Tim replied, since Ricky was probably right.

"Everybody else ate the cake and they're all perfectly fine." Ricky turned back to Tim again. "I wouldn't worry about it. Don't underestimate the after effects of adrenaline. She's had a massive shock. One she obviously had coming to her, but that's by the by. And it is four pm on a blazing hot Spanish August afternoon. That's siesta time in these parts. I definitely saw her necking the champagne as it was circulating too. No wonder the poor lass is tired."

"You're right," Tim agreed. Ricky certainly hadn't heard his earlier thoughts, even if he had softly voiced them. It couldn't just be a coincidence that their thinking was so aligned. "In that case, I'd better leave her to it and take Hannah to one side for a quick word, if I may?"

"Hannah's her own woman. You don't need to ask me for permission," said Ricky, giving Mervyn the evils as he tried to follow along to eavesdrop on their conversation, and swiftly thought better of it.

"Hmph. That's it. I'm done." Mervyn wrinkled his nose and eyeballed Ricky. "First I have the embarrassment of witnessing my bride and groom make a complete mockery of me, then nobody thinks to cut me a slice of cake, and now I have to endure the glares of the world's campest bully. Just look at the state of you, Ricky. That hair really wouldn't look out of place in a French portrait gallery – overlooking the lurid green."

"I couldn't ask for a greater compliment," snapped Ricky.

Mervyn snarled. "Give me a predictable bridezilla moaning about the rain any day of the week. You lot are the pits. I'm retiring."

"Chippety-chop, off you pop," said Hannah, giving Mervyn a round of applause as he sauntered off to count his millions. "It's well overdue."

"Right," said Tim. "Now we've hopefully seen the last of him, I've got something to ask you: where can I find Freya? Oh, and before I forget… it seems that Piper had one further trick up her sleeve prior to us not saying 'I do'… It's suddenly dawned on me that the Rob she got the message from earlier owed her a couple of favours. Piper's set him up with a glut of endorsement opportunities this year. Putting two and two together, and recalling the way I saw him dressed just before the ceremony, I'd wager this mission of his was to seize the other half of the cake. She was that narked about it, I'm almost certain she sent Rob over to snatch it."

∽

Hannah didn't stop to answer Tim's question about Freya. Her thoughts turned immediately to the Alice, River and their guests' safety in the finca at Mijas. She grabbed her own box of tricks, tugged at Ricky's shirt and told Tim she'd explain all in the van.

"Oh my God. Why didn't you mention your suspicions sooner? Say a speedy goodbye to your family and friends, Tim. Ricky and I can't possibly deal with this situation alone. Now you're a gooseberry at what was your own wedding, you'll have to come with us to another. If your hunch is right, your ex may have potentially wrecked Alice and River's day. It's our duty to catch this guy before things escalate and we need to call the police! Ultimately, this is all Mervyn's doing, of course. All of the double-booking is on him. I'd wring his neck if he hadn't had the sense to disappear on cue!"

Tim surveyed the guests. He saw that his parents, Brittany, and the lads were having a whale of a time and decided to leave them to it. He couldn't bear hearing at second hand about the potential fallout from yet another wedding mishap for Freya. Hannah was right. They had a duty to try to spare any further heartache and the clock was ticking. In a roundabout way, this stupid situation was as much Tim's fault as Mervyn's: if Tim had only had the guts to call the wedding off sooner, none of this would have happened. By trying to please people and fulfil his parents' expectations, he'd created a heap of unwanted trouble for another bride and groom and their guests. The ripple effect was an eye-opener and he vowed never to pacify others again.

Hannah, Ricky and Tim furtively made their way to the villa's sweeping driveway, the exhaust fumes of Mervyn's Jaguar still visible at the imposing double gates. After a further tip-off from the villa's security guards that a guy who looked like a fixer from a gangster movie had indeed been hired by Piper to retrieve the other half of the wedding cake, the trio sped off to Mijas in the quaint FOM van. Hannah messaged Alice en route, cringing at Ricky's snail's pace behind the wheel as they finally left the motorway and made their way inland to the tiny village next to Mijas. When she could take it no longer, she made Ricky pull over so they could swap seats, instructing him to watch her mobile phone like a hawk for news.

The conversation was sparse, nerves palpably jangled. Tim shivered in the back of the air-conditioned van, which had been heavenly for all of ten minutes in the wake of the afternoon heat, but had now rendered him an ice block. He didn't dare interrupt Hannah's focus to ask where the off switch was. At least the chattering of his teeth took his mind off the thoughts bouncing around his head.

"Something's just come in. I think Alice has sent a WhatsApp voice memo," Ricky finally cried.

"Turn up the volume and press play!" Hannah shouted. "We're almost there in any case but fingers crossed all of this is nothing but a false alarm."

"Give me a minute, will you? How many tabs have you

got open on your phone, love? I've got some random pie chart on the screen here now. Pharmacodynamic interaction? You are one mysterious wom—"

"Never mind that! Just press play," Hannah squealed.

"Oh, him?" Alice's southern lilt rang out around the van. "Please don't worry, Hannah. We've locked the idiot in the finca's bell tower and his limbs are bound. He's been fed and watered though. We couldn't bring ourselves to go too medieval on him. Luckily we got our wedding photos taken up there first but the drone has also captured some classic shots of my head bridesmaid, Hayley, putting Rob in a headlock when he tried to escape. The photographer said he wished every wedding was this exciting!"

A flurry of deep sighs echoed around the vehicle.

"It's still our job to deal with him," said Hannah as Ricky pressed the record button so she could send back a message. "No matter how dangerous and messy things get. The least we can do is take him back to Piper's villa and see if the security staff have any ideas on how best to handle this. Keep him where he is and don't take your eye off him."

ALICE

Word about the status of the Marbella wedding wended its way back to Alice via a speed of light WhatsApp voice memo from Hannah. Even Hayley was speechless.

"Wow," said River, wincing. "Talk about carnage."

"That's one way of putting it." Alice couldn't help but feel guilty that things had run *somewhat more smoothly* for them and their guests. "I think the ex-groom and the cake makers will need a long drink once they get here. Bruno and Zara, are you ready to make some Bellinis?"

"Coming right up!" Zara replied for the both of them, and set to chopping more fruit.

Before long, every single one of Alice and River's family and friends had heard the sorry tale of the unconventional celebrations further down the coast. Hayley, predictably, hadn't been able to keep her trap shut for long, and although Alice wouldn't dream of laughing at anybody's expense, some of the versions of the story doing the wedding party rounds made that impossible. They ranged from:

"The groom ran off with a super-fit guy on a yacht

THE WEDDING CAKE

who's taking him on a round the world trip with his pug," to "The bride was caught in the act with the wedding planner and a chef in the kitchen... plus an array of exotic fruits: make of that what you will," and "The bride married cardboard cut-outs of all the former members of One Direction, but she's decided she will mostly be living with Harry Styles since he's the best looking. The others are going to be relegated to her garage for occasional use."

Speaking of the gossip-in-chief, Hayley alerted everybody to the fact that their unexpected visitors had just arrived, and Alice and River rushed to the finca's entrance to welcome them, their own guests following behind like a flock of sheep, until River pulled a scary face and chased them all back into the garden. The last thing these poor people needed was rubberneckers.

"We really don't want to impose," said Hannah, rushing in to give Alice and River a kiss on the cheeks and congratulate them. "I can't tell you how sorry I am for such a terrifying ordeal. First the headache of the cake needing to be shared... and now this. We shuddered at the sight of the tower when we approached the finca. Lead us to the steps and we'll take the tyke off your hands."

"It's fine," said Alice. "And there's absolutely no rush. He can't go anywhere. We tried to call Mervyn but to no avail. Luckily we were able to improvise."

"Don't get me started on *that excuse for a man*." Hannah flashed her teeth.

"I can only apologise from the bottom of my heart, too," said a thoroughly attractive blond male, who hopped out of the back of the Freya's of Marbella van, practically vibrating. "I'm T-Tim... the g-groom. I mean the *ex*-groom. Mervyn should have split his time equally between the two weddings. He seemed so committed and competent when we decided to do business with him, but I'm quickly starting to realise it was all a bit of an act."

"Damn right he should have checked up on everything here," Hannah added, as a third person got out of the van, introducing himself as Ricky to a glut of raised hands and waves. Alice hadn't met him before and rightly assumed he was a behind-the-scenes employee at team FOM. Damn, she loved the grass green Somerset shade of his hair.

"Why doesn't he employ a *team*?" she asked, thinking of the decidedly dodgy Mervyn. "Clearly his professionalism and attention to detail was one giant façade, when we met him for all our supplier visits. He's happy enough to take everybody's money but all the old git really cares about is cutting corners so he can fill his coffers." Alice sighed. "Nice to meet you though, Tim." She held out her hand and Tim shook it in his decidedly cold one. Ricky moved in for a handshake too. No, she definitely wasn't imagining Tim's lack of body heat. Ricky was room temperature in contrast. "I'm sorry to hear about what must have been a truly tragic and disappointing day for you. There are no words to make it better, so I'm not even going to attempt to sugar-coat things. But we do have the cocktail bar up and running. So come on in, have a glass or two and then we can discuss how we're going to deal with the wedding crasher."

"I'm fine. Honestly," Tim replied in earnest. "The signs were there for some time that it wasn't meant to be. I should have called things off with Piper months ago… but then I wouldn't have met Frey…"

Alice's antennae perked up as Tim realised he'd lost his filter with that quirky statement. Oh, heck.

"I'm driving so it will have to be a mocktail, if that's okay?" said Hannah, intermittently glancing at her watch.

Tim, Hannah and Ricky followed Alice and River through the finca and out to the lawns, where a sea of people raised their glasses to them – some rather tipsily running over to Tim for a consolatory hug. Bruno and Zara filled their glasses and Alice led the visitors to a quiet nook half in the shade, half in the sun so that Tim could thaw out and gather his thoughts. River recounted the moment they realised they had a gatecrasher in their midst, and Alice shivered at the near miss, thanking her lucky stars for Hayley and her extreme heroics. Again.

As if on cue, Hayley sniffed out the clandestine meeting and introduced herself to Tim, Hannah and Ricky. Not before placing a platter of sliced wedding cake in front of them. Which was probably the last thing all three of their guests wanted to look at, even if they were hungry. Their friend had zero tact.

"Forget all the Marvel icons plastered around my bedroom," cried Ricky. "It's *you* I want framed above my four poster, you absolute legend of a woman!"

"That can easily be arranged, honey," said Hayley, quite seriously. "I'll have a quick chinwag with the photographer, like."

Ricky beamed and Alice cringed at her friend's lack of modesty and decorum.

"We can't thank you enough," said Hannah.

"Any day, chick. That's what I learned Krav Maga for."

"Oh." Tim perked up. "I've been hearing a lot about KM and how effective it is as a self-defence mechanism. It sounds like something I really need to add to my fitness instructor repertoire. You'll have to tell me more."

So Hayley did… And then half an hour later it was time to get down to business.

"That was fascinating," said Hannah, the first nanosecond anybody could get a word in. "I hate to interrupt you but we really need to take the numpty in the tower off the bride and groom's hands now. I'm sure you'll want to get back to your guests." She turned to Alice and River.

"Actually, we're in no rush. It's been lovely having everyone pile into the finca before and after the wedding – most of our family and friends are in Spain for a holiday – but it also means we've definitely had our quota of them!" River replied with a behemoth eye roll.

"I'll take Jack the lad over to the posh villa," said Hayley. She glared at the finca's tower where their intruder was hopefully still incarcerated, and wiped red velvet icing from her hands with a napkin. Alice had lost count of how many slices their friend had devoured – and rather impressively, too, since she'd been doing most of the talking.

River and Hannah went to protest at the same time but Hayley held up a hand to stop them saying another word. "I've got this. I've not had a drop of alcohol to drink, since I'm on guest-ferrying duty to and from hotels – hence cracking open your very best wine earlier in the week while I had the opportunity." Hayley sighed at her martyrdom. "I'll take the twit back to Marbella and we'll sort things from there. I could use a bit of muscle power to get him on board and off again though. Any volunteers? Hannah and Ricky: I'm looking specifically at you two. I know that Tim's no stranger to a gym but it wouldn't be fair to send him back to all that chaos. The poor bloke deserves to salvage some happiness from today."

"Of course we'll go," said Ricky, jumping from his seat. "I cannae wait to see you in action."

Hannah stood too and began to shift from foot to foot.

"Could you handle this on your own with Hayley?" she asked her colleague, her eyes not quite meeting his. "I should get the van back to FOM."

"Fair point," said Ricky and Hayley in unison, and Alice sensed she had witnessed the start of a beautiful friendship.

"Do you think you could dispose of a couple of extra nuisance wedding guests in the process?" River asked, cocking his head toward the sun loungers at the pool where Bear and Alex were sprawled out, knocking back a queue of cocktails.

"My pleasure," Hayley replied. "Just leave them to me."

"What about you, Tim?" asked Alice. "You're more than welcome to stay here but I don't like to think of your family and friends stranded over in Marbs. Want to coax them onto Hayley's coach once she's deposited the waifs and strays? They could finish the day in style with us. We can't offer caviar and Bollinger but we do have a churros cart."

"That would be awesome," said Tim. "I promise none of us will outstay our welcomes. I haven't had a chance to catch up with my family or friends properly all day – not without a camera lens pointing at us. But, erm, Hannah." Tim pivoted to talk to FOM's assistant. "I just want to check… if I did tag along with you now in the van, would that mean I'd get the opportunity to speak to Freya? Just quickly?"

"Oh, Freya's gone, Tim," said Alice, hating to be the bearer of bad news.

Tim, Hannah and Ricky turned in her direction en masse, eyes wide.

"I-I thought you knew? She muttered something about heading off to a mountain hiking retreat before she left us earlier today." Ricky began to shake at this news, eyes like saucers. "No idea where. I'm guessing she must be on her way there already."

Tim's face fell. Hannah's emotions were harder to read. Frankly the girl looked like she didn't know whether she was coming or going.

"Right, well," Hannah brushed imaginary crumbs off her clothes. She hadn't taken a bite of cake. "Thanks, Alice and River. All the best for the future to the both of you." She forced a small smile. "I'm sorry but there's no point in you coming with me, Tim." She turned to the ex-groom. "I'll take the van back to FOM's garage, dump my bits and pieces in the cakery and turn in for an early night. W-would you let me know if Piper's awake though, please? I mean, I'm sure she will be by now. But it would be good to know."

"It's the least I can do," Tim replied, downcast. "Oh, and thank you. For the pictures. Sometimes you have to be cruel to be kind, right?"

"You're welcome." Hannah whispered. Her face began to clash badly with her hair colour and she pelted out of the finca.

"What was that all about?" said Ricky. "I'd better go after her."

"Not until you've helped me transport our inmate, you won't," countered Hayley, and Ricky sat back down without protest.

"All I know is Hannah is a gem," said Tim, "and I'll tell you both why on the coach."

Alice wasn't sure she wanted to hear another word, at least not until the waste of space in the tower had been dealt with and her new friends had returned. Tim's disaster of a wedding had taken up enough of her special day. She chivvied Hayley, Ricky and the former groom into action so she could get back to the all-important job of partying with her own husband.

FREYA

Freya couldn't believe how gullible she'd been.
Twice…

Lars was Merv's stepson! It all made sense now. He had seemed to have a little too much insider information into her business all those months ago. Despite the queue of disasters that made up her previous dates, none of them had tried to worm their way into her affections to fleece her. Okay, Freya didn't have concrete evidence of the guy's intentions but the not-so-subtle hints he had dropped were enough of an alarm bell. It wasn't just Hannah who was worth her weight in edible gold. Ricky's undercover dating skills had come into their own. He'd purposefully copped off with 'one of Lars' fittest kitchen constructors' at a party and dated him for a few months once his sixth sense about Lars' motivations had been triggered, and his quarry had sufficiently rifled through his boss's errant office paperwork and its many mentions of Freya and FOM.

If only that had been the only time she had been duped. But no. Something much more sinister had come to light. She'd seen the signs along the way, she'd chosen to ignore them, and now FOM was officially screwed. After she'd left the Goldsmith-Jackson wedding, Freya had remembered she'd also left her house keys in the cakery. It was such a clumsy mistake but hardly surprising, given all the emotions today had dredged up. They must be in the finishing room where she'd overseen Ricky putting the final touches to both halves of the showstopper, before she and Alejandro had delivered one half of the cake to Alice and River in Mijas, and Hannah had accompanied Ricky to Marbella with Tim and Piper's side.

After scouring the room frantically, she made a last resort dive into the walk-in fridge. Bingo! They were twinkling at her from the middle shelf. Head full of Tim, Freya had never known herself to be such a klutz. She'd grabbed the icy cold keys and quickly made to walk out of the building so she could get back to the apartment and pack up her things for her much-needed few days away in nature. But just as she was leaving the finishing room, she did a double-take. Something caught her eye on the normally spotless floor. She walked closer to see what it was. A syringe. But this wasn't one of FOM's cake syringes. They were all white. This one had a purple plunger. This one had come in from the outside.

Freya dropped her keys in shock as she put two and two together, knowing that she had sadly come up with four.

"*Hannah!*" she yelled – despite the fact that her employee wasn't even on the premises – and so loudly that she couldn't believe the windows didn't shatter, littering the floor with glass confetti (bleugh) around her shaking form.

TIM

"They do say truth is stranger than fiction," said Hayley, taking the turning for Marbella after Tim had given the briefest possible version he could of the events that had led to Hannah sending him X-rated pictures of Piper. Having recently discovered that Hayley was a taxi driver, he'd no doubt provided her with some excellent fodder to breadcrumb to her clients during long journeys.

Ricky was equally gobsmacked at the revelations, eventually finding his voice to say, "We'd best not tell Freya. Much as I love Hannah, she's totally crossed the line. It's always the quiet ones. Hannah's always in her own little bubble in the cakery. She rarely joins in with our banter unless she thinks she has a valid point to make. Talk about double standards. It'll be a shame to see her go if Freya does find out what she's been up to. *I shan't say a thing, of course.* But now the secret's out, there's no telling how quickly the gossip will get back to the boss."

In other words, Ricky was totally going to break the news to Freya. Why hadn't Tim thought to keep his gob shut? Now poor Hannah would be out of a job. He'd created a bottomless pit of destruction! All the more reason to wait patiently until Freya came back from this mountain escape of hers, when he could hopefully persuade her that Hannah didn't deserve to be fired. Tim was booked to be in Spain for another week. He and Piper were supposed to be enjoying the perks of the villa before jetting off on honeymoon. From a work point of view, his clients and the hospital knew he'd be away. There was just the matter of trying to find alternative accommodation during August at short notice. But even if he had to kip on his friends' shared hotel room floor, it would be worth it. *Hopefully.* Hope was all he had now.

Once they'd arrived back at the villa, and had rung the bell to alert security, they then had to explain the complex logistics of Operation Transfer to the various members of staff. Tim snuck in through the side entrance of the property to check up on Piper in the bedroom. *Shit.* She wasn't there! The bed was empty, its crumpled silk sheets tossed to the floor – and not in a seductive way. Panic tugged at what was left of his heart strings and he willed away the wail of ambulance sirens in his head. Surely somebody would have notified him at the gates if his ex had been taken ill? If the sudden exhaustion had been a side effect of something serious? Or maybe not. Perhaps they wanted to damp down the drama so it didn't leak to the press. But whatever the situation, Piper's welfare was no longer his responsibility. Her parents were in Marbella and they would have to take care of her.

He packed his case as quickly as he could with shaking hands, rifling through drawers and wardrobes, swiping all his toiletries from the bathroom's plush shower and sink. The lack of a good square meal and the adrenaline of the long day had caught up with him and he looked more than a little jaded when he spotted his reflection in the mirror. Tim left his luggage by the bedroom door, ready to load back into the coach, while Hayley and Ricky oversaw the safe deposit of Rob, Bear and Alex. Tim would quietly round up his parents and friends, then everyone could be on their way. And then he could close the book on this chapter. But before he did that, he couldn't resist sneaking onto the balcony to watch the men reorient themselves down below in the garden. Bear and Alex thought they were still at the finca, apparently. They reclined on the pool's sun loungers and let the waiters bring them fresh cocktails, as they watched a woman straddling a unicorn lilo in her umpteenth outfit of the day.

~

"She slept for an hour and got a second wind," said Fergus, creeping up on Tim in the marble corridor after he'd tracked down his family, the boys, and their new friends, shepherding them onto the coach and slipping into the lift to the villa's first floor to retrieve his suitcase. "It was the strangest thing but then I guess it's been the strangest day."

On the subject of strange, a few of the other guests seemed to have caught Piper's earlier yawns and were scattered around the property themselves. Tim had passed them on his way outside. They snoozed on plush sofas and garden hammocks. And if he wasn't mistaken, Tim noted also that Mervyn was mysteriously back on the scene, chatting animatedly to a tall fair-haired male. Tim didn't have time to contemplate any of that.

"I'm glad to hear it. She deserves to enjoy her day and her night," Tim replied, relieved this man had never become his father-in-law.

"You deserve the best too, Tim." Fergus's words startled him and the two of them paused at the wide window that offered another bird's eye view of Spanish paradise. "I was wrong about you. I know Piper mucked you around but even after all that, you still had her best interests at heart and there's not many men out there who'd have been so forgiving... and, erm, visionary." Fergus tilted his head at Piper's double, who was now soaking up the last rays of the sun, Bear and Alex wittering away on either side of her. River had warned Tim that his former band members had probably consumed not so much an alcoholic-based cocktail, as a drug-based one. Yep, now that definitely figured.

"Thanks. It means a lot."

Tim shook Fergus's hand, walked to the lift with his case and then changed his mind and took the stairs. He wanted to feel life from this moment on. He wanted to be an active part in it. No more taking the easy way out – even when it was a struggle. No more glazing over things. No more meaningless luxury. Every action Tim took from this moment onward would be rooted in authenticity.

ALICE

Tim returned to the finca with Hayley, his family and his friends in tow. The sweet, balmy evening air and the pinpricks of stars grew ever more intense as the minutes ticked by and darkness fell upon the countryside. Now Jupiter glowed as bright as the golden lanterns flanking the pathways and lawns. The Spanish guitarist had swapped roles with a saxophonist, leading Alice and River onto the 'dance floor' for their first shimmy to *It Had to be You*. Alice was torn between savouring the moment with the love of her life – and all the heated anticipation of the things they were going to do to one another behind closed doors in a few hours – and trying to encourage her guests to grab cocktails from the bar.

When the last note sounded, Alice and River's friends whooped and cheered, and the musician got everybody onto the patio to dance to *Billy Jean*. The newlyweds bopped with everybody for half of the song before inching themselves away to check on the new arrivals.

"Hey! How'd it go?" River got to them first.

"Like clockwork," said Hayley, as she introduced Tim's

guests to the happy couple and Alice and River did the kiss-on-the-cheek-stroke-handshake routine all over again. "The Robster was given a firm verbal warning and a Will Smith-style slap."

"Erm, by who?" asked Alice, but Hayley chose to ignore that bit.

"And those good for nothing former band mates of yours have made themselves at home. We dumped their bags at the villa with them so you shouldn't be bumping into them again in this part of the world."

That was as maybe, but Alice noted there were now two extra guests in their midst. Hayley read her mind. "The lovely social influencer ladies here took quite a shine to Tim's friends." Hayley could say that again: Nath, Josh and Kyle looked like the cats who'd got the cream, and Alice didn't want to think about how things were going to pan out later romantically… "It would have been a shame to split them up."

Tim's friends appeared to have lost their voices – little boys whose wildest fantasies had finally come true – but one of the females did the talking for them. "I'm Sophia and this is Talia. We've known Piper for a while but to be honest, once you've been to one influencer wedding, you've been to them all. No offence, Tim."

"None taken," he replied.

"When Hayley said we could tag along, we jumped at the chance to move on to slightly less in-your-face surroundings. This place is perfect, and you look incredible, Alice. I'm sorry we haven't brought you a present."

"No problem," River said. "You can make up for it with a stint of promotional TikTok videos and Instagram reels down at our Somerset stables and eatery, when we get back to the UK."

"You've gone above and beyond inviting us back here to celebrate with you," Tim finally got a word in, peeping through his thoroughly-in-need-of-a-brush tufts. "We really appreciate it."

"It's our pleasure," Alice replied. "Isn't it, River?" River let out a yelp of agreement when she stood on his toe. "As luck would have it, there's a spare bedroom on the ground floor for your parents." Mrs Nutkins put her hand to her heart in thanks. "As for the rest of you." Alice pointed at the teepees, hammocks and mattresses dotted about the lawn and the lads' eyes looked like they were going to pop out of their sockets. "Just… you know… try to keep the noise down."

"It's very kind of you, Alice, but I won't be staying," said Tim, even though, quite unfairly, he was the last person she had been considering in this equation. "There's somewhere else I need to be."

FREYA

The rapping at the door wouldn't stop. But Freya was not in the mood for visitors. Tomorrow was her day off and she was packing a bag for a much-needed couple of days hiking in the mountains. She'd managed to get a space with a tour group in the Sierra Nevada. It would be just the tonic, taking her as far away from the lovebird activities in Tim and Piper's villa as possible – physically, if not mentally.

"Freya! Let me in if you're still there!" Hannah's voice screamed on the other side of the door. "Alice says you're running away. But you can't do that. There's stuff you need to know. *So much stuff you need to know.* The thing is that Tim—"

Freya couldn't take the weight of this conversation to the mountains with her. Not when Merv had literally just called her, delighting in relaying his suspicions. This could not be a coincidence. She opened the door on her colleague and Hannah practically tumbled into the apartment.

"Do *not* mention that man's name in my presence." Freya held her hands up in a desperate bid to repel the temptation.

"And the only reason I've let you in is to discuss the meaning of *this*." She pulled the purple syringe from the pocket of her shorts and held it up to the light as if she was inspecting a diamond.

Hannah gasped, and then shook, and then cried.

"What in the hell's going on, Hannah? I thought we'd agreed that you would remain as impartial as me. We had a job to do. A *professional* job to do. We said we wouldn't bring our judgement into this."

"*You* said we wouldn't bring our judgement into this. But I… I'm afraid I couldn't help myself."

Freya started to see spots before her eyes. She wilted onto the nearest chair, gripping its arms, waiting for some kind of explanation.

"It was just valerian."

"Ohhhh," Freya yelled. "That's okay then. Now we can all relax. It was just a sleeping draught! Christ, Hannah. We are not in some re-enactment of *Sleeping Beauty* or *Snow White and the Seven fricking Dwarves*! Karma doesn't work like that. It's the unseen forces which dole it out. We had one job, and that was to be Marbella's top wedding cake makers. Huh, not any more."

"It was a moment of foolishness, Freya. You have to believe me," Hannah cried as she looped around the coffee table, only making Freya feel dizzier still. "That day when we almost headbanged outside your office… I-I was eavesdropping on your conversation with Piper. Not that I particularly needed to. Do you realise you had her on speakerphone? I heard everything. That woman's attitude and foul manners towards you were unforgivable. So I sort of sent Tim the photos, too."

Freya put her head in her hands, unable to process how quickly this day was turning from bad to worse.

"I know I shouldn't have done it," Hannah pleaded, "but

there was no way I could let him go through with the wedding when I knew for certain what Piper was getting up to behind his back. Desperate times call for desperate measures."

"But this was taking things too far," Freya muttered, too apoplectic to face the woman standing in front of her. "Besides which, the cake is generally eaten *after* the ceremony!"

"Yeah, I know. In my haste I didn't exactly think that bit through but it doesn't matter because Tim…"

"Do not mention his name!"

"I'm sorry." Hannah let out a deep sigh. "I wish you would let me explain but I respect your decision. Listen." Freya peeped through the gaps in her hands to see Hannah taking a seat of her own accord. "I… what it is… there's something I need to tell you, okay? And it's something that very few people know because historically, when they've found out, they've treated me, treated *us* – differently."

Now Freya gave Hannah her full attention.

"I come from a family of witches."

Freya let out a gasp of astonishment and immediately regretted sounding so judgemental. The very thing she had reprimanded the woman in front of her for being, herself mere moments ago. "Oh, right. I see."

"We're the good sort. I promise. To cut a very long and gruesome story short, sadly, some of my ancestors were trialled at Lancaster during the atrocious witch hunts."

Freya's heart sank at this news. She'd recently read a historical women's fiction series that depicted the hideousness of that period.

"Unfairly and beyond inhumanely." Freya could see the pain in Hannah's eyes. A suffering that had been handed down the generations. "All we use is herbs and plants to help others." Just like the women in Freya's book. She felt queasy.

"But every once in a while the temptation to right wrongs on other people's behalf is overwhelming. I know I might end up paying the price if Mother Nature disagrees with my actions, but sometimes I have to take a calculated risk. What I did came from the heart. Tim needed rescuing. Can you imagine how messy his life would have been if...?"

"Hannah, I hear you," Freya cut her off. "But the cake knocked Piper out, according to Merv. What if it had gone to the other wedding by mistake and one of the children had eaten it?"

"I weighed the likelihood of that scenario up, believe me. As long as I went along with Ricky to assist with the delivery, I knew that couldn't happen."

"Valerian on its own is one thing, but valerian with alcohol is a potent concoction! I may not be into herbal remedies but…"

"That's where I completely screwed up. I kind of assumed clean eaters don't drink alcohol."

Freya remained silent. Clueless as to what to say next.

"I did what I had to do. But it was more than that, Freya. I've felt the chemistry between you and Tim. You're peas in a pod, made for each other. It would have been disastrous to let him marr—"

Freya put up a hand to stop Hannah in her tracks. There was no point dredging up the details of the day. She'd cut off Merv when he'd claimed on the phone the wedding had been a shambles too. Were Merv and Hannah in some kind of cahoots, trying to tell her what she wanted to hear, now Tim and Piper were loved up and embarking on their honeymoon? Nothing would surprise Freya anymore.

"I won't blame you for firing me."

Freya examined the cold hard facts: she was a hypocrite. If she'd conducted herself professionally when Tim visited for the taste test, none of this would have happened. "I don't think it needs to come to that."

"But how can you keep me on board? How can you trust me? I've let the whole team down."

"Do you know what, Hannah? The old Freya would have agreed with you, because she'd have brushed her own dodgy deeds under the carpet. But the new Freya's had a bit of an upgrade."

Hannah looked Freya up and down as if she'd missed a trick.

"Oh, not outwardly. But inwardly. I've made a decision. I'm stepping back from FOM to gradually hand the business over to Ricky, with the caveat that nobody discusses their love life (or lack thereof) on the premises ever again, that both members of the bridal party always show up for a taste test in person, all of my staff keep their current positions… and you are made general manager."

TIM

Tim banged on Freya's apartment door so hard and for so long that he couldn't believe he hadn't got *himself* banged up. Alas, there was no answer. He slid to the floor in defeat. And there he'd stay in a pathetic, lovelorn heap, until Freya came back from wherever she'd gone.

ALICE

All good things must come to an end, and that applies to all good – but totally roller coaster –weddings. Alice definitely needed a honeymoon to get over the last twenty-four hours.

Tim hadn't come back that night, or the next morning. She'd seriously hoped he hadn't gone off and done anything stupid, but his parents had reassured Alice of his safety, and the need for a few days away to regroup. And, at the end of the day, she could only control her own life. She might now be a married woman but it didn't give her any more influence over River (not that she was the domineering type), so how could she possibly have any impact on a relative stranger like Tim, and his movements? She had to let it go and be thankful that her own wedding had happened, appreciating every moment of the honeymoon without feeling guilty because others had been less fortunate.

Freya had sent her images of all the typically English traybakes she'd be providing, once she returned from her Sierra sojourn. Alice definitely wasn't hungry after the vast quantities of food and drink she'd enjoyed over the past few days, but just looking at the photos of Bakewell tart, flapjacks, Terry's chocolate orange brownies, St Clement's squares, and gin and tonic cake, her mouth couldn't help but water. Until then, she planned to enjoy the last few days with her family and friends at the finca, and her first few days as Mrs. Jackson…

FREYA

Freya checked into her rural accommodation at the stroke of midnight, just as the grumpy receptionist was about to clock off, and promptly fell backwards onto her double bed, trying not to think about the opulent one Tim would be lying in now with a certain woman on top of him. It was a bit of an extravagance running away like this at the last minute in peak tourist season (and peak wedding season) but if she didn't physically remove herself from the Costa del Sol for a couple of days, she'd lose the plot. Here in the mountains she could hike in conviviality with sensible people who probably did sensible things like rambling and eating organic granola for breakfast – as opposed to falling for their clients.

There were two choices of walks the next day. One left at the crack of dawn – *no, gracias* – and the other at five p.m. as the sun slowly started to weaken. Freya opted for the latter, enjoying a late breakfast of coffee, fruit and yoghurt on her terrace overlooking the forest – grateful she'd snuck a couple of pieces of the epic gin and tonic traybake she'd trialled into her rucksack. She'd already registered for the trek through wild boar country and would try to whittle down the stack of books on her Kindle in the meantime.

The group gathered at 4:45 in the garden, taking their snack boxes and water bottles from the guide and exchanging pleasantries. Freya found herself with a Dutch couple, two Japanese girlfriends and an older, grey bun-toting female who made it abundantly clear she preferred the old-fashioned ways, map at the ready, compass around her neck. She'd have loved the fricking green order book Freya had ceremonially burned last week – ensuring she'd gone through the remaining orders with a fine tooth comb first and adding them to a spreadsheet with Hannah and Ricky at her side, of course.

"We're waiting for a final person," announced Salvador, the guide. "Aha, the Englishman has arrived!"

Everybody turned to watch a coach pull into the driveway. *How many Englishmen were they expecting?* The sun was too dazzling to gawk and Freya looked away. No doubt they'd soon be joined by an uber-enthusiastic twit who thought he was the next Bear Grylls. But it wasn't a TV adventurer who dumped his backpack at the reception, shouting "thanks, Hayley" over his shoulder, before scooting over to the group to make his intro to the others. It was a thirty-something male with the kind of side-swept blonde hair that just begged to have your fingers running through it, and ever downwards…

Tim. *Tim!*

Now Freya wasn't seeing spots but stars before her eyes. She thought she would die. Her heart was in her mouth. And her mouth was as dry as that awful Rioja that Lars had tried to ply her with. How was she supposed to compose herself? This was so unfair. What the eff was going on? Clearly Piper would be along any minute. Great! No doubt she had a separate stretch limo to bring herself and all her paraphernalia.

But hang on. Why would Tim's bride agree to something as rural and unglamorous as this on day one of her honeymoon?

Tim's smile of an answer said it all as he panned the group and then stopped at Freya. He couldn't take his eyes off her. And now Freya wanted to dig a hole and hide.

"How did you know I was here?" she mouthed, body tensed.

But there was no time for Tim to answer so he teased her with a shrug and another knowing smile instead. He'd already made the group late and Salvador was keen to get going. Sensing the chemistry between Freya and Tim, their guide annoyingly asked Tim and Granny Bun to step out in front with him to set the pace as they went off down the dirt track which sloped into the forest. Now Freya couldn't even enjoy the peace and serenity of a simple hike, wondering what on earth Tim's game was.

She had so many questions. And none of them could be answered here with this group surrounding them. It was agony! The view of his extremely fit buttocks should have helped, but it only made things a million times worse because she couldn't stop imagining them freed from their layers of fabric. He'd come here for her. There was no doubt about it. She didn't want to get ahead of herself but evidently, somehow, some way, he really had called the wedding off with Piper. Just like Hannah had tried to tell her.

Tim glanced behind him every so often, throwing her deliriously heated looks that made her insides melt. He was like a sexy big bad wolf and Freya wanted nothing more than to let him snare her, carrying her deep into the forest where she'd be only too ecstatic to have him devour every inch of her. As the afternoon turned into early evening and the guide stopped them at the halfway point for snacks, careful to ensure Freya and Tim were once again not remotely within

THE WEDDING CAKE

touching distance, a wicked thought formed in Freya's head. As much as she loved chatting with Asami, Sakura, Marit and Dirk about their travels around Europe, and as much as she could tell Tim was trying to be equally polite in Granny Bun's presence, an infatuated woman could only take so much before she self-combusted. Freya tried to chew back the grin as the thoroughly naughty scene unfolded in her head. She had no guarantee it would work, but she also had nothing to lose.

As the group packed up to hike back up the hilly track to the accommodation, and Tim and Freya locked eyes for a tantalising appraisal of one another's physiques, Freya unbuttoned her khaki shirt a little lower than was necessary, shooting Tim one final lust-filled glance and biting her lip. Which was a little like a scene straight out of a porn movie but how the frick else was she meant to hint that she was up to something and that he should stay alert? Salvador insisted on the same regimented formation as everybody made their way back along the path through the forest and Freya bided her time, desperate for an awkward-looking obstacle to cross her path. Eventually her patience paid off and she let out a giant scream as she 'tumbled' over a small rock.

Effing hell! Actually, it really hurt.

She looked down at her grazed ankle and decided it presented enough evidence to suggest she might have sprained or even broken it. Thankfully, though, she'd used her hands to take the pressure off her foot as it had hit the earth, when she'd then dragged her outer left ankle along the gravel to achieve the grazed effect. It seemed everybody else shared her concern. Especially Tim and Salvador, who were both by her side within moments, assessing the damage, gently manipulating her foot as Freya faked being in far greater pain than she was.

"It could be broken. I have no way of telling until we can

call a doctor out. We'll walk slowly, one on either side of her, and take her back to the B&B," said Salvador decisively.

"Noooo!" Freya cried. "I really don't think I can!"

"I don't think so either," Tim begged to differ and Freya's heart fluttered. "Luckily, I'm a first aider, fitness instructor *and* an experienced orienteer with a gold Duke of Edinburgh award. I can stay here with our patient while you go get a stretcher. She shouldn't hobble such a long distance without any support for the ankle and we have plenty of daylight until you get back. I've got extra snacks and water in my backpack, too."

"*Me importa un pepino* about your qualifications! I am in charge and I shouldn't take my eye off the group." Salvador threw a massive spanner in the works. Unimpressed by Tim's CV, he literally couldn't give a cucumber about his credentials.

"This could be extremely serious and this lady could sue you," Tim insisted. "Go, now! Every minute we spend debating is costing us precious time."

With a heavy and reluctant sigh, Salvador eventually agreed. "But only if you are happy about this, Freya?"

"I-I think it might be for the best." Freya had zero problem surrendering to her fate.

"Okay. We'll walk as fast as we can." Salvador returned to the group, who were all nodding their heads in agreement. "Freya's in your hands now, Tim. I am trusting you to look after her."

"That will be my absolute pleasure," Tim whispered in Freya's ear as everybody pivoted flash-mob style and marched ahead. "Damn, you should be an actor." He grinned seductively. "I take it that's what all the body language was about earlier? You aren't seriously hurt, are you?" Freya shook her head and giggled. "Oh, my God, Freya. I want you more than you will ever know. I don't even know where to start and I hope you're not mad at me for following you here when you needed to get away. I just had to be with you. There's so much I want to explain. I…"

Freya clenched her fist around Tim's T-shirt and pulled him close to her, relishing the immediate hit of aftershave and masculine sweat. She'd pined for this man since the moment he'd stepped into her cakery. The words could come later. With a devilish smile, she pinned him with her hungry gaze, liking the look she saw reflected back at her, loving the groan that escaped his irresistible lips, where she now found her own mouth drawn with an unbreakable magnetic force as his sweet kiss sealed her expectations, exceeding every pent-up desire, and now she was completely drowning in lust. The skies could have erupted in Mediterranean forked lightning, they could have been in the middle of a wild boar migration, or they could have been lost in a pea-souper of a Saharan dust cloud. All of those things at once, but now they had found each other, nothing could tear them apart.

"We haven't got much time and there is *no way* I can contain myself until we get back to the accommodation. I know that makes me sound like a right slapper, but I've waited too long to care since falling into your lap that fateful day." Freya pulled away briefly, reluctantly, giddily happy to see Tim's eyes drugged on the tenderness of that kiss. "So, outdoor fitness instructor and orienteering expert, what are your cosy camp suggestions as you take in the immediate surroundings? I'm thinking somewhere we can get very intimate and be very naughty in a very short space of time."

"You are incorrigible." Tim tucked a strand of Freya's hair behind her ear, letting his thumb run enticingly across her jaw. "I should have locked you up in that kitchen when I had the chance. It's been torture thinking *what if* I'd played things differently for all these months. Why did Hannah have to come back when she did? The roleplay ideas involving you and that icing..."

The pair of them laughed as Tim scooped Freya up in his arms and carried her off the track and into the woods. It didn't take them long to find a clearing that opened onto a meadow of botanical jewels; its carpet of pink and yellow flowers taking her breath away.

Tim lay Freya down and ducked in for a tender kiss before standing to pan the horizon, making pretend binoculars with his hands.

"I think we're all right. I mean the birds and the bees might get inspired by our actions but other than that, we're completely alone. And, oh, my God, Freya... I am going to let you know it."

"Good!" Freya grinned, feeling thoroughly aroused and ridiculously rebellious. "Now where were we?"

"Right about here?"

Tim pressed his lips to hers as she bucked her hips to meet his. Freya would never normally get in so deep so quickly, but this was different. It had always been different with this man and now they had lost time to make up for she wasn't going to waste a precious second of it. Tim deepened the kiss, his tongue sensuous yet famished. Slow-burning then fast. A blissful indicator of all the pleasure that was to come.

The shade of the trees on the outskirts of the meadow might have provided a little cover from the heat of the sun, but Freya couldn't wait to shed her clothes. Side note – thank gawd she'd de-fuzzed last night! Now it was her turn to groan as she guided Tim's fingers over the buttons that weren't yet revealing her skin. His touch was fire. Ecstasy and agony as his palms slid over her chest, caressing her bust beneath the white satin, teasing her nipples. Meanwhile his hot lips tasted her neck, working their way expertly and deliciously down to the tops of her breasts. Tim slid his hand behind her back and whipped Freya's bra off within seconds, rocking back on his knees for a few moments to admire her curves.

"I'm the world's biggest idiot to have let you drive away that day in the carpark."

He shook his head, his pupils dilated, his smile full of intent.

Any insecurities Freya might have had about what she could offer this man in comparison to Piper vanished in a Spanish heat haze. Tim had it as bad as she did it. He almost ripped his top off in his excitement and Freya pulled him on top of her. She didn't want to feel a millimetre of space between them, but soon she would have to let him peel away for another excruciating few moments when they tugged off the rest of their clothing. His erection was massive and that was all she needed to know, to remind herself that the anticipation between each piece of the action was just as big a turn-on.

But then her thoughts turned to practicalities: a) she was rusty as… well, she couldn't think of a suitable simile without killing the passion, but she was massively out of practice between the sheets (and on top of the grass), whereas this hunk of a male who was currently sending her senses into overdrive as he his tongue flicked against the sensitive patch of skin at the side of her neck, had definitely been getting his regular fix and b) she didn't have any contraceptive on her.

Tim ramped up the intensity of his neck nuzzles and Freya surrendered to the pleasure. This had to be a sure sign they were made for each other. Sid had never been this tuned into her needs. And as for the men who showed up on the scene after him, the less said the better.

"Are you sure you want to take things further? I don't

want to rush you." Tim mumbled deliciously into her ear. "I have condoms but I don't want you to think that I came here to find you with one thing on the brain."

"How did you find me, by the way?"

"Hayley." He grinned. "That woman is incredible."

Freya donned a fake jealous expression and Tim laughed. "Alice and River's bridesmaid."

"You know the other couple? What the...?"

"So as I was saying, Hayley and I swapped numbers when we dumped the unwanted guests at the villa. It's a *long* story and there's no way I'm telling it now when we have more important business to attend to." Tim winked. "Alice let slip to us all that you were on a hiking retreat in the mountains, and Hayley called around a few places, narrowing them down to this very dot on the globe."

"Useful friend."

"Wait until I tell you what she did with the cake snatcher!"

"The what?"

But Tim refused to be drawn into lengthy explanations once again. He stopped to gaze into Freya's eyes and she pulled him back in for a sensuous kiss, unable to bear looking at him without touching, her hands roving all over his body, feeling their way along the length of his penis, breathless at the thought of it inside her, until he pulled away again.

"Freya? My...erherm... earlier question?"

"Wasn't that kiss answer enough?" she laughed.

"Hell, yes." Tim arched a brow and pulled down Freya's shorts, following that up with a slower and raunchier removal of her matching black satin panties. He closed his eyes dreamily as Freya helped him with his zipper before she lay back to thoroughly enjoy the view of his crotch, unable to believe how much her life had changed in twenty-four hours as he rolled the condom over his erection and gently trailed his fingers along her inner thigh. "As much as I want this to last forever, it's going to have to be fiery and fast. Once the others are back at the inn, Salvador will stride down that hill in no time with a stretcher."

"Let's do it. It's the perfect excuse to over-exert myself to make my injury look even more credible," Freya giggled naughtily.

She wrapped her legs around Tim, guiding his hardness inside her. His first thrust was as meaningful as it was ecstatic, the waves of pleasure building as they explored one another until Freya was tugging at the blades of grass in the absence of a pillow. "Later we'll do this properly. Over and over and over. Without the worry of getting caught," he groaned.

"Doesn't that just add to the thrill though?" Freya had never felt so alive. So bold and alive. She knocked Tim's hip with her knee, hinting that she wanted to go on top, and he gently manoeuvred her into position, eyes glazing over at the uninterrupted view of so much of her body.

"You are sooooo hot!" he moaned. "I've dreamed about doing this to you since the moment I laid eyes on you. Never did I dare to think it could become a reality."

"And yet here we are." Freya moved sensually, loving the effect she was having on this man, hungering for his kisses once more. She pinned Tim's arms to the ground, splaying her hands to run them along the length of his muscles, clamping his thoroughly capable hands in hers as she slowly and tantalisingly let their lips meet, savouring the sensation of her breasts pressed to his chest and the throbbing of him inside her.

"Can I take you from behind for the finale, baby?"

"Are you a mind reader?" she giggled.

Freya couldn't believe how relaxed Tim made her feel. At most she might have contemplated an outdoor fumble with

Sid if they were drunk and on holiday. It had happened once on a secluded beach. But then everything had been so authentic with this man since the moment she'd met him. They could probably get away with one final act of passion in the great outdoors without getting kicked out of the group for lewd behaviour… and if luck wasn't on their side, so what?

Tim expertly twisted them both so as not to break the delicious contact and Freya closed her eyes and revelled in the mounting waves of bliss, letting herself melt into the greatest orgasm of her life, before collapsing in a deliriously happy heap.

∽

"Well, waking up to this is as much the stuff of dreams as it is unexpected," said Tim, rolling over to snuggle into Freya as they both took in the sunrise from their bed.

"If this is a dream then don't you dare wake me up."

Freya bit her lip as Tim's fingers traced her nipple and she wondered how she would be able to resist round five. Or was it six? She'd lost count. Epic didn't do the past few hours justice. Once they'd caught their breath in the meadow, they'd quickly dressed, raced back to a grassy patch beneath the trees at the side of the track where Salvador had left them, and waited no more than five minutes to spot him pounding toward them with a stretcher. Talk about taking risks! The journey back to the accommodation had been the most surreal of Freya's life, her mind unable to stop replaying her brazen actions whilst enjoying furtive body language from Tim over the top of the stretcher as Salvador took the lead. She could have hobbled along and announced her remarkable recovery but after all that exercise, she really did need a lie down.

"Where do we go from here?" asked today's Tim as he wrapped his arms tighter around her and they marvelled at how quickly the sun moved in the mountains.

"We put on our hiking boots and we sneak crafty snogs when Salvador and the rest of the group aren't watching."

"Sounds heavenly."

"And, Tim?"

Freya tried not to come on too strong... but failed spectacularly. She unpeeled his arms, put his hand in hers and looked at him in earnest.

"*Yes?*"

"I know it sounds ridiculously premature, but it has to be said – because this isn't like anything else I've ever experienced and..."

"I love you, Freya Ashcroft," Tim cut in. "I totally and utterly, head-over-heels love you. And I don't care how much people scoff at love at first sight. You were it for me. You *are* it for me. There's nothing you can say that will change my mind."

"Okay then. I'm just going to come out with it..." Freya's heart skipped a beat as she replayed that little flurry of words. She felt the same but she wanted to find her own moment to announce it. "I don't expect either of us to contemplate marriage again. And I think I should be straight about that from the start. I do believe in HEAs but I am so over the whole bridal business, including... probably... being one. FOM's been an amazing journey, most of the time, and if I hadn't set it up, I'd never have met you, but it's time for a whole new adventure now. A complete life overhaul."

"Oh?"

Tim looked a little wounded and Freya wished she could reassure him how strong her feelings were too, but she didn't want it to sound like she was simply parroting back his words. "But I do absolutely want to build a life with you. The sooner the better. I still can't get my head around the circumstances that brought us together... But then again, don't most people meet *the one* at work?"

"Overlooking the time I met Piper."

"Erm, yeah. And I'd totally like to erase the time I met Sid."

"Anyway, what would this new life of yours entail? You live in Spain. I live in Manchester."

"Well, that's where it gets interesting."

EPILOGUE

TIM

*T*im moved into Freya's Marbella apartment right after the mountain retreat and only left once; to pack up his life in Manchester and never look back. Until they both left together… for Nerja. His fitness students were made up for him that he'd managed to escape his toxic relationship with Piper. Social media had typically broken the news to them before he could. But they were gutted when he announced his relocation to a whole other country. Luckily, he quickly found somebody to take over the classes and buy all his equipment.

The glitz and glamour of Marbella had been fun for Freya for many years, and for Tim for many weeks, but the town wasn't who they were as individuals or as a couple, and a new life together called for a totally new start. Cosmopolitan but down to earth Nerja was further east along the Spanish coast, and just what they'd both been looking for. From that pin on the map (and their blissfully cosy apartment with its terrace overlooking the Mediterranean Sea) things happened really fast, and before they knew it, they had registered their joint business, Awesome Andalucía Adventures. AAA was a tour company with a difference. It offered all the usual active tourism activities but it revved them up, throwing a little more excitement into the mix: horse trekking in the Doñana National Park complete with a churros picnic breakfast served by a chef; sherry-sipping hot air balloon flights over the city of Granada with the backing of a Spanish guitarist, and paddle board racing on Seville's river Guadalquivir followed by a sangria-fuelled pottery session in the city's Triana district. The latter always produced questionable works of art!

It was no wonder Tim had procrastinated forever over his Pennines pursuits. He was never meant to be there. He'd swapped those uplands for the majestic mountains of the Sierra Nevada, and he'd exchanged the lakes of the North for kayaking around Nerja's sparkling turquoise coves. Of course one wasn't better than the other, on paper. But his life in Spain included Freya. And it was so much easier to stop all the people-pleasing here; to start living for himself. He'd started Spanish lessons too and was learning fast so he could talk to local clients and providers. For now that was Freya's job.

In the quiet season, Tim and Freya put on team building workshops for companies. The first stop was FOM and a tame (but wild enough for Ricky) vineyard tour, followed by a hilarious flamenco lesson. Freya was making considerably less money while Tim was making considerably more. But finally they both had the balance and opportunities they had always dreamed of. And they had found happiness.

Tim thought back to their wild behaviour in the meadow and realised how jammy he was that things in that department had definitely continued. Barely a day went by when one of them wasn't jumping on the other. Freya's ideas were particularly spontaneous; his favourite being the 'secret cove' they'd tandem-kayak to for a very steamy afternoon most weekends when the weather was good, taking a massive picnic with them so they had the energy to get back to the beach.

As for Piper, the video clips of her wedding day infiltrated every corner of the media. She even ended up making guest appearances on daytime TV. *Loose Women* couldn't get enough of her, and she graced their panel a handful of times. She could say what she wanted about Tim's lack of get up and go, but the fact could not be disputed; this turbo boost to her career would never have happened if it hadn't been for his moment of ingenuity on their wedding day. That said, her self-marriage had soon fizzled out. In a surprise but very fitting twist, she'd ended up dating Mervyn's stepson, Lars. The Costa del Sol's dodgiest wedding planner had apparently encouraged things along after a brainwave during the reception, which seemed to have coincided with nabbing a gigantic wedge of the cake and eating it on his drive to 'retirement'. Tim had to wonder what else Hannah had put in the villa's half of the bake. He'd not long ago read a story about a Colombian wedding where the bride and groom had laced their multi-tiered cake with cannabis, to spectacular effect!

"Look at us," said Freya as she snapped Tim back to present-moment February. She let the instructor strap her up, ready to time-travel an hour into the past over the River Guadiana, thanks to Portugal being an hour behind Spain. This was the world's only cross-border zip line, 720 metres long and offering speeds of up to 80kmph. "Who'd have thought that, exactly one year on from me de-icing your nose, we'd be doing *this* together."

Today they were checking out a brand-new trip on their itinerary. Oaks and olive trees flanked the river, which was actually a former smuggling route from Africa into Europe, while little whitewashed houses flecked the landscape. Their clients would absolutely love this. Tim could totally imagine the idyllic start to married life that River and Alice had had in this beautiful countryside, as they handed Freya's amazing traybakes out to the people who crossed their camper van's path.

"It's corny and it's cliche but it's definitely been a ride! In every sense of the word."

Freya eye-rolled Tim. "Sometimes you've just got to take a riiiiiisk!" she cried as she was launched from the stage. Tim watched her fly free as a bird from one whole country to another, marvelling at how utterly perfect his life had become the moment he'd started following his heart

The Arabs, the Romans, and the Greeks had come to this land beneath his feet. And now it was Tim from Manchester's turn. Okay, he'd actually been living here for six months and a day, but the idea was the same. Travel broadened the horizons, making life bigger and better.

Tim patted his pocket to check that the small box was still there. Hopefully Freya's diamond solitaire engagement ring wouldn't fall into the waters beneath him as he made his own flight along the wire to Portugal. Asking her the question he was about to pop was yet another risk, based on a certain conversation they'd had in a cosy mountain retreat bed last summer as they watched the sun rise.

But no matter what Freya's decision was today, Tim couldn't lose. She'd been his world since the moment he'd first set his eyes on her, three hundred and sixty-five days ago, and he would happily meet Freya Ashcroft halfway, until the end of the world.

THE END

ABOUT THE AUTHOR

Isabella May lives in (mostly) sunny Andalusia, Spain with her husband, daughter and son, creatively inspired by the mountains and the sea. She grew up on Glastonbury's ley lines and loves to feature her quirky English hometown in her stories.

After a degree in Modern Languages and European Studies at UWE, Bristol (and a year working abroad in Bordeaux and Stuttgart), Isabella bagged herself an extremely jammy and fascinating job in children's publishing... selling foreign rights for novelty, board, pop-up, and non-fiction books all over the world; in every language from Icelandic to Korean, Bahasa Indonesian to Papiamento!

All of which has fuelled her curiosity and love of international food and travel - both feature extensively in her romantic comedies, along with a sprinkle of magic.

Isabella is also a Pranic Healer and a stillbirth mum.

FOODIE ROMANCE JOURNEYS

You can follow Isabella May's Foodie Romance Journey series at the following hang-outs:

www.isabellamayauthor.com
Twitter - @IsabellaMayBks
Instagram - @isabella_may_author
Facebook - https://www.facebook.com/IsabellaMayAuthor/

Would you like to read the first of Isabella's novels - The Cocktail Bar - for free, and would you like to be a part of her mailing list for exciting news about her books?

Simply click the link: hbit.ly/3GgI4ZZ

You can unsubscribe at any time

ALSO BY ISABELLA MAY

The Cocktail Bar

Oh! What a Pavlova

Costa del Churros

The Ice Cream Parlour

The Cake Fairies

The Chocolate Box

Bubblegum and Blazers

Twinkle, Twinkle Little Bar

The Custard Tart Cafe

Spin the Bottle

Coming soon:

An exciting spin-off trilogy for three of the female characters in Oh! What a Pavlova

and…

Christmas at the Keanu Kindness Cafe

Made in the USA
Middletown, DE
10 April 2023